"I wish we

Nick said huski...

Leanne leaned into him, and his arms tightened around her in a possessive gesture that intensified the longing that tormented her.

"There will be a time for us," he said softly. "I'm not a patient man, and I want to make love to you. But I want the time to make it good for you."

She found it impossible to breathe. She was intensely aware of his body: the hard muscles of his thighs, his firm stomach pressed against hers, his powerful chest crushing her breasts. When he lowered his mouth to hers she met it eagerly, thrilling at the groan that came from deep within his chest.

He stood back, panting. "I hope you know what you're unleashing here, Lee. I'm not sure I can be a gentleman much longer."

"I hadn't noticed you were one before," she answered.

His eyes roamed over her, savage and hungry. The look of naked passion on his face was so intense it scared her as he said, "I'd better go while I still can."

Dear Reader,

When two people fall in love, the world is suddenly new and exciting, and it's that same excitement we bring to you in Silhouette Intimate Moments. These are stories with scope, with grandeur. These characters lead the lives we all dream of, and everything they do reflects the wonder of being in love.

This month we're pleased to bring you a new line of books, Silhouette Classics. These titles are "something old, something new" for your bookshelf. Over the years, you've asked us to reissue early books by your favorite authors, and with Silhouette Classics we'll bring you two titles every month, representing the best of the Silhouette Intimate Moments and Silhouette Special Edition lines. This month we're featuring *Dreams of Evening*, by Kristin James, and *Intimate Strangers*, by Brooke Hastings. We hope you'll look for them wherever you buy books, and that they'll bring back memories for some of you and provide new adventures in love for others.

In coming months, look for *new* Silhouette Intimate Moments novels by Maura Seger, Parris Afton Bonds, Linda Howard and Nora Roberts, to name just a few. And whenever you buy books, look for all the Silhouette Intimate Moments, love stories *for* today's women *by* today's women.

Leslie Wainger
Senior Editor
Silhouette Books

Doreen Roberts

Gambler's Gold

Silhouette Intimate Moments

Published by Silhouette Books New York

America's Publisher of Contemporary Romance

SILHOUETTE BOOKS
300 East 42nd St., New York, N.Y. 10017

Copyright © 1987 by Doreen Roberts

ISBN: 0-373-07215-5

First Silhouette Books printing November 1987

America's Publisher of Contemporary Romance

Printed in the U.S.A.

DOREEN ROBERTS

lived in England until she immigrated to the U.S. with her British husband more than twenty years ago. Having been an avid reader of romances for most of her life, and an intermittent writer for even longer, she decided to settle down and try her hand at combining both.

She now lives happily in Oregon with her husband and teenage son, and has discovered her greatest joy comes from mixing romance and danger.

Chapter 1

From the shadows at the back of the barroom, Nick Garrett watched the slender, elegant woman cross the worn carpeting to the bar. He'd seen plenty of women like her. One too many. But he'd never seen one here in the Blue Bucket Saloon. He knew money when he saw it. That cream silk blouse and tan skirt had never graced the pages of a Sears catalog, and he'd bet his best pair of boots that those were diamonds flashing at her ears.

He recognized the type, all right. He'd had more than his fill of that kind of trouble. Not that he actually had anything against money. After all, without it, he would never have hung on to the Blue Bucket, every last weather-beaten, broken-down timber of it. No. It was the people who had too much of it that he despised. The people who used it and abused it and sold their souls for it. He forced his mind off his memories and concentrated on the woman instead.

She was attractive, if you went for that fine-boned, delicate look. Personally he preferred them a little more robust, and hungry. Wry amusement flicked across his rugged features, softening the hard planes of his face, as he imagined her cool elegance lying warm and eager in his bed.

No way, José. Stick to your own kind—you knew where you were with them. One night of hot passion and on your way. No commitments, no regrets, and no one gets hurt. And, if a part of him deep inside suggested that he could be missing out on something important, he ignored it. To listen to it could mean exposing himself to risks, and Nick Garrett no longer took any risks.

His hard, navy-blue eyes narrowed as he saw her say something to Dan, her voice inaudible against the throbbing beat from the radio. Dan, his barman and longtime friend, sent him a quick warning look that Nick interpreted immediately. The woman was looking for him. Above his prominent nose his dark brows drew together.

It was barely five-thirty, but already the ranch hands were wandering into the tavern. Men in grubby jeans and torn, grimy T-shirts, hot and sweaty from hours spent under the burning sun, sprawled at the beer-stained tables. Nick saw that they eyed the slim figure at the bar with undisguised curiosity. More than one gave her a second glance, weighing their chances, undaunted by her apparent indifference.

She was arguing. She had her back to Nick now, but he saw the toss of her head, the impatient gesture of her hand. Again Dan caught his eyes, his brows raised in question.

Nick hesitated, then eased his long, muscular body away from the wall and prowled across the floor.

Lee stared at the pudgy-faced, balding barman in frustration. The last thing she wanted to do was sit in this stuffy, smoke-filled room, breathing in fumes of stale beer and body odor. She could feel the calculating stares directed at her back, and sensed the knowing nudges of the coarse-looking men crowding the bar.

More than anything, she wanted to turn around and walk out of this sordid little shack and breathe the hot summer air outside until she purged her lungs. But she couldn't do that.

Simon needed her, and she wouldn't let him down. She struggled to regain the courage that had allowed her to walk into the bar in the first place.

"All right!" she said, raising her voice against the thump of country music. "If he's not here and you don't know where he is or when he's expected, then I'll sit here and wait for him. Or are you going to object to that, too?" She glanced up irritably at the speakers hanging on the yellowed walls. Her head throbbed with every foot-stomping beat. She snapped her eyes back as the barman spoke again.

"Suit yourself, lady. There's no law says you can't sit there all night if that's what you want. Till two a.m., that is. Then we close." And you're out, his expression implied.

Lee's chin lifted defiantly. "Then I'll come back tomorrow. And the next day. Sooner or later your Mr. Nick Garrett will have to show himself."

"And then what?"

The deep drawl had come from behind her, and Lee swung around, her pulse quickening as she met the probing eyes of the man who towered over her. He wasn't quite what she'd expected, though she wasn't sure what she had expected. Someone older and, she realized with a quiver of awareness, someone not quite so attractive.

This man had to be somewhere in his mid-thirties and was wide-shouldered and lean-hipped, with a face that would definitely turn heads. His shirt and his close-fitting jeans were clean, and she could forgive the shadowed jaw.

"You're Nick Garrett?" She almost wished he weren't.

"I am."

"You're a difficult man to find." He made no comment, and Lee fidgeted with the strap of her purse. "I'm Leanne Coulton," she announced, and, when that elicited no response, added, "My brother is Simon King."

She'd surprised him, she saw. The expression was fleeting but unmistakable. "I'd like to talk to you," she said, "someplace where I don't have to shout to be heard."

At first she thought he was going to refuse, then he twisted on his heel, beckoning her to follow. He led her into a small office and shut the door, muffling the noise from the bar.

A scarred desk littered with papers stood before a narrow window. Lee saw Nick's brief gesture and sat down on the aging chair, resisting the impulse to brush off the dust. The faded curtains diluted the sunlight, shading the room, and she felt a sharp longing to be back in the plush security of the Royal King. Damn Simon. What had he gotten her into?

She watched Nick move away, and she took the opportunity to run her eyes over his body. He was in peak condition, judging by the lack of surplus flesh. His long legs, confined by the faded jeans, displayed muscles that were well developed. Aware that she'd been staring, Lee looked up hastily as his legs disappeared behind the desk.

Nick ran a hand through his thick hair and looked at the woman seated opposite him. It was hard to believe this elegant creature was Simon's sister. Brown eyes, olive skin—a direct contrast to Simon's blond, blue-eyed looks, though it had been hard to tell what Simon looked like beneath that beard of his.

Coulton, her name was. That meant she had to be married. What the hell was her husband doing letting her wander into places like this on her own?

He allowed his gaze to slide over her well-shaped body. She was taller than most women he knew, and pleasantly curved in all the right places.

When he met her eyes again, he knew she wasn't entirely unaffected by him, and unexpectedly, desire curled its fingers low in his belly.

"Does your husband know where you are?" he asked abruptly. The words were out of his mouth before he'd realized he intended to say them.

"I don't have a husband. I'm divorced."

The little lift of relief he experienced disturbed him. "You don't look much like Simon," he said.

Lee struggled with her breath. His scrutiny had bordered on insulting and had left her in no doubt to what he'd been thinking. Her skin still tingled with the shock of it.

"That may be true," she said stiffly, "but I assure you, I am Simon's sister. His twin, in fact. I'm here to find out what happened to him."

"Happened?" Nick's eyebrows lifted in surprise. "Why do you think something's happened to him?"

"He was supposed to meet me in Portland last week. It was the anniversary of our mother's death. We always visit the grave together on that date."

She paused as Nick leaned back and put his hands behind his head. The movement widened the gap at the neck of his blue denim shirt, revealing an expanse of tanned chest that was generously covered with fine, dark hair.

"Simon hasn't missed that date in the past eighteen years," she went on, determined to keep her eyes firmly fixed on his face. "I've known him to trek through an African jungle to make it home on time, yet last week the anniversary came and went without so much as a word from him. The last time I talked to him was two weeks ago."

She paused, meeting the dark eyes with disapproval. "He told me you were taking him up into the mountains to look at some old gold mines. He promised me he would be back in Portland for the sixteenth. No one has heard from him since."

"Is that supposed to be my fault?" Nick lowered his hands and sat up. "Simon came to me a couple of weeks back. He said he was a photojournalist, working on an article about ghost towns in Oregon. Someone had told him that I knew the area well, and he asked me to show him. I did. That's it."

"Why did he need you to take him?" Lee demanded. "I thought there were tourist maps of the mines."

"There are. Your brother didn't want to see the tourist mines. The ones he was interested in are farther back in the mountains, unreachable by a car and out of range of Forest Service areas."

And out of range of the law? Lee wondered. She thought of Simon's words, of fragments of sentences she'd overheard in his apartment that night when he hadn't known she was there. *Keep the law off my back.* Dear God, she thought, what kind of trouble is he in this time?

Anxiety made her voice sharp. "So you just left him up there? Alone? How did you think he was going to get back?"

"He followed me as far as the parking lot in his car. I figured if he could hike in with me from there, he'd be quite capable of hiking out again." Nick scowled. "He asked me to show him the mines, Ms. Coulton, not hang around as his bodyguard. Besides, he's not alone. There are plenty of prospectors to keep him company. The location of the mines isn't exactly a secret."

She ignored his emphasis on the *Ms.* It wasn't worth arguing about. "Then why hasn't he come back?" she demanded.

Nick's broad shoulders lifted in a shrug. "How do you know he hasn't? Or maybe he's enjoying himself up there. He could have found some dust. It wouldn't be the first time a man has forgotten a woman for gold."

"That's ridiculous." Lee raised her chin a fraction. "You obviously don't know my brother very well. Nothing would prevent him from being with me for that anniversary. Not by choice, anyway."

"Okay. If you think he's had an accident or something, I suggest you call the sheriff. In fact, I'll get him on the phone right now."

As he lifted the receiver, her voice cut across the room. "No!"

He paused, giving her a measuring look. "No?"

Lee twisted the strap of her bag around her fingers. "I can't call in the authorities."

Nick replaced the receiver, his expression thoughtful. So, his instincts had been right. He could sense trouble lurking ahead like an assassin in the shadows. What was it that she wasn't telling him?

"It's strange that Simon didn't mention you," he said, keeping his voice casual. "You don't look like him at all. I spent three nights with Simon. I'm surprised he didn't talk about his twin."

"Simon doesn't talk about his family much," Lee said shortly.

"All right." Nick propped his chin on his hands, his eyes dark and intense on her face. "So why don't you tell me what this strong aversion to the law is all about?"

Lee met his gaze steadily. How much could she afford to tell him? If only she could trust him with all of it, all her doubts and suspicions. But that was a chance she couldn't take.

"Have you heard of the Royal King Hotels chain?" she asked.

Nick nodded. Who hadn't? "Of course. There's one in Portland—the Royal King I believe. I know there's one in most of the big cities in the country."

"Right." Lee hesitated. Her palms felt damp, and her blouse stuck to her back as she leaned forward. "They're all owned by Jonathan King."

She thought she saw a flicker of distaste cross Nick's face.

"The hotel baron of the Northwest. Yeah, I've heard of him." His expression changed as the significance of her words sank in. "Are you telling me that Simon is *that* King?"

"Jonathan King is our father."

Nick let out a soft whistle. It was hard enough to associate Simon, that animated free soul, with this sophisticated woman. It was almost impossible to believe that Simon was the son of one of the wealthiest men in Oregon.

"Mr. Garrett," Lee said quietly. "You've met Simon. He's a little...unorthodox. He's a terrific photographer, but he takes enormous risks to get his pictures. They get him into trouble sometimes."

She stood up and moved restlessly over to where a small bookcase held several volumes, all of which looked well handled. Her eyes widened as she took in the authors inscribed on the leather spines—Shakespeare, Chaucer, Hemingway—hardly the kind of books she would have expected to find in this environment. She fingered them thoughtfully as she continued.

"There was the time," she said, "when Simon covered a drug bust on the Mexican border. He posed as one of the gang and ended up getting arrested himself. It took the best lawyers in town to sort out that one."

She dropped her hand and turned back to Nick. "Then there was the time the local police raided a male strip club. Simon heard of it from one of his contacts and got himself hired as one of the dancers."

She frowned as Nick smothered a grin behind his hand. "I'm not trying to be funny, Mr. Garrett."

Nick straightened his face. "Sorry. I was just wondering where he hid the camera."

Lee came back to the chair and sat down. "I'm telling you all this so you'll understand." She arranged her thoughts with care. What would it take to convince him? "Our mother died when we were quite young," she went on. "Father was devastated, of course, and took out his pain mostly on Simon. I had to work hard to keep the peace between them, which was shaky at best. My brother's escapades have infuriated Father. The publicity is embarrassing, especially for someone as prominent as Jonathan King. My father is convinced that Simon is deliberately trying to cause problems."

Lee looked past Nick at the rectangle of sunlight between the curtains. "I'm afraid that if Simon is in trouble again and Father hears about it, there will be a breach between them that nothing will heal."

Maybe that's all there is to it, she thought. Another of Simon's escapades. Maybe she'd misunderstood that one-sided conversation she'd overheard that night. But if that was so, why had Simon become angry when she'd questioned him? He'd denied ever saying those words and had more or less told her to mind her own business. That had hurt. They'd been so close. She came back to the present as Nick spoke.

"I still don't see what all this has to do with me."

In spite of her efforts to control it, her voice shook as she said, "I want you to show me where you left Simon. I'm going to look for him myself."

Her heart sank when he shook his dark head. "Sorry. There's no way I'm taking you up there."

"But you took my brother!" The determination on his face dismayed her.

"Taking a man into those mountains to show him around is one thing. Taking a woman like you is something else entirely. You don't know that your brother is in trouble."

"I know my brother. This is one date he would have kept. He must be in some kind of trouble, and I'm going to help him. Unfortunately, I can't do it alone. Doesn't it matter to you that there's a man out there who may desperately need your help?"

Nick leaned back in his chair, his dark eyes warning her. "There are only two things that matter to me, Mrs. Coulton. One of them is this building you're sitting in."

"And the other?" She expected him to say "money," giving her the opening. Instead, he shocked her by dropping his voice to a seductive drawl.

"Something tells me you wouldn't be the least bit interested in the other."

She refused to give him the reaction he was looking for. She'd met men like him before; she'd even married one. She was an old hand at dealing with that attitude.

"Mr. Garrett." She was proud of her cool, disinterested tone. "How much did my brother pay you to take him to those mines?"

"What makes you think he paid me?"

"I'm quite sure that's the only reason you agreed to take him."

Nick lifted his wide shoulders in a careless gesture. "Your brother was in a generous mood. There's not a lot of profit in beer, and this place eats money."

Lee resisted the smile of satisfaction. "Just how generous was he?" She winced when Nick named a figure. Simon must have been drinking again, she thought. "I'll double it," she said firmly.

There was a long pause while Nick's dark blue eyes probed hers, and she had the uneasy feeling that he could see right into her mind. Through the closed door she could hear the muffled laughter competing with the heavy twang of guitars. She held her breath as Nick leaned forward.

"Lady," he said softly, "you've just made me an offer I can't refuse."

A shiver slid down her spine and shimmied all the way to her toes.

"There's one condition," Nick added before she could speak. "I go alone. I'll find out what I can, and I'll contact you as soon as I have anything definite. Give me a number where I can reach you."

"No!" Lee's face was a mask of determination. "I'm not sitting around this seedy town twiddling my thumbs, wondering what's going on. It's a package deal, Mr. Garrett."

Nick tapped on the pitted surface of his desk. "How much hiking in the mountains have you done?" he asked abruptly.

"None." Lee looked at him steadily. "That doesn't mean I can't do it."

She noticed a reluctant smile tugging at his mouth—a sensual mouth, Lee couldn't help but observe. A firm, full-lipped mouth, hardened by a trace of bitterness at the edges. She lifted her eyes hastily and was disturbed by the gleam in his.

"Maybe not," he agreed, "but it does mean that you have no idea what you're up against. This isn't a Boy Scout camping trip we're talking about. We can only go so far on wheels. The rest is on foot over some of the roughest territory in the Northwest. The trails are rugged, even dangerous in places. Frankly—" he swept his eyes over her "—you don't look the type to rough it."

"I'll manage." Again she felt the impact of his probing gaze.

"You got a sleeping bag?"

This time she couldn't hide her apprehension. "A sleeping bag?"

Nick sighed. "It's at least a day's hike to the mines. We'll have to spend at least one night on the mountain—more if we don't find your brother right away."

Lee's stomach lurched sickeningly. Why hadn't that occurred to her? She had assumed it would only take a couple of hours to reach the mines. She stared, wide-eyed, at Nick's face, which was now drawn into grim lines.

"That's not all," he added. "The mountains are a refuge for all kinds of people, and some of them don't take kindly to strangers."

Lee took hold of her galloping nerves. He was deliberately trying to frighten her. Well, he'd find out that Leanne Coulton didn't frighten easily.

"Then you can understand why I'm worried about Simon. I'll buy a sleeping bag in town this evening," she said.

In spite of himself, Nick felt a grudging admiration. She might look delicate, he mused, but there was nothing fragile about her mind.

He knew what he should do. He should tell her to forget it. To go hire a private detective to track down her wayward brother. Or, better yet, insist that she call in the law. He didn't believe for one minute that bit about family arguments. The lady was hiding something. All his instincts were screaming at him to leave it alone. So why was he sitting here considering it?

It wasn't just the money, though he couldn't deny it would come in handy, especially since the air-conditioning was showing signs of going on the blink. Still, it was more than just the money.

He'd taken a liking to Simon in the short time he'd known him. Simon reminded him of himself before he'd decided he was getting too old to tilt at windmills. Whatever had happened to the friendly, likeable photographer, he felt partly responsible. After all, he'd taken Simon up there.

He refused to listen to the tiny voice that insisted the woman sitting opposite him just might have something to do with his decision. So maybe she intrigued him. It had been a long time since anything had intrigued him. With a sense of misgiving, he defied his instincts.

"Don't worry about the sleeping bag," he heard himself saying. "I'll bring two. Just make sure you bring enough food and drink to last a couple of days or so. Supplies are hard to come by in the mountains." He tried not to notice the delighted relief in her eyes. Wide brown eyes, he thought. Eyes a man could get lost in. He stood up, pushing his chair back with a protesting screech.

"Bring some warm clothes," he ordered. "It's fairly warm up there this time of year, but the nights can get cold. Have you checked into a motel?"

Lee gave him the name of one of a few blocks away. "It's the same one Simon stayed in," she said. "He called me from there." She swallowed past the sudden lump in her throat. Something must have showed in her face, because she saw Nick's expression soften.

"If it's any consolation, I doubt that anything serious has happened to your brother. There are plenty of people roaming around up there. Someone would have heard if there'd been an accident, and word would have gotten back to town."

"I hope you're right." Lee was horrified to hear the tremble in her voice, and she cleared her throat. Now was not the time to break down. She stood up. "I'll write you a check as soon as we get back to town, if that suits you."

His mouth twisted. "Whatever you prefer. Which brings me to a point. Technically, I may be working for you, but I don't take orders well. From anyone. I make all the decisions. You do all the agreeing. Deal?"

"Deal." At least for the moment, Lee told herself. Right now she'd agree to anything as long as he accepted her proposal.

"Okay. I'll pick you up at eight-thirty tomorrow morning." Nick walked to the door. "With any luck, you could be talking to your brother tomorrow night."

"I hope so." Lee grimaced as he pulled the door open, letting in a blast of pounding music and smoke. She moved to pass him, but he stopped her, his hand on her arm.

"Where do you fit into the picture?" he asked loudly above the din.

Startled, she gave him a blank look.

"The hotels, Jonathan King—all that."

"Oh!" Lee gave a nervous little laugh. "I work for my father. I run the Royal King Hotel." When he didn't answer, she slipped through the door.

Nick frowned after her, all his misgivings rising to the surface. What the hell was he doing? He had to be crazy letting himself get talked into this setup. He was walking into a loaded situation, in more ways than one.

Why was the elegant Leanne Coulton going to such great lengths to keep Simon's disappearance a secret? Just where did she fit into all this? And, more to the point, why was he getting mixed up with someone who belonged to a life he'd put behind him forever?

Money. Everything about her shouted the word. Her clothes, her perfume, those diamonds flashing in her ears. It was people like her who had almost destroyed him. People like his mother, who had used her money to manipulate his life, and people like Laura, who had betrayed him for it.

He had decided long ago that if that was what wealth did to people, he would stay away from it and everything that could remind him of it. He hadn't been near a city since then but had buried himself in the backwoods where money was something you used in order to survive, not to destroy.

With a muttered oath, he strode out to the bar and flung an order at Dan. He'd made a deal, and he wouldn't back out. But that didn't mean he had to like it. He took the bourbon Dan placed in front of him and tossed it back in one long draft, wishing heartily that he'd never set eyes on Simon King.

Lee stepped out into the fading sunlight, thankful to be leaving the suffocating atmosphere of the tavern behind. She lifted her face, allowing the pine-scented breeze to cool her warm skin. In the distance the mountains rose against an apricot sky, their lower slopes shadowed by the blue-tinged carpet of ponderosa pine.

Simon was up there somewhere. Alive. She refused to think otherwise. She walked slowly toward the Lincoln parked beside the chipped sidewalk, her eyes scanning the long, narrow street.

A few hundred yards of decaying buildings comprised the entire business district of the town. Shored up in places by weathered beams, the buildings sent long shadows across the dusty street, poignant reminders of a century ago when Gambler's Gulch had been a thriving, bustling mining town.

Lee reached for the heavy car door and pulled it open. Once, long-skirted women had made homes in this neglected town for tough, determined men who had only one real love. Gold.

The white leather burned her skin through her clothes as she slid across the seat, and she rolled down the window, her eyes on the dark, stained walls of the tavern.

Whatever Nick Garrett might think, Simon would have made it for their mother's memorial if it had been humanly possible. Even gold wouldn't have prevented him. It was too important to him. To both of them.

She sighed as she fitted the key into the ignition. She hoped fervently that the tavern owner had been right and that she'd be talking to Simon tomorrow night. She had no desire to spend the night alone in the wilderness with that man Garrett. With a fluttering of nerves that had nothing to do with Simon, she pulled away from the curb.

Chapter 2

Nick was early the next morning, but to Lee, impatiently waiting for him, it seemed an eternity before his tall figure strode into the foyer, looking impressively virile in khaki shirt and pants. He inspected her with unabashed thoroughness, but she said nothing, aware of the scowl that darkened his hawklike face. If her guess was right, his second thoughts must have kept him awake half the night.

"Those sneakers are going to last about five minutes in the mountains," he said. "Don't you have any boots?"

"No. It's not a necessary item in a city wardrobe," she said dryly.

"I guess they'll have to do." Nick picked up her backpack from the floor.

This was going to be no picnic, she thought as she swept past him and stepped out into the morning sun.

Her spirits took a further plunge when she caught sight of the Jeep parked at the curb. It looked as if it had been in an argument with a bulldozer—and lost. Nick threw her pack into the back, and she scrambled into the front seat, hoping fervently that they didn't have far to go. They took off in a cloud of blue smoke and a series of jolts that had her clinging to the dash with both hands.

Was he being deliberately provoking? she wondered as they rattled at a brisk pace up the main street.

He caught her baleful glance and returned it with a smug look. "I'm sorry if you were expecting a Rolls-Royce."

"What I was expecting," she said, "was a responsible driver. Not some show-off." She was relieved to see that that had the effect of slowing him down.

The scenery claimed most of her attention for the next hour. They rose rapidly up a gravel road, winding through a dense forest of pines. Occasionally she caught a glimpse of the quiet green valley dropping away below, and the blue sparkle of a mountain lake. Twice she saw the decaying remains of ghost towns and would have asked Nick about them if not for his uncompromising expression.

He hadn't spoken to her since they'd left town. She saw that he certainly didn't intend to be sociable. But then, he hadn't pretended to be thrilled at the prospect of taking her with him. She wasn't exactly overjoyed herself. Now that she had time to think about it, she hadn't been too sensible.

She'd been a fool to set this up without telling anyone where she was going. Her father had been surprised when she'd told him she needed a short vacation, but he'd accepted her explanation of a sick friend in California.

Lee stole another glance at Nick Garrett's face. His mouth was compressed in a tight, hard line, the muscles in his jaw tense. His nose, she noticed, was on the large side, and slightly hooked. Not a handsome man, she thought, but there was a certain tough aggressiveness about him that a lot of women would find attractive.

What did she really know about this man, she wondered uneasily, except that Simon had hired him as a guide? She was charging off into the wilderness with a total stranger. In

an effort to prevent her imagination from running away with
her, she attempted to start a conversation.

"When you left Simon," she began, "did he mention
anything about his plans?"

His sideways glance was brief. "Not much. I spent a day
showing him the area, then left him at one of the mines.
When I left, he said something about finishing up his film,
but I don't know how long that was going to take him."

Lee's gaze wandered down over his shoulders. The rolled-
up sleeves of his shirt seemed to restrict the bulge of tanned
biceps, and below them, his forearms were sprinkled with
dark hair. He held the wheel with confidence, his hands
resting lightly on the spokes, and Lee looked away as a tin-
gle moved down her spine.

"Are the mines dangerous?" she asked.

He took his time answering. "If you want the truth, yes.
The timbers are rotting, and there's always the danger of a
cave-in. But I don't think that's what happened to Simon."

"Why not?"

"There were men working the mines. Word spreads
quickly up there. If there'd been a fall or some kind of accident, word would have gotten back to town, as I already
told you."

"You can't be sure of that."

"There's a way we can make sure." He swore suddenly as
a rabbit darted out from the trees and streaked across the
road in front of them. He braked sharply, and Lee held her
breath as the Jeep swerved violently on the gravel.

The movement swung her against Nick, her shoulder
bouncing off the hard muscles of his upper arm. She
straightened at once, disturbed by the contact. To her relief, the rabbit vanished into the forest, its tail flashing in the
sun.

"Damn fool thing," Nick muttered as he righted the ve-
hicle.

"You said there was a way to make sure," she prompted when they resumed their steady pace.

"We're going to pay a visit to a friend of mine."

"A friend?" He hadn't mentioned anything about a friend before, Lee thought nervously. It had taken all her courage to deal with one stranger; the last thing she wanted was to face another. If only she knew who she could trust.

Nick slowed the Jeep to a crawl when the road began to climb even more steeply.

"About a mile and a half," Nick said, noting her expression, "and we start walking."

"How far?" She couldn't quite keep the tremor out of her voice.

"Never measured it." Nick shot her a quick look. "Still want to go on?"

"I'm not in the habit of changing my mind once it's made up." She sat up a little straighter. "Tell me about your friend."

"He's a prospector. Got a campsite not too far from the mines. He knows everyone on the mountains, everything that goes on. If there's any news of your brother, Midge will know it."

Lee digested his words in silence. Would this Midge know if Simon was into something illegal? She could simply be overreacting, she admitted. Simon's end of the telephone conversation had been brief. *Keep the law off my back.* Why would he say that if it was a simple photo assignment? Why would he deny it afterward? Most important of all, why hadn't he shown up for the anniversary? Something had happened to him; that much was certain. She hated the thought that there was enough doubt in her mind to propel her into this crazy situation.

One thing was clear. There was no way she was going to lead the law to him, at least until she knew what was going on. And she wouldn't voice her suspicions to Nick; she was quite sure that if he knew what was on her mind, he'd insist on calling in the authorities.

She was jolted back to the present when the Jeep pulled off the road into a large clearing and slid to a stop in a cloud of dust. Nearby, several vehicles were parked in the shade of the trees. She turned to say something but was stopped by the grim expression on Nick's face as he stared straight ahead.

"What is it?" Her voice echoed her anxiety.

"I hate to rain on your parade, but it looks as if you were wrong about your brother."

"What do you mean?" She followed his gaze but could see nothing except for the half-dozen pickups and cars in front of them. "I can't see anything."

"That's exactly what I mean. Simon's car. A blue Chevy? Banged up on one side?"

"Yes." She gulped as it dawned on her what he was getting at. "You mean it was parked here?"

"It isn't anymore. Looks as if he went back to town after all."

"No." Lee pushed down the panic that threatened to overwhelm her. "I tell you, if Simon had left the mountain, he would have called me at least. If the car is gone, someone must have stolen it."

His dark gaze rested on her face. "Stubborn, aren't you? I guess you're telling me you want to go on looking for him up here."

"I was under the impression that that's what I'm paying you for." She saw that she'd gotten to him.

His eyes darkened, and a muscle moved in his jaw. "Don't worry. You'll get your money's worth." He shoved the door open on his side and jumped out. "I just hope you know what you're getting into."

So do I, thought Lee grimly as she climbed out of the Jeep. Her uneasiness grew as she caught sight of the trail ahead. It climbed steeply, twisting through the lofty pines that shouldered for room on either side. Thick shrubs and clumps of coarse grass bordered it, and here and there a gray boulder poked through the earth, moss clinging to its smooth sides.

Lee pulled in a deep breath, filling her lungs with the moist, earthy fragrance of the forest with all the appreciation of someone more used to inhaling traffic fumes.

"You'll have to carry your own sleeping bag," Nick told her, his voice coming from the rear of the Jeep where he was hauling out the backpacks. "I'll strap it to your pack."

"Thanks." Lee walked around the hood to join him. He was bending over her backpack, fiddling with the straps.

"I take it you brought food with you," he muttered. "Or did you stuff this thing full of clothes?" He stood, his expression disapproving, as his gaze skimmed over her designer jeans and blue oversized shirt.

Even in that outfit, he thought irritably, she managed to look elegant. She was still wearing the diamonds, for crying out loud. What the hell was he doing? He had to be crazy. It was bad enough that he had to drag a woman all over the mountains, but taking one who was so obviously out of her element was asking for trouble, not to mention the fact that she was a constant reminder of someone he'd rather forget.

He hoisted his pack onto his shoulders. If Simon King was up there somewhere, having himself a ball, he'd personally wring the man's neck.

"I brought something of everything," Lee said, recalling her frantic shopping trip of the night before and the odd assortment of supplies she'd packed.

Nick grunted and lifted her pack.

It looked enormous to her with the bedroll strapped to it. She managed to keep her face neutral as Nick helped her slide the straps over her shoulders. It weighed a ton. How was she going to haul this thing up a mountain? Gritting her teeth, she gave Nick a good imitation of a smile.

"Lead on, pardner. If the pioneers could manage it, I'm sure I can."

Nick's sarcastic snort brought a flush to her cheeks. "You have about as much in common with the pioneers as a debutante with skid row bums."

As he moved away from her, Lee wondered who had done such a good job of putting a chip on his shoulder. She'd bet it had been a woman, though it was hard for her to imagine any woman getting the better of Nick Garrett. A smile played across her mouth as she followed Nick's tall, striding figure toward the trail. Maybe he wasn't as tough as he liked to make out.

In spite of the cool breezes that ruffled Lee's hair, after an hour of trudging along the rocky trail, her clothes were clinging to her damp skin. Perspiration beaded the bridge of her nose and prickled on her forehead, and her legs were solid columns of pain. What rankled even more was Nick's apparent oblivion to their strenuous exertions. He'd tolerated her frequent rests only with ill-concealed impatience.

Lee had always considered herself to be fit. Her aerobic sessions, combined with a game of racquetball twice a week, kept her in good shape. It galled her to be sweating and struggling for breath, heart pounding and knees reverting to babyhood, while the unsympathetic monster up ahead bounded along like an overgrown puppy. No, that wasn't it, she amended. He was more like a racehorse: powerful, athletic and incredibly smooth. He made her feel like a penguin on dry land.

She looked up and saw him waiting for her at the top of a sharp incline, and longed to wipe the smug look off his face.

He held out his hand as she staggered up the last few feet. She would have loved to ignore it but knew that would have been childish, so she let him grasp her hand with his strong fingers. She clenched her jaw as he hauled her up, then forgot her resentment as she looked down on the panorama before her.

They'd broken out of the trees and were on a wide ledge that jutted out from the side of the mountain. The valley plunged below them, cool and green, dotted with yellow wheat fields and blue ribbons of water. Beyond, smoky blue ridges of mountains dozed beneath the late-summer haze.

Small figures dotted the bank along one of the larger streams, and Lee squinted, trying to see more clearly.

"What are they doing down there?" she asked, pointing to the miniature people.

"Panning."

"For gold?"

"Well, they're not panning for trout." He examined her with a critical eye. "You all right?"

"Fine," she said, but it didn't come out quite the way she'd intended.

Nick frowned. "If you can hang on a little longer, we'll break for lunch. There's a stream up ahead where you can stand your drink to cool it. I take it you brought something."

"Yes."

"Fine. If you get too tired, yell."

I'd die first, Lee mouthed silently at his back. Even so, she was glad when Nick called a halt. She'd heard the stream for the past several minutes, which had aggravated her thirst. Now she could actually see it, tumbling noisily over huge boulders and rushing alongside a meadow bordered with tall dark firs. She sank to her knees in the spiky grass, relishing the shade of the lacy branches.

"I have to hand it to you, Nick. You sure know how to pick a restaurant." She grinned at him and was intrigued by the odd look on his face.

"Glad you approve."

For an instant the expression in his eyes warmed her, but then it was gone, leaving her to wonder whether she'd imagined it. She slipped the pack off and eased her shoulders up and down, convinced she'd have permanent scars from the straps. She watched as Nick swung his pack easily to the ground and then knelt beside it to untie the pockets.

"If you give me what you brought to drink," he said, "I'll stand it in the stream." He pulled a can of beer from his pack and stood.

Lee rummaged around until she found the packets of fruit punch. She handed a box to Nick, who looked at it with a grimace before walking away in the direction of the stream. At least it wouldn't give her a beer belly, she thought in response.

The punch tasted delicious and was almost worth the long wait, Lee decided as she drank thirstily some time later. She'd already polished off most of her chicken legs and was looking forward to the cheese croissants she'd bought the night before.

"It's so beautiful up here," she remarked as she looked for them in her pack. "Clear blue sky, warm sun, cool breezes and fresh mountain water. What more could you ask for?"

"Don't let it fool you." Nick finished off his thick beef sandwich and reached for his beer. "The mountains are like beautiful women—great to look at but treacherous. They'll turn on you without any warning."

She looked up to find his eyes challenging her as he lifted the can to his lips. She refused to let him spoil her enjoyment.

"I can't imagine this place being anything other than perfect."

"Wait till it rains. You can get lost in a storm up here, especially when you can't see a foot in front of you."

"I didn't think it rained much in eastern Oregon."

"It doesn't in the valley. It rains at least a third of the year in the mountains, though." Nick crushed the can in his hand until it was flat, then poked it in the side pocket of his pack.

"It rains twice as much as that in Portland," Lee said, wondering if that little display of strength was for her benefit.

"Must be as depressing as hell."

"Not at all. There are a lot of compensations. Portland is a wonderful city to live in."

"If you like cities."

"And you don't, do you?" She jerked her pack closer toward her. "You don't like women, you don't like cities, and you don't like the rain." She stopped, annoyed with herself for letting him get to her.

"I never said I didn't like rain." He was laughing at her, his eyes crinkling at the corners, and her exasperation melted.

The sudden stillness between them was almost tangible, a gossamer net of unspoken communication that made her breathless. A squirrel chattered in a burst of noise somewhere nearby, and in the distance a jay wheeled above the forest, its harsh shriek echoing off the mountain.

Flustered, Lee dropped her gaze and took out a white square box from the pack. Placing it on her lap with intense concentration, she opened it and lifted out one of the pastries, which she bit into without tasting the creamy sweetness. When she could look up again, she saw that Nick was engrossed in peeling an orange. His fingers fascinated her; they didn't seem to go with the rest of him. Long and slender, they were better suited to a concert pianist than the rugged tavern owner.

She watched him work expertly at the orange, removing the peel in one, long continuous piece. She couldn't seem to look away, and when she did, back to his face, it was to find his eyes on her, dark and enigmatic. She felt the blush spread up from her neck.

Damn the man! And damn herself for being so susceptible. She jammed the croissant into her mouth, scattering crumbs across her lap. She was surprised when he spoke, his tone mildly conversational.

"How old were you and Simon when your mother died?"

"Twelve," she replied, barely noticing the familiar twinge of pain in her voice.

"It must have been hard on you both." His expression was sympathetic, and she relaxed.

"It was. Especially for Simon. Father buried himself in the business, and I dealt with my grief by concentrating all my energies on the house. We had a housekeeper, of course, but I wanted to continue all the family traditions, to keep things the way they'd always been as much as possible."

He watched as Lee flicked a crumb from her lap, her face pensive, then said, "I decorated the house for all the holidays, even Valentine's Day and Easter, and I hung seed bells on the trees in the backyard for the birds at Christmas." Her smile warmed her face, he thought.

"Simon and I made a pact on the first anniversary of our mother's death that we would spend that day together, no matter what, as long as we lived."

Her voice broke, and she cleared her throat. "Anyway," she went on, "except for the holidays, I didn't have much time to spend with Simon, and neither of us saw Father more than a few minutes at mealtimes, if then. Simon felt left out, I guess. He got a little wild. Nothing serious—playing hookey, joy-riding in cars, all schoolboy stuff—but it was worrying. He's always been a bit headstrong."

She frowned, staring down at the remains of the croissant, which had crumbled in her hand. Headstrong enough to get into something he couldn't handle this time? she wondered. It was hard to believe, yet she couldn't deny the doubts were there.

"When Simon finally graduated from high school," she said, "Father told him he was expected to join the family business. There was an awful argument. Father should have known that Simon would be miserable, cooped up in one place. The only thing that interested him was his camera, and he insisted on taking off and doing his own thing. Father was terribly disappointed, but then I suggested that he let me try. He wasn't too excited about it at first, but now he says it was the best idea he ever had.''

She flashed Nick a grin and filled her mouth with her croissant crumbs.

"How do you like managing the hotel?" Nick asked, shaking his head as she picked up another croissant, which promptly disintegrated in her hand.

"I love it. It's hard work, and sometimes frustrating, but I meet a lot of interesting people. I enjoy the challenge. I get a lot of satisfaction out of organizing a convention, or a ball, or maybe just a simple club lunch, and seeing it all come out the way I planned. It's the people, though, that make it exciting. You never know who's going to walk through that door.''

"Is that where you met your husband?"

Lee paused in the act of popping a piece of pastry in her mouth. "Yes. Steven's a computer consultant. He was living in Seattle and often came to Portland on business trips. He moved down permanently when we got married.''

"What happened?"

She felt she should have resented the question, but oddly she didn't. "I was busy at the hotel, and Steven was always traveling. I guess we weren't together enough to make it work.'' It was a laundered version of the months of arguments, suspicions and accusations, but it was all she was prepared to tell him. She stuffed the remains of the croissant into her mouth and finished by delicately licking her fingers one by one.

Nick watched her, conscious of a tight feeling low in his stomach. "What are you trying to eat?" he said abruptly.

Lee gazed down at the mess of crumbs in her lap. "Croissants. They got a bit crushed. They're not usually so crumbly.''

"Croissants!" His tone mocked her as he looked at her. Her eyes were wide velvet orbs beneath the arched brows. The sun glinted off the diamonds in her ears, and he felt something soft squeeze his heart. "All dressed up in diamonds and eating croissants. Is this your idea of camping out?"

"The earrings belonged to my mother," Lee said defensively. "I always wear them when I need an extra boost of luck."

Her chin came up in a gesture that he was beginning to know well. "And what's wrong with croissants?"

Her lips were dusted with crumbs, and on an impulse Nick leaned forward and gently brushed them off with his thumb. Her eyes were huge above his hand, and he read something in them that stirred his blood. He dropped his hand as if he'd touched poison ivy.

"If you're finished," he said brusquely, "we'd better get moving." Without waiting for her answer, he scrambled to his feet and strode back to the stream.

Lee brushed the crumbs from her lap with trembling fingers. Her mind reeled from the sensual gesture. His touch had been feather light but had seared her lips. He'd made it clear that he resented her, yet twice she'd felt the magnetism between them like an invisible, vibrant thread. She sighed, gathered up the remains of her meal and stuffed the trash into her pack.

She had no idea why she should be attracted to Nick Garrett. He was nothing like the men she normally dated. He was so different from Steven. She smiled, trying to visualize Nick's powerful build squeezed into the neat, gray, pin-striped suits that Steven had a fondness for.

It was hard to imagine Nick striding into a corporate boardroom or closeted in a stuffy office. Even the smoky confinement of the tavern seemed wrong for him. This was where he belonged, she thought, in the freedom of the mountains and the open sky. She gave herself an impatient shake. She was getting fanciful. She'd better cut it out, she told herself, before she made an idiot of herself.

She heard Nick's footsteps and jumped up, her breath catching as he came toward her. He'd washed in the stream; water still clung to the dark ringlets of hair plastered to his forehead. His shirt was unbuttoned, and Lee's gaze slid away from the sight of dark chest hair reaching clear down to his navel. She stooped for her pack, wincing as the straps bit into her shoulders again. At least the pain would give her something else to think about, she thought wryly as they moved back onto the trail.

The sun had begun a rapid descent before Nick halted again. Although they didn't gain much altitude, the trail worked its way around the mountain, dipping and rising with unexpected twists and turns, and Lee could feel her muscles cramping with pain. Her legs no longer seemed to belong to her. Her shoulders cried out for release from the chafing straps, and she was fast losing her enchantment with the scenery.

She wasn't even able to manage any enthusiasm when Nick pointed out an abandoned mine, a skeletal structure of sun-bleached timbers leaning drunkenly against the ugly black hole in the wall of the mountain.

Why her brother had wanted to photograph anything so depressing was beyond her, she thought. The niggling reminder that something else could have brought him here was firmly suppressed. She wouldn't let herself dwell on vague possibilities. Soon they'd find Simon, and he'd have a perfectly good explanation for everything. She had to go on believing that.

She was almost in tears from exhaustion when Nick stopped in front of her.

"How you doing?" His expression changed when she tried to tell him she was fine but her voice croaked on the words.

"Here. Sit down." He hauled the pack off her shoulders, and she tried not to grimace as pain burned into her flesh. She dropped wearily onto a boulder at the edge of the trail and attempted a smile.

"Are we nearly there?"

"Just a few hundred yards. You'd better take a breather. You look a little frayed at the edges."

"I imagine that's a vast understatement." Lee touched her hair, groaning as she felt the spiky tangles. She reached for her pack, but Nick was there before her.

He found her packets of punch and pushed a straw through one of them before handing it to her.

She took it with a murmured word of thanks and drank it down, wiping her mouth with the back of her hand when she was finished.

Nick grinned. "You're learning."

"I am indeed," said Lee dryly. She pulled her pack toward her and started rummaging through it.

"What are you looking for?" Nick stuck his hands in the pockets of his pants and stood watching her with a quizzical expression.

"My comb," she replied. "That's if I brought the darn thing," she muttered under her breath as she pulled various packages out of the pack.

"Why don't you use mine?"

Lee looked up to see him holding out a small black comb. She found it extremely difficult not to ogle his flat, bare stomach. Wishing fervently that he'd button his shirt, she dragged the comb through her hair, dislodging several strands by their roots in the process.

Her feet felt like clay, and she seriously doubted they would carry her another step. Never again would she complain after an aerobics session.

She handed the comb back to Nick and watched him run it through his dark hair. Apart from the faint shadow on his jaw, he looked no different than he had that morning.

"How do you do it?" Lee asked in disgust.

"Do what?"

"Look so damn vigorous. You look like you've been out for an afternoon stroll."

"I'm used to it."

Amusement gleamed in his eyes as Lee frowned at him.

"You must come up here a lot."

"Not as much as I'd like. The tavern keeps me busy." He'd dropped his pack to the ground and was digging out a can of beer. "I spent almost five years up here. I guess you never lose the knack, or the stamina." He moved over to a boulder a few feet from Lee and sat down on it, stretching his long legs in front of him.

"Five years?" Lee said in amazement. "You lived up here?"

"Yep. Prospecting. I owned a mine up here. I got to know the area pretty well."

"I imagine you did." Lee studied him with interest. "Did you find any gold?"

"Enough to keep looking." He lifted the can and drained it in a series of long gulps.

"What made you give it up?" she asked, shuddering as she imagined the warm beer sliding down his throat.

He lowered the can and looked at her. "The Blue Bucket."

"But why a tavern?"

"My camel came first."

Lee stared at him in confusion. "Your what?"

"Camel." He drew a line in the dust with the heel of his boot. "It was a side bet on a camel race in Reno. I won."

"You *won* the Blue Bucket?"

She sounded incredulous, and he nodded, amused by her expression.

"Lock, stock and barrels."

"That's crazy! Who would bet a business on a camel race?"

"Someone who thought I had a pot of gold and was figuring on taking it from me." He shrugged. "It wasn't that good a deal. The Bucket was beat-up and loaded down with debts. It took everything I had, plus a lot of sheer muscle, to pull her out of it."

Lee couldn't stop the smile of admiration spreading over her face. "You're quite an enigma, Nick Garrett."

His eyes held hers, dark and challenging. "So are you, Mrs. Coulton," he said softly.

Her immediate response, strong and compelling, shook her, then he was standing, and the spell was broken. She watched him swing his pack onto his broad back with no apparent effort, then he bent to take hold of hers.

"I'll take this for now," he said briskly. "It's not far to the camp." Before she could thank him, he spoke again. "By the way, I'd better warn you about Midge and his men. They'll probably seem a little rough to you. They're not exactly members of the social register."

Lee flushed. Was he trying to get to her again, or was she being oversensitive?

"I'll try not to let it ruin my day," she said with more than a trace of sarcasm.

His mouth tightened. "Not that I'm apologizing for them. I'd trust them with my life. They're good people."

Meaning I'm not? Lee wondered, trying to ignore the resentment nagging at her. What was it with Nick Garrett that he seemed to regret even the slightest softening in his attitude toward her? Whatever pain he'd been dealt, it had gone deep. She followed his striding figure, full of burning curiosity about Nick's past and more than a little apprehensive about meeting Midge and his "rough" friends.

Chapter 3

The aroma of woodsmoke and barbecued meat tormented Lee when they finally reached their destination. The camp was laid out on a small plateau, she saw, bordered by the stream that plunged by on its way to the valley.

Tents huddled in a haphazard pattern, most of them weather-bleached and worn. A group of men stood by an enormous grill, chatting idly, while two poorly dressed women tended the hamburgers spread across it.

Nearby lay a pile of dirt bikes, and a small dog, its coat matted with mud, stood over the heap, barking furiously. Lee saw the men turn as she and Nick drew near. Their eyes flicked over Nick and lingered with appreciation on her. Neither woman at the grill gave any sign of noticing their entrance.

Lee watched with rising apprehension as a man stepped from the group, a rifle tucked under his arm. A red bandana held his long, stringy hair back from his unshaven face. His hold on the rifle was casual, but the barrel was pointed in her direction, and Lee tightened her fingers on the straps of her pack.

The man walked toward them, and although Nick called out a friendly greeting, it didn't do a lot to reassure her.

The man's foxlike face nodded in answer. ''Hi there, Nick.''

Nick was about to speak again when he was interrupted by a roar from the direction of the stream.

Lee turned her head, her skin prickling as she saw another man lumbering toward her. He roared again, and she knew in that moment how David must have felt facing the mighty Goliath.

He was built like a battleship. Dressed in a plaid shirt and jeans, he lumbered forward on thick tree trunk legs, his face half hidden by the wide-brimmed hat pulled low over his eyes. The rest of his face was covered by a frizzy bush of gingery beard that reached his chest.

''Yo, Nick!'' he thundered as he approached. ''Twice in one month? You must be getting sick of town living.''

''Don't kid yourself, you ugly tub of lard.'' Nick dropped both packs to the ground and grinned at the huge man, who grabbed Nick's hand and pumped it with undisguised enthusiasm. Letting it go, he turned to Lee, his pale gray eyes sliding over her body with a boldness that angered and revolted her.

''This your woman?'' he roared, and the women at the grill twisted their heads in Lee's direction.

Eyes sparking with embarrassment and temper, Lee was about to make a hot denial when Nick took hold of her arm and pulled her forward.

''Lee, meet Midge. Short for Midget. No one knows his real name.''

Nick's grip on her arm bit painfully, and Lee looked up to protest. His expression stopped her. He moved his head in faint warning, and she stared at him in bewilderment. What was he trying to tell her?

"This is Leanne Coulton, Midge," he said, still looking at her.

"Well, I'm mighty pleased to meet you, miss," Midge rumbled.

Lee looked with distaste at the large hand stretched toward her.

"Midge," Nick cut in hurriedly, "you remember that photographer I brought through here a couple of weeks back? The guy with the blond beard?"

"The greenhorn? Sure. You said something about taking him up to the mines."

To Lee's relief, Midge had turned his pale eyes back to Nick.

"Right. He should've been back in town a week ago, but no one's seen him."

Nick let go of Lee's arm, and she rubbed it, sending him a reproachful look.

"I figured if there'd been an accident," Nick said, "you would've heard about it."

The big man shook his head. "Ain't heard nothing. You sure he ain't back in town? I thought he went back down a few days ago. Seems to me somebody told me he left the mines."

"Who told you?" Lee said sharply. She felt her skin crawl as his colorless eyes fastened on her again.

"Well, now, I don't rightly remember, Miss Coulton." He lowered his gaze to her breasts, where it remained. There was something about his expression beneath that tangled mess of beard that chilled her blood.

"I wouldn't worry none about your brother, ma'am," he added. "He's probably back in town getting drunk somewheres." He paused. "You a widow woman or divorced?"

"That's none of your business," Lee snapped. Where did this big ape get off asking her a question like that?

"Whoa!" As he spoke, the red beard parted, revealing uneven and heavily stained teeth. "We got ourselves a spitfire here. I like a woman with spirit—makes it more interesting."

Again his eyes crept over her, and Lee clenched her fingers.

"How about you and the little lady spending the night here?" He was talking to Nick, but his eyes never left Lee. "We got a delivery today—fresh meat and beer. Plenty for both of you. You won't get off the mountain before dark, anyways."

"We're not going back," Lee said. "We're going to look for Simon."

The pale eyes glinted at her with sudden alertness. "Take my tip, little lady." The hearty voice dropped to a mutter. "This ain't no place for someone like you. The mountain's dangerous to people who don't know how to handle her. You'd do better to get back to town where you belong."

Lee watched with loathing as the tip of his tongue protruded far enough to slide over his bottom lip.

"How about it, Nick?" Midge said without shifting his gaze. "I'd sure enjoy your company."

Lee looked imploringly at Nick, who'd been watching the exchange with an odd expression on his face.

"Sorry, Midge, old buddy." Nick laid an arm across Lee's shoulders. "I've got plans for tonight. Big plans. Private plans, if you get my meaning."

There was a short silence while Lee glared at Nick, pulling away from his grasp, then Midge's laugh rang out, shaking his enormous body.

"Well, why didn't you say so, m'boy?" he bellowed. "I might have known a hot-blooded son of a gun like you wouldn't pass up a chance like that. Go to it, pal, and more power to you." His eyes slid back to Lee's outraged face, and once more his laugh rolled into the ravine. "You're a lucky guy, Nick," he said, still chuckling. "This one's gonna be fun to tame."

"Now, just you wait a damn minute—" Lee began, and was interrupted by Nick.

"We'd better be on our way, Lee," he said loudly. "Midge, if you should hear anything about Simon King, I'd appreciate it if you'd get word to the tavern. I'll be checking back there tomorrow."

Not without Simon, Lee vowed silently. She knew there was no point in saying anything now, since Nick was determined to shut her up. But once they were out of earshot she was going to set Mr. Nick Garrett straight—on a couple of things.

Seething with fury, she kept her mouth shut as goodbyes were said. She allowed Nick to lift her pack onto her shoulders and managed to suppress a cry of pain. She even ignored, with a stoical expression, Midge's offer to fill in if Nick's performance failed to come up to scratch.

Just wait, she promised herself. Once she got him alone, she'd let him have it. With both barrels. That thought gave her the strength to stalk across the coarse grass to the trail, even if her back was bowed beneath the weight of her pack.

She said nothing as Nick caught up with her, gave her a quick glance, then strode ahead of her to lead the way again. As if she were one of those Eastern women who have to remain five paces behind their men, she thought, furious.

When they'd put some distance and a fair amount of solid rock between them and the camp, she stopped walking and dragged the pack off her shoulders.

"Wait a minute!" Her voice rang out with cold authority, bouncing off the rocks and echoing into the valley.

Nick slowed his steady pace, but he didn't stop.

"I said hold it!" she yelled. Her stomach lurched as Nick came to a halt and slowly turned. Even from that distance she could see his irritated scowl.

"Come back here," she commanded through gritted teeth.

"If you've got something to say to me, Ms. Coulton, then you come here and say it."

She should have been warned by the lethal softness of his voice, but she was far too angry to care.

"You bet I've got something to say to you." Breathing fire, she marched forward until she was close enough to see the pupils of his eyes.

"What in the hell," she said angrily, "were you doing giving that barbarian the idea that we had something going on? How can you have the nerve to even suggest I'd be interested in you?"

She clenched her fists as she trust her jaw forward. "You get this, Garrett. I'm not some floozy that hangs around that hovel you call a tavern."

She saw his mouth thin to a dangerous line, but she was on a roll and wasn't ready to let up.

"Let me assure you," she said with all the contempt she could muster, "even if I *were* that kind of woman, I wouldn't let you touch me if my life depended on it."

She paused for breath, then stepped back as Nick leaned toward her, a ferocious frown on his face.

"If you're finished," he said, pronouncing each word with deliberate care, "I'll tell you why I did it."

"I'm waiting with bated breath," Lee said nastily. She could almost hear his teeth grinding.

"I was doing you a favor." He was obviously making an effort to stay calm. "If I hadn't given Midge the idea that we were involved—to use a delicate term—he would have made a move on you, and I wouldn't have been able to do much about it. He was itching to get his hands on you."

"Well, Mr. Busybody," Lee retorted, "in the future, you can mind your own business. I don't need your protection. I'm perfectly capable of taking care of myself." She caught her breath when she saw his expression change.

"Is that so?" he said softly. "Well, let's find out for sure."

Lee's heart began to thump heavily as he drew first one arm and then the other out of the straps of his pack. With his eyes riveted on her face, he lowered the pack to the ground.

Lee backed away. "What are you doing? Garrett, I warn you..." She gasped as he grabbed her arms and hauled her against the hard wall of his body.

She struggled to get free, but his arms held her locked against him. She jerked violently when the solid muscles of his thigh collided with her hip. She lifted her knee, but he was ready for her and sidestepped it neatly, twisting so that his body imprisoned hers against the side of the mountain.

Her hands, trapped in his, were crushed between her breasts and his chest. Humiliated, she knew she was powerless to move.

He murmured into her ear, "You were saying?"

The smug amusement in his voice goaded her into heaving against him. He answered with a slight movement of his hips that sent heat surging throughout her body, shocking her.

She became intensely aware of his knuckles, which were pressing into the soft flesh of her breasts, and of his strong legs, which pinned hers to the wall.

"All right, damn you," she muttered, "you made your point. Now let me go."

"Have I?" His voice sounded husky, and she looked up, then wished she hadn't. He was staring down at her and no longer looked amused.

She drew in a shaky breath, and found that he smelled of the outdoors, an exciting, intoxicating male scent. His eyes, the color of the night sky, held her mesmerized. She felt her body responding to his touch and despised herself for her weakness.

He must know what she was feeling, she realized with embarrassment. He must be aware of her breasts, the nipples hardening against the back of his hands.

Her pulse leaped as he dropped his gaze to her mouth, and he brought his head down, until his mouth hovered just above hers. She no longer felt any desire to fight him. Every pulse in her body echoed the pounding of her heart, and she went limp, her eyes closing with the unbearable tension of waiting for his lips to touch hers.

"You're not a very good liar, Ms. Coulton."

His warm breath fanned her face, and it was a moment before the shock of his whispered words penetrated. Her eyelids flew open. Even in the fast-fading light she could see the amusement in his face. She was sorely tempted to hit him.

He let her go and stepped back. "Before you go ranting off again," he said mildly, "think how easy it would have been for me. Then think how easy it would have been for Midge."

"That would have been rape," Lee said in a trembling voice. "There are laws to protect women, you know." She was having a great deal of trouble controlling her emotions. She was still shaking from the force of her reaction to Nick's body on hers, and hated herself for it.

"Laws don't count for much up here," Nick said. "These mountain men live by a different code. They take what they want, whenever they want it."

"Well, he wouldn't get away with it with me." Lee brushed the dust from her jeans. "I'd report him so fast he wouldn't have time to blink."

"Wouldn't do you any good," Nick said cheerfully. "The sheriff has enough trouble keeping the valley in line."

"I can't believe that."

"That's mountain law."

He was laughing at her again, and her temper got the better of her. "Well, you should know. You're one of them. You're no better than that bloated hillbilly back there." She had gone too far. She saw it in his eyes and took a step backward.

"That bloated hillbilly," Nick said in a dangerously controlled voice, "once saved my life." He lifted his pack. "Just keep this in mind, lady." His voice sliced through her with icy disdain. "You're not in your nice, cozy, rich world now, where everyone caters to your whim." He turned his back on her. "Now, get a move on. We've got to find somewhere to bed down before it gets too dark, and we're wasting time standing here arguing."

"Bed down?" Lee stared at him in dismay. "But I thought—I mean—I want to go to the mines tonight."

"We're not going anywhere tonight," Nick said over his shoulder.

"But what if Simon's there? We could find him tonight and then—" She broke off, and he turned sharply.

"And you wouldn't have to be alone with me," he finished for her. His eyes looked almost black, and his mouth was set in a forbidding line.

"Look, lady, that little demonstration back there was to prove a point. I wanted you to understand what you're up against out here in the wilderness. You don't have to worry about me." He moved his gaze over her, much as Midge had, but with the opposite effect.

"If it makes you feel any safer," he drawled, "you were right about one thing. You're definitely not my type."

Angry tears pricked at Lee's eyes as she trudged back to where her pack lay. What riled her the most was that he was justified. Her remark, degrading him to Midge's level, had been spiteful as well as inaccurate.

He might have spent a few years bumming around the mountains, but she had to recognize the fact that Nick Garrett was well educated. His manners, his speech, his whole bearing, not to mention the type of books she'd seen in his office, pointed to a man used to a different style of living.

What had brought a man like him to this primitive, untamed territory of the mountains? she wondered. She dragged her feet along the trail, her mind on the peculiarities of the man striding ahead of her.

He confused her, overwhelmed her at times, and infuriated her far too often. Her biggest cause of discomfort, though—and it was one she couldn't erase—was the realization that she'd wanted him to kiss her, desperately, and he'd known it.

The orange sky had paled into thin ribbons of light by the time Nick stopped once more. Sheer exhaustion was taking its toll on Lee, and she felt like a zombie, moving automatically without any real sense of feeling.

She barely acknowledged Nick's inquiry about her state of health. As he lifted the pack off her shoulders, she stood meekly, then sank to the ground, groaning as she stretched her aching legs.

Part of her mind registered her surroundings. A small clearing circled by bushy firs and tall, straggly pines enclosed them in a secluded refuge. Several feet away stood a broken-down shack, part of its roof missing and one wall leaning crazily inward. Lee watched with heavy eyelids as Nick piled twigs and small branches into the rough stone fireplace that stood in front of it, then set them alight.

She was vaguely aware of his voice as he explained that the shack had once been a prison and the fireplace had been built by the pioneers. But the last thing she remembered before she closed her eyes was Nick's face, set aglow by the crackling flames, his eyes dark and brooding.

She awoke when she felt his hand on her arm. Her first conscious thought was to find the source of the most delicious aroma that was wafting past her. Nick knelt beside her. In his hand an aluminum plate was filled with something dark and lumpy that smelled like heaven.

"What is it?" she said, struggling to sit up.

"Stew. Eat it. It'll make you feel better."

Giving him a quick smile, she took it from him and tried a mouthful with the spoon he'd given her. He was right; it tasted marvelous, and she did feel a lot better.

"How did you manage this?" she asked between mouthfuls.

His half grin improved her spirits even more than the food had.

"It wasn't that difficult. It's canned. I only had to heat it up."

Lee spooned some more into her mouth and sighed. "I never realized canned stew could taste so good."

"Hasn't anyone ever told you, Ms. Coulton, that everything tastes better when it's eaten outdoors?"

Lee looked at him across the flames. He sat cross-legged, his plate balanced on his knee. The firelight threw his face in shadow, silhouetting his hair, which tumbled over his forehead in untamed curls. He looked like part of the forest, a mysterious, unpredictable being, and just a little dangerous. Yet, beneath it all, there was a man who she suspected had once known sophistication.

She wondered if there was a wife somewhere in the picture. He'd never mentioned one, but it was hard to believe a man like him hadn't been—or still was—married.

"I wish you'd call me Lee," she said, sending him a tentative smile.

"I didn't think you'd want me to be that familiar."

She sighed. "All right, I guess I asked for that. I'm sorry for what I said back there. If we're going to be in each other's company for a while, we should at least try to get along. Truce?"

Her stomach muscles tightened when his eyes met hers across the fire.

"It's a deal. Want some more stew?"

"Yes, please." She moved over to him, wincing as her muscles protested violently.

"It's going to hurt even more in the morning, but it'll gradually wear off."

Did he ever miss anything? Lee wondered as she watched him fill her plate from the battered saucepan that was balanced on the rocks. When she returned to her seat, she was surprised to see how dark the forest had become. She could barely make out the outline of the trees.

"How long was I asleep?" she asked as she placed her plate on the ground and reached for her pack.

"About an hour." He sounded amused, she thought. "You were out like a light. You seem to be adapting to this life pretty well."

Lee laughed. "The way I felt, I could have gone to sleep on a barbed wire fence." She looked up. "Would you like some wine?"

"Wine?" His astonishment made her smile. "You brought wine?"

"Just a little."

Nick groaned. "Don't tell me. Beaujolais, '78."

"Sorry. California jug, '86." Lee held two small bottles in the air. "I found some sample bottles. I thought we might celebrate when we found Simon, but . . ." Her voice trailed off into a bleak silence.

Nick put his plate down. "Don't worry. If he'd had an accident, Midge would have known it for sure. Unless there's something else you're worried about."

She was almost tempted to tell him. If she could only be sure he wouldn't go rushing back for the sheriff. It would be a relief to talk about it, maybe have him reassure her that she could have misunderstood the whole thing— No, not until she was sure Simon wasn't involved in anything criminal.

"Isn't the fact that he's missing enough?" she said lightly. He gave her a hard look that made her heart beat a little too fast. Then he took the bottle from her and twisted off the cap.

"Maybe he's not missing," he suggested. "Tomorrow morning we'll reach the mine where I left him. Simon will probably still be there, happily taking pictures and swearing he didn't know where the time had gone."

She couldn't help smiling. "I'll drink to that," she said, and took the wine from him. *And I pray you're right,* she added silently, lifting it to her lips.

The second plate of stew tasted every bit as good as the first, and Lee cleaned her plate with a satisfied sigh. When Nick leaned forward and poked at the fire with a thick branch, she watched the golden sparks dance in the air. She knew then that she'd never forget the aroma of woodsmoke and pine, and a dark-eyed man who was beginning to command more of her attention than was sensible. But then she hadn't done anything sensible since Simon had failed to come back.

She reached over, unlaced her shoes and pulled them off her feet. After a moment's hesitation, she followed with her socks, and she wriggled her bare toes in the cool, prickly grass. The sensation was quite wonderful, she thought.

"Tell me something." She pulled her knees up under her chin. "How did Midge save your life?"

Intent on piling more branches onto the fire, he didn't answer right away. Flames crackled and spat, leaping high in the air before settling down to a steady flickering.

"It was around six years ago," he said so quietly she had to strain to hear him. "We were in the mine. We'd hit a small vein. Nothing much. But we were anxious to milk it. We'd been working down there day and night for three days. We were tired, and I guess we got careless. We should have seen it coming. I was the farthest one in, with Midge about fifty yards behind me. The other two men were closer to the entrance."

Cold prickles crept along Lee's arms as she watched Nick's face. He was staring into the flames, his eyes seeing only his memories.

"Carlos must have seen the first showering of stones and realized what was happening. He yelled at Billy to get out, then ran forward to warn us. He never saw the beam that killed him."

Lee felt sick and wrapped her arms more tightly around her knees.

"Midge was right in front of him when it happened," Nick continued. "He looked up and saw the beams caving in on either side of Carlos. Midge could have run for it, but he chose to come back for me. We went through that passage like a pair of hunted rabbits, and we almost made it."

His voice died away, and Lee stared at him, hardly daring to breathe. Somewhere behind her, the wind rustled the branches of the pines and disturbed the long grass.

"Can you believe that idiot tried to brace the beams with his arms?" Nick said, almost in a whisper. "He couldn't hold them, of course. Even his strength wasn't enough. What he did manage to do was give me a few extra seconds. I made it out." He rubbed his forehead as if trying to erase the frown there.

"Billy and I got him out of there eventually, more dead than alive. Luckily for him he has the constitution of a bull elephant. He was back on his feet in just under a year. He's never been down a mine since. He'll only pan the streams now."

Lee swallowed, trying without much success to visualize the uncouth giant in the role of hero. "I can see why you feel the way you do about him," she said, "but frankly, he gives me the creeps."

"It would be a pretty boring world if all of us were the same." He shifted away from the fire and leaned back against a tree. "What about your brother? He marches to a different tune, doesn't he?"

"Very much so, I'm afraid. Simon is a restless soul, never happy unless he's on the move. That's why his job suits him so well. He's traveled around most of the world taking pictures. He loves it."

"He's lonely."

Lee looked up in surprise. "Lonely? I'd never describe Simon as lonely. He's always seemed happy with his way of life."

"Maybe he doesn't know it himself. Some people don't."

His expression was pensive, and Lee wondered if he was talking about himself. Her heart stirred, and she looked down.

"Simon is never short of companions," she said. "Just about everywhere he goes, he has women hanging on his every word."

"You sound as if you don't approve," he remarked.

"I just wish he would settle down, find someone to spend the rest of his life with. Then I could stop worrying about him."

"Isn't he a little old to have a keeper?"

She was on dangerous ground here, she knew. "I made a promise to my mother that I would take care of both of them—Simon and my father. I sometimes feel I haven't done a great job with either of them. Father spends his time working. He doesn't know how to relax and enjoy himself. And Simon—well, he's Simon."

She picked up her socks and started pulling them on. She was getting used to using the shrubs and bushes as a bathroom, but it embarrassed her to explain where she was going. When she had her shoes laced, she looked up and found Nick watching her.

"I have to go for a little walk," she said, avoiding his eyes.

"Don't go too far—it's easy to get lost in the dark."

She heard the smirk in his voice and flushed. "Don't worry," she said shortly. "I won't be long."

Nick watched the slim figure disappear into the woods, his face a mask of doubt. She confused him, and he didn't like being confused. Something heavy was going on behind her refined features, he knew, yet there was a straightforward honesty in the way she looked at him and in some of the things she said.

He was reluctant to question her, to get at the truth, and he wasn't sure why. Maybe he didn't want to know the answers. He ran a hand through his thick hair, his eyes on the flames weaving between the logs. Her uncomplaining efforts to keep up with him had impressed him. It wasn't what he would have expected from someone like her. In fact, there were a lot of things he hadn't expected.

He couldn't rid himself of the feeling that Simon King was involved in something far more serious than an "escapade" with his picture-taking. His gut feeling was that he was getting involved in something he should stay out of, and he'd learned long ago to trust his instincts.

That wasn't all. He had a new problem, and he wasn't sure how to deal with it. In spite of the certainty that he was making a hell of a mistake, he wanted her.

It wasn't the way it usually happened, either. This afternoon when he'd had her pressed against him, a gut-wrenching need had slammed through his body and left him shaken.

He recalled that it had taken considerable control to force a smile onto his face. It had been even more difficult to propel himself away from her soft, supple body and ignore the invitation of her parted lips. He'd actually had to forcibly remind himself of who she was and what she represented.

Nick heaved a sigh and stood. The fire was dying, and he'd used up all the branches. He moved away toward the trees, searching the ground. This whole thing was getting too damned complicated. He'd allowed his curiosity, and his constant need for money for the tavern, to override his common sense. He'd be glad when it was finished and he could get Lee and Simon both off his back. He didn't need any more complications in his life.

Lee was forced to feel her way along at first, hands outstretched to ward off a low branch or some other hidden obstacle. Her eyes soon adjusted to the dark, and she found she could move with some confidence. When she was finished, she made sure she knew in which direction the fireplace was, then started back.

The damp darkness seemed to be closing in as the forest hung over her. An owl hooted somewhere in the distance, and a terrible feeling of isolation swept over her. What would it be like, she wondered, to be alone in this eerie blackness, where every sound was magnified in the imagination?

She heard a faint scuffling close by. Was it a night creature hunting for food, or something evil creeping up on her? Impatient with her unfounded fears, she quickened her pace, heedless now of the crawling tendrils of undergrowth snatching at her ankles. It seemed imperative that she get back to the warmth of the fire and the comforting security of Nick's solid figure.

When it came, it was almost as if she'd been expecting it, her nerves forewarning her. Shattering the silence of the forest, the deadly crack of a gunshot split the air, then echoed away.

She froze, her heart beating wildly. She clamped her hands over her mouth in an effort to smother the scream that threatened to escape. Forcing down the urge to run, she moved with careful steps toward the fire, her mind spinning.

Someone was out there with a gun. Shooting at her? At Nick? Why? She was close enough to hear the crackling hiss of the flames, their yellow tips visible through the silent trees.

Who could possibly want to hurt her? The same person who was responsible for Simon's disappearance? Or was it Nick they were after? What did she know about this man, anyway? She was alone in the forest with a total stranger.

Her heart jolted when a twig snapped under her foot. To her it sounded almost as loud as the gunshot.

Palms cold and damp, knees shaking, she waited, but nothing moved. Again she went ahead, a step at a time, and now she could see the campsite. The fire sent a glow of flickering light in a wide arc. Everything looked the same as when she'd left, except for one thing—Nick had disappeared.

Panic seized her, cutting off her breath. Where was he? She heard Simon's words again, pounding in her brain: *Keep the law off my back*. Dear God, Simon, what have you done?

She struggled to get her mind working, to push away the fears clawing at her. She had to get out of here, get help. They had Nick now. It would only be a matter of time before they found her. Had they shot him? She buried the thought, unable to deal with it. Somehow she had to find her way back to town and tell the police. What a fool she'd been, thinking she could handle this without them.

She backed away from the firelight, her body tensed for flight. There was no warning. She heard nothing until arms clamped around her from behind. A hand covered her mouth, stifling her scream of cold terror.

Chapter 4

Lee's first reaction was sheer relief when she recognized the voice, but when Nick still continued to hold her, his hand covering her mouth, the doubts rushed back. Her indignant mumble of protest was cut off as he hissed in her ear, "Ssh! Hold still if you don't want a bullet through that pretty head."

Shock held her motionless in his grip while she wondered for a crazy moment if she'd trusted the wrong man, then he spoke again in an urgent whisper.

"I'll let you go, but you make one sound and you'll be sorry. Got it?"

She nodded, then spun around to face him when he loosened his hold. She could just make out Nick's features. He glared at her, his eyes as black as the night, and he was breathing hard, as if he'd been running.

"We're going to get out of here," he whispered grimly, "and then you're going to talk."

Stunned, Lee realized that his anger was directed at her. Surely he couldn't think that she was responsible for that gunshot.

"Nick, I…" Unthinking, she had spoken aloud, and once more he covered her mouth with his hand.

"For God's sake, do what you're told. Whoever shot at me is probably still around somewhere, and if you don't keep that damn mouth shut, we could both end up getting killed."

Wide-eyed, she stared at him, pulling in a trembling breath when he dropped his hand. "What are we going to do?" she whispered, her lips barely moving.

"We're going to find a new camp. You and I have a lot of things to get straightened out, and I don't want to be interrupted."

He moved away from her, and she knew he was listening for sounds of movement in the darkness. She realized her shoulders were hunched with tension, and she made an effort to relax them.

He came back to her, close enough to murmur, "You stay here. I'm going back for the packs."

Lee grabbed at his arm. The solid muscle beneath the cool, bare skin was reassuring. "Nick, I'm coming with you. Don't leave me alone out here."

"You'll be safer here in the dark, as long as you keep still and don't make a sound." He pulled his arm gently from her grasp. "I'll get in and out of there a lot quicker on my own."

She watched him slip away from her, surprised a man of his size could move so silently. No wonder she hadn't heard him come up behind her. She shivered as she relived the moment his arms had locked around her. She had sensed the cold, lethal power of his body, and she felt a vast relief that he was on her side. He would make a formidable enemy, she knew.

The big question was, of course, just who was the enemy? Who would want to shoot Nick? Surely it couldn't have anything to do with Simon.

Anxiety gnawed at her. It looked as if her worst fears were being realized. Had she been wrong about Simon? At once her thoughts sprang to his defense. She would not believe the worst of him; there had to be some explanation.

Lee sank to the mossy ground and leaned against a tree. She was shivering now, and for the first time she realized how cold she was. She thought longingly of the heavy sweater tucked in her pack. She hugged her body, aware of her jumping nerves, and expected to hear another shot ring out any minute in the dense quiet of the forest.

When Nick's tall figure suddenly appeared in front of her, she gasped with shock. She hadn't heard so much as a rustle. Scrambling to her feet, she shot him a look of resentment. "You keep creeping up on me like that and I'll go into cardiac arrest."

"That'll save us both a lot of trouble." His voice was at its normal level, and in answer to her questioning look he shrugged. "I guess he's gone for now. He would have taken another potshot if he'd still been around." He dropped the pack at her feet. "You'd better put something warm on. It'll get cold fast now."

Lee noticed he was wearing a light jacket, and she gladly pulled her sweater out of the pack and slipped her arms into its comforting warmth.

"Where are we going?" she asked as he helped her on with her pack.

"Higher up, to a place I've used a few times. It'll be safer than the woods." He turned to go. "Just in case," he said over his shoulder, "no talking unless absolutely necessary. And stay close to me."

Lee needed no second bidding. She stayed close on his heels all the way. They left the main body of the forest, and there the ground was more open and rocky. Huge boulders blocked their path, but Nick skirted them easily as he climbed surefootedly over the rough terrain.

Long before Nick halted, Lee's sore muscles reminded her of the abuse she'd given them. Ahead of them, the mountain soared, stark and forbidding against the starlit sky.

Nick waited until Lee had reached him, then caught her arm, pointing with the other hand. "Straight ahead."

She blinked, trying to see in the darkness. "But that's a solid wall!"

"No, there's a cave, behind that big rock over there. It's small, but quite comfortable and sheltered. It's also hidden. Not too many people know about it. We'll be safe there till we get things sorted out." There was a grim note to his voice that made her wince.

She followed him toward the rock and was surprised to see a small gap down one side of it that was just large enough to allow a man to slip through.

Nick went first, then held out his hand. She took it, feeling the warmth of his strong fingers spreading up her arm. Thick darkness met her inside the cave, and Lee stood quite still, apprehension prickling at her scalp. She was relieved when, after a succession of shuffling sounds, a beam of light played over the smooth walls, and she realized that Nick had a flashlight. Something scuttled in a dark corner, and Lee shuddered, taking a step closer to Nick's big body.

"It's better than a bullet." His voice came out of the darkness, and she caught his relentless undertone.

Her heart skipped as it dawned on her that now their positions were reversed. He didn't trust her. She could hardly blame him. He must be wondering what she'd gotten him into. That was something she'd really like to know herself. Somehow she had to convince him that she was almost as much in the dark as he was.

As if he'd read her mind, he spoke. "You've got a lot of explaining to do, lady, but it will have to wait till morning. Apart from the distinct possibility that I'll fall asleep in the middle of it, I want to see your face when you talk." She heard him move away from her. "I don't know what your brother's into, but I have a feeling you know more than you're telling. We don't move another step until you fill me in. I'm not setting myself up for target practice without at least knowing why."

She swallowed, glad that he couldn't see her face. There was a small ledge about waist high, and he set the flashlight on it to illuminate the tiny area.

"I'm going to to leave this on long enough to get the sleeping bags down," he said gruffly, "so you'd better get a move on."

Lee did as she was told; she wasn't about to argue with that tone of voice. She managed to get the straps of the sleeping bag undone and the fabric rolled out in record time, obeying Nick's orders to place it at the back of the cave, with his bag lying across the entrance. He wasn't taking any chances, she thought wearily. Well, it would all have to wait till tomorrow. What with the shock and excitement, not to mention the incredibly long day, she was ready to drop.

She wondered just how much she should take off before getting into the bag. Her dilemma was solved when Nick snapped off the light. She removed her socks, shoes and, after a moment's hesitation, her sweater and jeans. Pulling her shirt closer around her, she slipped into the folds of the sleeping bag.

After a minute or two of wriggling around to get comfortable, she forgot about the hard ground, the unfamiliar night sounds and the unsettling presence of the man lying a few feet away. Sleep, deep and obliterating, overtook her.

The hoarse laughter of the crows woke her the next morning. Pale light filtered into the small cave, and she turned her head carefully.

She could barely make out the hunched shape of Nick, who lay as still as a statue. She waited, letting her senses catch up one by one. Her body felt stiff and sore, and something sharp dug into her right shoulder blade. Outside, the song of a bird she didn't recognize welcomed the morning. The air smelled earthy and touched her face with its damp fingers.

She moved her toes experimentally, grimacing as her calf muscles tightened with pain. Feeling the need to answer the call of nature, she looked over at Nick's huddled body.

If she were very quiet, she could slip out and be back before he knew she was gone, she thought, and wouldn't have to give him any awkward explanations.

Holding her breath, she eased her body out of the bag. Nick's sleeping form didn't even twitch. Gathering confidence, she rose silently to her feet and stood, waiting. Still no movement. She looked at her jeans, lying at the bottom of her bag, and decided not to risk putting them on.

Tiptoeing on bare feet, she approached the still figure. It would be tricky, she saw. She'd have to step over him into the narrow gap between the rock and the mountain wall. She lifted her foot and almost overbalanced as his hand flashed out and grabbed her ankle.

He turned onto his back and stared up at her, his face taut with suspicion. "Where do you think you're going?"

Lee glanced at his bare shoulder emerging from the bag, then looked back to his face. "I have to go to the bathroom," she said with as much dignity as she could muster.

He saw the color rush to her face and realized what he was holding on to. He moved his gaze from the slim ankle clutched in his hand all the way up her bare legs to the lacy briefs that clung to her slim hips. Abruptly he let her go. "I guess you won't go far dressed like that," he said wryly.

Just as she'd almost recovered from the impact of his touch, he destroyed the little composure she had left by sitting up. The quilted fabric of the sleeping bag, which barely covered his hips, exposed a great deal of his upper torso.

There was nowhere else to look, Lee thought helplessly, and she gave in to the temptation. His shoulders were smooth and tanned and heavily muscled, and they more than confirmed her impression of his superb physical condition. Dark hair curled down his broad chest, narrowing over his flat stomach to his navel and beyond.

She found herself struggling to breathe naturally as she met his deep blue eyes and saw amusement gleaming in them.

"You'd better turn your back," Nick said with a hint of a grin. "I don't want to offend your sense of propriety."

She looked at him blankly, her entire body a mass of confusion.

"Okay!" His hand gripped the edge of the bag. "If you don't care that I'm naked, it's all right with me."

Lee gave an embarrassed squeak and whirled around. "Where are you going?" she asked, mortified to hear the wobble in her voice.

"I'm coming with you," he replied.

She could hear him moving around behind her, and she clamped her eyes shut in a vain attempt to erase the image of his nude body from her mind.

"Oh, no you're not!" she said more firmly. "I don't need your assistance."

"You might, if our friend is still out there with his peashooter. Or is it *your* friend?"

"Don't be ridiculous." She swung back, forgetting her consternation. "You can't really believe that."

He was zipping up his pants, his eyes dark and brooding on her face. "Lady, till you tell me the whole story, I don't know what to believe."

Knowing what the sight of his bare chest did to her, Lee locked her eyes on his. "Right now, all I can think about is a little privacy, and it's not going to wait much longer."

"Right." He stepped back and gave her a mock bow. "This way, your ladyship. Don't worry. I won't peek. I'm more interested in preserving my hide."

"Thank heaven for small miracles," Lee said stiffly, edging past the expanse of his bare skin to emerge into the chill morning air.

He was waiting for her at the cave entrance when she came back, and this time he didn't hide his interest in her legs. By the time she reached him, her knees were shaking, and she felt as if she were trying to balance on stilts.

"Feel better?" He was leaning against the mountain wall, his ankles crossed, his thumbs hooked in his belt.

Damn that smirk, Lee thought furiously. One of these days he'd get his. It didn't help that she noticed the sunlight playing across his bronzed shoulders.

"I'm fine," she said shortly, and waited for him to move away from the gap in the wall. He edged sideways, giving her a few scant inches to slip through, and her arm brushed the hair on his chest as she passed him. It might as well have been an electrified fence. Shock waves bounced off her arm to every nerve ending in her body. She stumbled into the shadowed cave, grabbed her jeans and hauled them on.

"Won't be long!" He almost sang the words, and she gritted her teeth.

"Take your time." Damn him! She kicked at the sleeping bag, and her foot caught one of her shoes and sent it skidding toward the back of the cave. She swore loudly, and felt much better.

After dragging her socks and the remaining shoe on, she limped over to where the errant shoe had come to rest. She had to stop this adolescent mooning over him, she chided herself. Lost in thought, she jerked when she heard his footsteps behind her.

"It looks as if we're alone," Nick said as he bent over his sleeping bag for his shirt.

Lee looked at him suspiciously, but his face was serious when he looked up, and she relaxed. "Good. Then we can go on to the mines?"

"Yep. It's going to take us longer, though. We'll have to stay off the trails and go in the back way. I don't want to take any chances."

The grim look was back on his face, and Lee's stomach lurched. "You think he's still after us?"

"That guy meant business. He's not likely to give up. Which brings us to where you and your wayward brother fit into all this."

Lee swallowed nervously. "Can we eat first? I don't think well on an empty stomach."

He gave her a dark, brooding look. "All right. But no more excuses. You're going to stay here until you spill it all. Every word."

She nodded. There wasn't much else she could do. Besides, she wanted to tell him. She trusted him now, and it would be so wonderful to tell someone, especially someone as capable and as strong as Nick Garrett.

The granola bars and punch tasted better than she'd expected, considering her stomach was still tied up in knots. Nick barely hid his impatience as he waited for her to finish, and the minute she had drained the last of her punch, he pounced.

"All right. From the beginning. And don't leave anything out."

Lee packed away the wrappers in her pack with unsteady hands. "I don't really know a whole lot . . ." she began tentatively.

Nick sighed. "How about telling me what you do know?"

She stared down at her hands and started to speak in a low voice. "Two weeks ago I went over to Simon's apartment. I'd picked up some prints for him, and I wanted to drop them off. He'd told me he wouldn't be home, so I let myself in with the key he'd given me. He was talking on the phone in the bedroom and didn't hear me come in, so I picked up a magazine and started to read." With her finger, Lee absently traced what was left of the crease in her jeans.

"I could tell by his voice that he was angry," she went on. "I heard him mention something about money, then he said he wasn't interested." She started to work on the other leg. "I heard him say, 'All right. I'll do it. But it's the last time.'" She paused. "He said he was getting too old for the risks." When she didn't say anything else, Nick shook his head.

"Is that it?" he said, sounding exasperated. "He could have been talking about the photo assignment."

Lee looked at him in desperation. "He also said, 'If I get caught in those mountains, you know what will happen to me. You'd better make sure you keep the law off my back.'"

Nick groaned. "Terrific. Why the hell didn't you tell me all this before?"

"Would you have brought me here if I had?" She met his gaze, unflinching.

He twisted his mouth wryly. "No way."

"That's what I figured."

"Okay." Nick stretched out his legs. "So, did you ask him what it was all about?"

Lee shook her head. "I didn't get the chance. I didn't want him to know I'd been eavesdropping, so I went out and pretended I'd just gotten there. He didn't mention it, of course, and I couldn't. He left the next morning, and when he called me from Gambler's Gulch, he said he was going to take pictures of the mines and that he'd found someone to show him over the area—you." She frowned. "I should have been more persistent when I questioned him that night in his apartment. Maybe I could have stopped him."

"And maybe he would have lied to you anyway."

Lee sighed. "Whatever it is, I won't believe that Simon is into anything illegal. He may be a little crazy, but he's not a criminal. I'd bet my life on it."

"You may be doing just that," Nick said dryly. "I admire your loyalty, but your prejudice is showing. People don't get shot at for no reason. Someone out there doesn't want us pushing our noses in their business, and something tells me their business might also be your brother's business."

Lee's temper flared. "Surely you're not suggesting that it was Simon shooting at us!"

"It's a possibility." Nick rose and stretched his arms over his head.

In spite of her anger, Lee was glad he'd put on his shirt. "What are the other possibilities?" she demanded. The idea of Simon shooting at them was utterly ridiculous. Just about anything would make more sense than that.

"I haven't formed any conclusions yet." Nick looked down at her. "When I do," he added grimly, "I'll let you know."

Lee's stomach lurched. She twisted onto her knees and began to roll up her sleeping bag. "You're still going to take me to the mine, aren't you?" she asked, afraid to look up at him and see his expression. The question hung in the air for several seconds.

"That's what you paid me for. That's what you get," Nick said finally. "I'm not going to pretend I like it or that I'm convinced your brother is as innocent as you make out. But now I'm curious. I want to know—badly—why someone is out to get me."

Lee gasped when he suddenly leaned down and grasped her arm, hauling her to her feet.

"I'm going to make two things very clear, Ms. Coulton. Number one, if your brother isn't at the mine when we get there, we go straight back to town." Lee flinched as his fingers bit into her arm. His eyes seemed to be boring right through her soul. "Number two, if I find out that Simon King is the enemy, all bets are off. I'll take care of this in my own way. Got it?"

He was so close to her she could feel the heat of his body. Something tugged at her in the most intimate recesses of her being. She forgot to be angry or afraid. She forgot everything except that she was standing close to a man who seemed able to create an overwhelming response in her at the slightest touch.

His eyelashes, she noticed, were long and thick beneath his dark, furry brows. Her gaze drifted down his wide cheekbones and strong nose to his mouth. Need, hot and urgent, raced through her body.

Nick went very still and loosened his hold on her arm.

Still staring helplessly at the hard lines of his mouth, Lee whispered, "I thought you were going to call me Lee." She looked into his eyes, and a small surge of triumph swept through her as she saw the sudden flame there. His jaw was clenched, and she watched, fascinated, as a tiny muscle twitched just below his cheekbone.

"Lee."

It came out in a husky whisper, and her pulse leaped.

"That's better." She was still whispering. She didn't have the strength to do anything else. She leaned forward, her heart thumping. She heard the swift intake of his breath, then disappointment gripped her as he let go of her and stepped backward.

"I don't know about you," he said a shade unsteadily, "but I could use a shower. The stream may not be as comfortable or as private as a suite at the Royal King, but it's the best I can offer."

Lee fought to control her frustration. What on earth was she doing? She'd almost made a colossal fool of herself. It must be the mountain air or something, she thought. How could she possibly throw herself at a man? Especially such an arrogant one as Nick Garrett.

"That's sounds great." She managed to say it in the crisp tone she used with her staff at the hotel. "I feel as if I haven't washed in a week."

"It's something you get used to in this environment," Nick said, and dropped to his knees to roll up the sleeping bag.

Lee watched him for a moment, her emotions warring with one another. Finally, with a determined shake of her head, she finished packing up her belongings.

The stream was a ten-minute hike from the cave, and though the water was icy, Lee enjoyed the exhilarating feeling of being skin-tingling clean. Nick had disappeared around a bend and was completely hidden from her by the bushy shrubs. Even so, she hurried her wash, excruciatingly aware of him several yards away. She heard him splashing around, and then he was quiet. By the time she quickly dried herself with the hand towel she'd tucked into her pack, she was shivering, though she couldn't blame it entirely on the cool air.

Once she was dressed, she felt much warmer. The sun was already high in the cloudless sky. It was going to be another hot day, she thought. She prayed she wouldn't have to walk far; her shoulders still ached from carrying the pack, and her body felt as if it had been run over by a truck.

The familiar fragrance of pine and dried grasses reached her, and she sniffed with appreciation. She understood how Nick could fall in love with the mountains, she thought as she made her way back to where they'd left the packs. It was a far cry from her life at the hotel, with its constant problems: disputes in the kitchen, overbooked rooms, lost keys and mixed-up baggage—all part of the hectic pace of hotel management. She smiled ruefully.

It had been a while since she'd thought about the hotel, she realized. It seemed so far away, a distant world. As distant as Leanne Coulton, hotel manager, seemed right now. Her hair was a mess. She'd washed it in the stream, and now it clung damply to her head. She wore no makeup, and her skin felt tight with sunburn. Her nails were jagged and broken from clawing up steep, rocky slopes.

Simon would have a fit when he saw her, though he'd probably prefer the new Lee.

Her thoughts were blasted out of her head as she negotiated a clump of small trees and came out into the clearing. Nick stood—naked—with his back to her, rubbing his head vigorously with a towel. He seemed absorbed in drying his hair and apparently hadn't heard her.

Lee's first impulse was to spin around and creep back behind the trees, but her feet refused to obey her. Her blood surging through her veins, she succumbed to the inevitable and took her time surveying his body. His tan reached down his back, ending abruptly above his pale, tight buttocks. Farther down, his powerful thighs were the same mahogany color as his back and were furred with dark hair.

Lee drew in a slow, strangled breath. Her only coherent thought was that he swam a lot. Only a brief swimsuit would leave such a narrow band of pale skin. It dawned on her that the reason Nick hadn't heard her coming was that his ears were covered by the towel. Any minute now, he would drop it and turn.... The image that evoked almost brought forth a moan from her lips. Holding her breath, she stepped back until she was hidden by the trees.

"Are you decent?" she called out when she was sure her voice would sound natural.

His muffled "Wait a minute" did a few more uncomfortable things to her stomach, and she took a firm hold of herself. He was sharp—if she didn't watch it, he'd realize she'd seen him.

It took all her self-control to walk casually toward him when he called out again. He was getting into his shirt when she reached him, and she did her best to avoid looking at him. The image of his virile body was too fresh in her mind.

She was relieved when he picked up his backpack and pushed his arms through the straps, saying, "All set?"

She nodded, glancing at him, then slid her eyes away from his face.

They had been moving about ten minutes when Nick stopped, his hand in the air.

"What is it?" Lee asked anxiously, her heart hammering. Nick shook his head and spread his fingers out in warning. She waited, fear churning her stomach. Then she heard it. The low, muffled roar of an engine. No, several engines. She raised her eyebrows questioningly.

"Motorcycles," Nick muttered. "Somewhere up high." He turned his head, listening. "They're going away from us."

"Who do you think they are?" Lee asked nervously.

"I'm not sure." His tone matched his face, and Lee shivered in spite of the heat.

"One thing I do know," Nick said, moving forward again, "is they're not supposed to be there."

Well, that was something Simon wouldn't be involved in, Lee thought with relief. As far as she knew, Simon had never been on a motorcycle in his life. But then she was beginning to wonder just how well she knew her brother.

The journey was far more difficult than it had been the day before. Nick was keeping to the trees as much as possible, and at times they had to fight their way through the undergrowth. She began to take rest stops more and more frequently. When she'd reached the point where she was quite certain she couldn't take another step, Nick halted and took hold of her arm. She jumped, and he looked at her in surprise.

"Take it easy. We're safe as long as we stay off the trails."

"Well, I don't feel safe. I'll be glad when we get to the mines and find Simon." She heard the irritation in her voice and silently cursed herself.

"Just hold out a little longer. We're almost there."

Good grief! Lee thought desperately. Was that sympathy in his deep voice? She must be hallucinating in her exhaustion.

"We've got to cross the trail here," Nick said, leading her forward. "I don't expect any problems, but we'll go fast just in case. Okay?"

"Okay." She took a deep breath, then forced her legs to pump as Nick half dragged her across the uneven ground. They reached the trees on the other side, and to Lee's surprise, Nick eased her down to a sitting position beneath a tall fir.

"Stay here," he said. "I'm going back to the trail for a minute."

Chest heaving, Lee could only nod as she watched him move away from her. Curious, she edged forward to keep him in sight. He was crouching at the edge of the trail, apparently examining the ground. He stayed there for several seconds, then returned. His expression sent new flurries of fear to her stomach.

"What's the matter?" she asked sharply. "What were you looking at?"

Nick seemed to look through her. "Let's go," he said, already treading away.

Lee shoved her aching body upward, incensed and afraid.

"Damn it, Nick, I'm not a child. Tell me what's going on!"

He looked at her, and there was an odd expression in his navy-blue eyes. "Lee, I'm trying to put this all together. I know what you must be going through, but until I get the answers myself, I can't tell you much."

He didn't have to tell her anything. Right then she couldn't care less about the answers. Except for that strangled whisper in the cave, it was the first time he'd used her first name. It was incredible how good that made her feel. She followed him without another word until, fifteen minutes later, he motioned for her to stop.

She crept forward and peered at where he was pointing. The trees had thinned out considerably, and she and Nick were at the edge of a flat, grassy area. Fifty yards away, where the mountain swept toward the sky, an ugly black hole gaped in its side.

Excitement grabbed at Lee as she stared at the dark, forbidding opening. She could sympathize with Midge, she thought with a shudder. If it weren't for Simon, nothing could induce her to go into that thing.

Nick was squirming out of his pack when she looked at him. "I want you to go back into the trees," he said, gesturing to the firs. "Wait for me there."

"No." Lee struggled to push the straps off her shoulders. "I'm coming with you."

"You're staying here."

She was amazed at how much force he could inject into a low voice.

"I'm the decision maker, remember? You'll do as you're told. There's no sense in both of us taking chances." As he opened his pack and took out the flashlight, she stared at him, fear prickling down her back.

"You don't think Simon—"

"I don't think anything," he cut in. "I have no idea what's waiting in there. Probably nothing, but if there is trouble, I'll handle it a hell of a lot better if I don't have to worry about you. Now get going."

She couldn't seem to stop shaking. "Nick?" She grabbed his arm and held on to him. "Please be careful."

A grin flicked across his face. "Don't worry. I intend to be." He gave her a long look. "Lee, if something happens, or if I'm not back in half an hour, I want you to promise me you'll go back as quickly as possible. Find the stream and follow it down—it'll eventually lead you back to the road."

"But—"

"But nothing." He gripped her shoulder, giving it a comforting squeeze. "More than likely, this is all unnecessary. I like to cover all my bases, that's all."

"Sure." She managed a smile. "Go find my brother, Garrett."

His hand moved to her forehead and gently smoothed her dark hair back from her brow. "I'll do my best," he said softly, and then he was gone.

How long? Nick wondered as he paced carefully toward the mine. How long would he have the strength to keep his hands off her? He didn't need this now. He had to concentrate, to keep his mind squarely on what he was doing. He didn't need this urgent response of his body every time he got near her, looked at her. He would have to do something about it soon, or he'd go out of his mind. Why her? She was everything he'd sworn he would never touch. She'd gotten to him. Those huge brown eyes and that soft, warm mouth had gotten to him. He couldn't keep his eyes off that supple body. Its soft curves were driving him crazy.

He swore silently. You don't have time for this now, Garrett. He concentrated on the dark, jagged opening in front of him, his senses finally responding to the demands he was putting on them. He was alert now, his ears straining for the slightest sound.

He hadn't told her everything. A lot of it didn't make sense, but now he was fairly sure of one thing: that shot last night had been a warning. If the gunman had been intent on killing him, he wouldn't have given up so easily.

Nick had hoped to make it to the mines without being noticed, but he'd seen dirt bike tracks back there on the trail. Fresh ones.

Somehow they had second-guessed him and were ahead of him now. Waiting. Was it Simon King? He desperately hoped not. Lee would hate him for what he would have to do, and that was something he didn't care to think about.

He took hold of his jumping nerves, molding them into the cold, hard mental alertness that had served him so well in the past. Expertly and with a minimum of sound, he slipped out of the sunlight into the gloomy bowels of the mountain.

The passageway went back farther than he remembered. Ben must have worked like a mole since he'd bought the claim from him six years ago, Nick thought. He paused every few feet to listen, but the silence hung around him, and the musty air lay still, every bit as depressing as he remembered.

He marveled that he had stayed down as long as he had. Five years in this miserable hole now would kill him. That it had taken him so long to work through them was an indication of how deep his problems had been.

Impatiently he forced his mind back to the present. Concentrate, Garrett, if you want to stay alive. Even then he almost walked into it.

His sixth sense, the elusive instinct that he'd relied on so many times, wasn't quite as sharp as it had once been. He smelled the danger an instant before it exploded in front of him, and it was almost too late.

Sheer reflexes hurled his body backward, and he dug his heels frantically into the soft earth to give him momentum as the bullet ricocheted off the wall and plowed into one of the beams. The flashlight dropped from his hand and rolled, bouncing off the wall before it went out. There had been enough light to give him a blurred image of a man crouched low on the ground, a rifle jammed against his shoulder. Then Nick was moving. Sideways, then forward, just as the second bullet burst from the gun.

Chapter 5

Relief surged through Nick's body as his forearm, held taut in front of him, collided with flesh. The rifle clattered to the ground, drowning out the explosive gasp from his assailant, and his strong fingers found the throat with unerring instinct.

Nick squeezed, and the body beneath him thrashed in a frenzied effort to escape the deadly hold. Nick moved his foot in a stretching half circle until he felt the welcome roll of the flashlight. He trapped it with his foot and drew it closer. When the flailing arms weakened, he reached down and flicked the light on.

The old man's eyes were closed, his thin lips parted in agony.

"Ben!" Nick snatched his hand from the prospector's throat, his alarm subsiding as a raspy cough and a muttered expletive reassured him. The eyelids fluttered open, and pale blue eyes stared at him, focusing with difficulty.

"Goldarn it, Nick!" the prospector wheezed. "Get off my stomach."

Nick grinned and climbed to his feet, dragging the old man up with him. "I'd apologize," he said, "but you shot first."

Ben shook his scraggly head. "Thought you was one of them White Devils."

"What in the hell are White Devils?"

"You don't wanna know." With pale eyes he squinted at Nick. "What're you doing here, anyways? Thought you'd had enough of digging."

"I have." Nick leaned down to pick up the rifle, then stood it against the wall. "I'm looking for Simon King, the photographer I brought up a couple of weeks ago. Is he still here?"

Ben opened his mouth to answer, then shut it again as a rattling sound echoed down the far reaches of the passageway. Nick turned off the flashlight, and once more the shaft was plunged into darkness.

The first muffled report had brought Lee to her feet, horror swirling through her stomach. The hope that she'd misinterpreted the sound barely had time to form before the second dull crack stopped her heartbeat.

She took a step forward, then hesitated as she remembered Nick's words. If something happened, he wanted her to go. It took her two seconds to make up her mind. Nick was in there—maybe Simon, too. But Nick hadn't been carrying a gun. Surely Simon... No! She shook her head to dispel the unthinkable.

She wasn't going to find out anything by standing there. She shoved the packs into the undergrowth until they were hidden, then turned toward the mine. She tried not to think of the murky blackness waiting for her inside that ominous gash in the mountain. She refused to accept the image of Nick's body lying on the ground. She went quickly, before she could change her mind, and then it was there, in front of her, like a huge, sinister black mouth.

She could smell the dampness and decay oozing from it, and her stomach churned. She was breathing too fast. Easy, Lee. Don't hyperventilate. Deep breaths. That's it. She willed her muscles to relax and felt the blood easing back into her fingers.

Her foot scraped on a loose rock, sending it rattling down the slope to the mine. Her heart jerked, and she stepped more carefully, her eyes glued on the dark nothingness ahead. She paused a few feet from the entrance, wondering which would be worse—the darkness beyond that black hole, or the eerie silence.

Even the birds seemed to have stopped singing. She waited. Ten seconds, twenty, thirty. Then, taking a last look at the sun, she slipped into the mountain's belly.

It was darker than she could have imagined. The soft earth deadened her footsteps as she crept forward, her hand on the wall to guide her. Nick's words tormented her mind. *The timbers are rotting...a danger of cave-ins...we got him out eventually, more dead than alive.*

The musty air seemed to clog her lungs, and it smelled of dying wood. She could hear a steady dripping somewhere ahead of her, and she almost cried out as her searching fingers touched something cold and clammy. She pulled her hand away, and it bounced against the rough edge of a beam. A shower of loose rock spattered down. Her heart pounded as she was overwhelmed by the urge to run, to race for the entrance and the glorious safety of the open sky.

Terror held her motionless. She waited for the walls to collapse, her eyes squeezed tight. The seconds ticked by, and gradually she relaxed. Silence had settled over the shaft, and she was still alive.

She must have been holding her breath; she was gasping. She struggled to hold down the panic as she filled her lungs with the foul air. She felt as if her head were floating above her shoulders, and she called on all her resources to regain a measure of control. When she felt capable of moving again, she edged forward on quivering legs.

The passageway curved to the left a little farther down, and she followed it, feeling in front of her with each foot before setting it down. She heard a slight movement behind her, but by then the hands had grabbed her, and her scream reverberated in a piercing crescendo before it was cut off by the arm jammed cruelly across her throat.

She clawed at muscled flesh until bright light flooded her eyes. Her vision cleared, and she plunged farther into nightmare as she found herself staring at the wickedly gleaming blade of a knife held less than six inches from her face. She fixed her eyes on it in terror, then her senses reeled as her captor swore in a tone that was wonderfully familiar.

Lee cried out and staggered forward as the arm fell away, then she whirled on her attacker. Nick's strained face, bathed in the glow from a lantern, looked pale, his eyes glinting like dark sapphires.

"What in the hell are you doing in here?" he said in a harsh voice.

In her intense relief and delight at finding him apparently unharmed, she resorted to flippancy. "Why, Mr. Garrett," she said more throatily than she'd intended, "we really have to stop meeting this way."

Nick was not in the least amused. "For God's sake, Lee, I came damn close to knifing you."

He looked desperate, and Lee's eyes shifted to the knife clutched in his hand. "Where did you get that?" she asked faintly.

"It's mine. I never go anywhere without it."

Lee swallowed. "I've never seen it before."

"You've never seen me without my pants."

She looked up at him, heartened to see the stormy look fading from his eyes.

"I keep it in my boot," he said gently.

"Oh!" She gave him a weak grin, then spun around as he added, "It's all right, Ben. This is a friend of mine, Leanne Coulton. She's Simon King's sister."

Lee blinked in confusion and wondered why it hadn't occurred to her that someone else had to be holding the lantern. The light reflected back along a plaid-sleeved arm and splashed across a face that resembled a neglected peach. Two light blue eyes glowed beneath wispy gray brows, and the old man's chin sprouted hairs that must have escaped a roughly wielded razor.

"This is Ben," Nick said. "He bought this mine from me a few years ago."

"You never told me Simon was at your mine," Lee said, giving Ben a smile.

"You never asked."

Ben gave a dry cackle. "I'm sure glad you didn't use that knife, Nick," he said. "Would have been a heck of a waste."

"Thank you. I think," Lee said.

"She was damned lucky," Nick muttered. "I thought I told you to go back to town if something happened."

"Now that would have been a waste, seeing as how you appear to be all right." She ran her eyes over his body. "You are all right, aren't you?"

He nodded. "Ben is a lousy shot, luckily. This being shot at all the time is getting to be a habit I could do without."

"So what happened?" Lee looked at Ben as he cackled again.

"I almost killed your boyfriend. Came barging in here, so I figured he was one of them White Devils."

Nick cleared his throat loudly. "Let's get out of this dungeon. I could use some fresh air." He moved past Lee and took the lantern from Ben. "I've got a few questions that need answering, and this isn't my idea of a place for a cozy chat."

"Ain't much I can tell you," Ben protested as Nick took Lee's arm and began walking back to the entrance.

"We'll find out about that when we get up top," Nick said, and Lee glanced at him, alerted by the gruff tone.

"Who are the White Devils?" she asked. "And where is Simon?"

"That's something I hope we'll find out." He glanced back at the old man, who shuffled along reluctantly a few paces behind them. "That's if I can get any sense out of him. Ben's always been a little closemouthed."

"You mean he may not tell us everything he knows?"

"If he chooses not to."

"But why would he do that? Doesn't he want to help?"

"It pays to keep your mouth shut in the mountains."

Lee sighed. "I forgot. Mountain law."

"Right."

"Do you think he knows where Simon is?"

"I was just getting to that when you came creeping down here. I figured you were our friend from last night." He tightened his grip on her arm. "You don't know how close you came to getting a knife in your guts." His voice sounded ragged, and the look he gave her went straight to her knees. "That was a crazy stunt to pull," he said quietly.

"I thought you were hurt." Lee dropped her gaze and concentrated on the patterns of light leaping over the walls from the swinging lantern. "I couldn't leave without knowing. I had to do something."

"At the risk of your own life? Or didn't you consider that?"

"I considered it." She still couldn't look at him. "There wasn't much time to weigh the pros and cons."

"Remind me," Nick said softly, "to thank you properly the next time we're alone."

She couldn't think of a thing to say. To her vast relief, the shadows disappeared as the faint pool of sunlight spread out to welcome them, and then they were standing in the bright warmth of clean mountain air.

Lee spread her arms and lifted her face to the sun. Never had it felt so good on her skin. How could anyone choose to spend their days buried in that horrible black pit? she wondered with a shudder as she watched Ben stumble out into the sunlight, blinking his watery blue eyes.

It was even more unbelievable to imagine Nick down there. She remembered their conversation of the day before. Five years, he had told her. What had happened to him in the past to make him take such desperate measures to escape from it?

She watched him turn off the lantern and set it down near the mine entrance. His shirt was black with dust; he must have rolled on the ground. His dark hair drifted across his forehead, and black stubble covered his chin. He looked unkempt, roguish and intensely male. She was engulfed in such a wave of tenderness that she had to turn away.

"All right, Ben," Nick said as Lee found a flat rock to sit on, "let's start with Simon. I want to know everything that happened after I left."

Lee craned forward to hear the mumbled words.

"He hung around for a day or two, took some pictures and then he left."

"Did he say he was going back to town?"

The old man looked stubbornly at Nick, his lips clamped shut.

"Ben, this is important."

Nick's voice was dangerously quiet, and Lee looked at the prospector anxiously.

"Don't know nothing," he muttered.

Nick folded his arms as he drew his brows together. "We go back a long way, you and I. I wouldn't want anything to ruin that."

Lee thought Ben looked as if he were about to throw up. For agonizing seconds he seemed to struggle with indecision, then blurted out, "He went to find the ghost town."

Nick's frown grew deeper. "What ghost town?"

Ben waved a bony arm in the direction of the mountain's summit. "Up there."

"You know there's no ghost town up there, Ben," Nick said. "You know these mountains as well as I do."

Ben nodded vigorously. "That's what I told him. There ain't no such ghost town. He went looking anyways. Probably gave up and went home after a while."

"He didn't come home, Ben," Lee said firmly. "Where did he hear about this ghost town?"

"Good question." Nick leaned against the wall and stuck his thumbs in his pockets. "He didn't mention it to me."

The old man looked scared, Lee realized. Nick's voice was abrupt but not threatening. She wondered what the prospector was afraid of.

"The White Devils," Ben mumbled. "He must have heard it from the White Devils."

"Aha!" Nick folded his arms again across his broad chest. "I was wondering when we would get to that."

"Who are they?" Lee asked. She was beginning to get frustrated with this whole conversation; it seemed to be leading nowhere.

"Bikers." Ben was practically babbling. "They come in off the mountain and come down the mines and try to scare us off. Some men been hurt real bad 'cause they wouldn't pay no mind to what they said. They steal the gold, supplies—they're real bad news."

"How many?" Nick pulled away from the wall and stood, watching the old man with narrowed eyes.

"Dozens!"

"Have you seen them?"

Ben shook his white head. "Not me! They come anywheres near me, I'll shoot every last one of 'em."

"Oh, Nick!" Lee's voice was a cry of anguish. *Keep the law off my back.* Surely Simon couldn't be mixed up in anything as bad as that. Or had he run into this gang and, Simon being Simon, challenged them? She couldn't bear to think of the consequences.

Nick's eyes were sympathetic as they met hers.

"Okay, Ben," he said. "If that's all you can tell us, we'll be on our way."

"No, wait." Lee pushed herself up from the rock and hurried over to the prospector. "Ben. Did Simon tell you where the ghost town was?"

Ben's faded blue eyes darted from side to side. "A mile and a half into the morning sun on the high plateau." Fear etched his face as he seemed to realize what he had just said. He grabbed Lee's arm with a strength that surprised her. "It ain't there," he said in a high-pitched voice. "I told your brother it ain't there. He wouldn't listen. You gotta listen, though. You get off this mountain, you and Nick both. As far as your legs'll carry you."

Before she could recover, he grabbed the lantern and shuffled into the mine shaft.

"What did all that mean?" Lee said, turning in time to catch Nick's worried expression.

"It's very good advice."

"No, not that. I mean all that about the White Devils and the ghost town."

"I think," Nick said, coming toward her, "it's probably the ramblings of a senile mind. That's all."

"But we heard the bikes!"

"We heard some bikes. Could be just a bunch of kids horsing around. Rumors get exaggerated in these parts. There's not a lot around here to get excited about."

"You don't believe that for one minute," Lee said angrily. "Stop patronizing me, Nick."

He arched an eyebrow skyward. "I don't know about you," he said, "but I'm starving. How about lunch?"

She voiced her exasperation with an angry growl at his back, which he blithely ignored, striding away from her toward the trees. She noticed the flashlight jammed into his back pocket and hoped they wouldn't have to use it again. She never wanted to see the inside of another mine. Ever.

They lunched on soft crackers and cheese and Nick's last two apples. The good thing about the dwindling supply of food, Lee reflected, was the lightened weight of her pack. Maybe her shoulders would survive after all. She was unprepared when Nick fastened the pocket of his pack and looked at her.

"At least we can say we gave it our best shot," he said. "We'd better get moving if we're going to make it back before dark."

Dismay hit her like a shower of hail. "Make it where?"

He couldn't miss the caustic tone of her voice, and his jaw set with matching obstinacy. "Back to town."

He was openly challenging her now, daring her to protest. Well, she was going to protest, all right. With great care she stashed her litter, then stood and looked down at him.

He sat in his usual crossed-legged position, his arms resting on his knees, his eyes intent on her face.

"We're not going back to town," she said clearly. She felt the familiar plunge of her stomach when his mouth thinned in an expression she recognized.

He rose in a fluid movement that she was forced to admire in spite of her apprehension. She was struck again by his powerful build. She wasn't used to looking up that far at a man, and his shoulders, outlined against a backdrop of graceful firs, seemed wider than ever.

She was tempted to back away from him. He was much too close, less than an arm's length away. She wouldn't give him that satisfaction, though, and she lifted her chin and met his gaze squarely.

"And I say we are." His voice carried a note of authority that she knew from experience was dangerous to oppose.

"I'm not going to give up now," she said.

His brows clashed above his nose. "So what are you proposing to do?" His emphasis on the word *you* was ominous.

"Look for Simon. In the ghost town. It's our only lead."

"There's no ghost town up there, Lee."

"Simon thought there was."

"Simon was mistaken."

Her control snapped so fast it took even her by surprise. "You don't know everything. Simon went to look for the ghost town, so it seems perfectly logical to me that that's where we should be looking for him."

"Lee."

He was trying to pacify her, she thought angrily. If he touched her, so help her, she'd hit him.

"I know these mountains," Nick said evenly. "Well enough to be sure that there were no towns built this high up. The buildings were erected around the old railroad, which ended far below where we are now. The miners that came this high camped out—it was impossible to get supplies, so they didn't build houses."

"I don't want a history lesson," Lee said sarcastically. "Someone gave Simon directions. You heard Ben—a mile and a half, he said, into the morning sun, which is east. That should be simple enough to work out."

"I know where the high plateau is," Nick said in a voice that suggested his patience was running out. "There's nothing up there except wheat grass and spruce and a few rabbits."

"Fine. Then it should be easy to spot Simon."

The gleam in his eyes spelled danger. "I told you this morning. If Simon wasn't at the mine, we would go straight back."

It was getting harder for her to stand her ground. He was starting to breathe more heavily. It was like facing a smoldering volcano, she thought. "I see. You've fulfilled your contract. Is that it? Or are you waiting for me to up the price?''

She noticed that his hands were clenched, and now she stood back, awed by her own recklessness.

''We're going back now. Your brother is a big boy. Big enough to take care of himself. I've been shot at twice. The next time they may get lucky. Or they may get you. I'm not going to be responsible for that.''

''You don't have to be,'' Lee yelled. ''I don't need you. Go back to your nasty little tavern. I'll find Simon on my own.''

He stepped forward and grabbed her arms. ''You're going back to town with me,'' he said fiercely, ''if I have to drag you kicking and screaming all the way.''

''No!'' She fought with everything she had—hands, feet. She even butted her head against his chest. ''Let me go!'' she screamed at him when it became apparent that her struggling was useless.

When he did so, abruptly, it shocked her. ''How far do you think you'd get,'' he said, ''out here on your own? You can't stand up to me. How are you going to deal with a gang of bikers?''

She refused to cry. She blinked the tears back and looked at him. ''You don't understand,'' she whispered brokenly. ''I promised my mother. She'd never forgive me if I didn't at least try.'' In spite of her efforts, the moisture welled up, and she dashed at her eyes with an angry hand.

Nick muttered an oath, closed his eyes and raised his face to the sky, raking one hand through his hair. How was he going to argue with that? he asked himself, knowing he couldn't.

''It's all right,'' Lee said stiffly. ''I release you from any responsibility for my welfare. You can go back to town. I'll mail you a check as soon as I have this all cleared up.''

She turned her back on him and took a step toward her pack. Her foot was still in the air when he reached for her with his strong hands and twisted her around. She pounded on his chest with her fists, speechless with fury.

He grabbed her hands and twisted them behind her back, pulling her against his solid chest.

She gasped as her breasts collided with his hard muscles, and she jerked her face up. Whatever she was going to say was smothered by his mouth as it came down on hers with an intensity that took the strength from her knees. Her angry protest dissolved into a moan as his mouth moved on hers, insistent and demanding. His beard grazed her skin, but she was heedless of it as he released his hold on her hands and folded his arms around her, his hand moving up to grasp the back of her neck.

Lee felt as if every nerve ending in her body had burst into flame. She slid her hands up the sinewy contours of his arms and shoulders, then curled them, at long last, through the thick waves of his hair. She knew she'd been longing for this moment ever since he'd pinned her against the mountain wall. Maybe longer.

She felt the thud of his heartbeat against her breast, and she strained for her body to meet his, desire cutting through her with sweet intensity as he groaned deep in his throat. He lifted his head, and the hunger in his eyes created an answering passion that was impossible to deny.

Inside her head a voice whispered a warning. *You'll get hurt. It'll be that much harder to walk away.* She dismissed it as his mouth opened and covered hers, his tongue probing her lips open with a gentle insistence that compelled her to submit. The fire raging inside her was melting her resistance. The voice in her head faded as his hands slid to her hips, and he pulled her against him, making her undeniably aware of his urgent need. Her resolve crumbling, she returned his kiss with a fever that matched his.

She was shocked when he lifted his head and pulled away from her. His breath rasped in his throat as he stood motionless, his eyes still blazing with a hungry fire. Then Lee heard it, too. A faint rumbling in the distance, rapidly intensifying.

"Bikes." Nick's terse explanation chilled the flames smoldering in her body.

"Are they coming here?" she whispered.

"They're coming damn close." He stooped and lifted both packs, signaling for her to follow with his head.

She obeyed without question, staying close behind him as he plunged into the haven of the forest.

They didn't stop until the sound of the engines had faded, leaving only the birds to interrupt the silence. They were back at the stream, Lee realized with a sense of shock. She hadn't thought it was that close.

She watched Nick drop the packs and sit down on a fallen tree trunk. After a moment's hesitation, she perched on the other end. She was out of breath, and it wasn't entirely due to the scramble through the trees. She was still shaken by Nick's kiss, and by the intensity of her own emotions. She didn't know what to say, or whether she should say anything at all. She'd wanted his kiss, and now she wished it hadn't happened. It complicated things. She stared miserably at the stream and waited for him to speak.

Nick stretched out his legs and contemplated his boots. He had a few decisions to make, and he didn't like any of them. There was no doubt in his mind of the most sensible course to take. He should get her back to town in the fastest time possible. He was convinced that every minute they spent on the mountain put them deeper in danger.

He must be slipping. He'd let his needs take control, something he never did. He knew only too well what the outcome would have been if the bikers hadn't intervened. He still wanted her, dammit. His body was an agonizing furnace of need. Her response had far exceeded his expectations; she'd given him a tantalizing glimpse of a passion he hadn't suspected. It scared the hell out of him.

He wanted to take her back, to get her out the way of whatever was waiting for them out there. But he couldn't get the image of her face out of his mind, desperate, pleading and stubbornly fighting tears.

He could understand what was driving her. He'd felt the same way once, before he'd been betrayed. He frowned at his boots and crossed his ankles. How could he refuse to help her when it was so damned important to her? He desperately wanted to find Simon and put an end to her misery. Not to mention his determination to find out what was going on, for his own sake. He glanced over at Lee, who was watching the stream splash over the rocks.

Her hair was a dark, fluffy cap framing her face, and her delicate cheekbones glowed from the sun's touch. Her mouth curved in an enticing arc; he remembered vividly how it felt under his, and his body responded in an urgent reminder.

He shifted to a more comfortable position and took hold of his racing emotions. From now on, he'd have to keep a lid clamped tight on his desires, he decided. He couldn't afford to be this distracted; it would take all he had to finish the job. Surprised, he realized he'd made up his mind.

"There are a few things you should know before we go on looking for your brother," he said.

Lee's face blazed with relief and delight. In order to stop his hands from reaching for her, he had to press them into the knotted wood on either side of him.

"First," he went on doggedly, "we're in a tight spot. We know there's danger out there, but we don't know what it is or where it will come from. That makes it all the more deadly. Second . . ." He paused, then forced himself to continue. "You have to face the possibility that Simon may already be dead."

He hated what he'd done to her. She looked as if he'd hit her.

"No!" Lee jumped to her feet, her eyes wide with fear. "He's not dead. I would know it. He's not dead, I tell you."

"Lee!" Leaning forward, Nick grasped her arm and pulled her down beside him. "I said it's a possibility, that's all."

She stared up at him in the defiant way that he knew was so much a part of her.

"You can think what you like," she said. "I know what I know."

He shrugged, hiding his concern with a smile. "All right. If he's on this mountain, we'll find him. But it could take days. Weeks. You're not used to these conditions, and it's going to get rougher. The climb to the plateau is a tough one, and we're running out of supplies. The supply camps are way below us. We should go back down and stock up before we attempt to go on. Wouldn't it make more sense for me to get help and leave you in town?"

"No." She looked at him with determined eyes. "I'm not going back."

It was the answer he'd expected, but he had to give it one more try. "All right. We'll go on. We'll take a chance on the supplies and go up to the plateau, even though I know there is no ghost town up there. Maybe we'll find Simon, or at least find out what happened to him." He looked at her, his expression grave. "There's something else I haven't told you."

"What is it?" She was almost afraid to ask.

"I think I know who's been following us," Nick said. "I'm pretty sure he has been ever since we left Midge's camp."

Lee stared at him, a growing fear clutching at her. "You think it's someone in Midge's camp?"

"I think it's Midge himself."

"Oh, no." The look on his face tore at her heart. "What makes you think it's Midge?"

"There were bikes at the camp. They're illegal on the mountain. Any vehicles are."

"Are you saying you think he's part of this gang?"

"I think he's connected in some way."

She could see what it was costing him to condemn his friend, and she felt sick. "If you think he's been following us, that means..."

"He's also the one who was shooting at me in the woods."

"Why Midge? It could be anyone from the camp." She knew she was clutching at straws, but she would have done anything to take that look off his face.

"I saw the bike tracks. It had to be someone pretty heavy to make tracks like those."

"There must be lots of heavy men in the mountains," Lee said desperately. She hadn't liked the man, but she hadn't thought of him as an enemy. Not in the way Nick was suggesting.

"Then how do you explain," Nick said heavily, "the fact that Midge knew Simon was your brother? I didn't tell him, and I know you didn't."

It took a while for the implications to sink in. She reached out and laid a hand on his arm. "I'm sorry."

"No, *I'm* sorry." He pulled away from her and stood up. "I'm sorry I brought Simon up here in the first place. I'm sorry I let you talk me into bringing you. I'm sorry I didn't turn back when I first got suspicious, and I'm damned sure I'll be sorry for not going back now." He jammed his hands in his pockets and looked at her. "But now I've got a personal stake in this and, since you're so intent on coming with me, so be it. We've come this far. We might as well see it through."

Lee stood up, her smile lighting her eyes. "I'm ready if you are."

Nick drew in a sharp breath. "You'd better stop looking at me like that," he said, "or we won't be going anywhere."

Relief at his quick change of mood made her widen her smile. "What's the matter, Garrett? Losing that iron control?"

"You'd better pray I don't." Nick hoisted his pack onto his shoulders and helped her on with hers. "You won't get away so easily next time."

"What gives you the idea there's going to be a next time?"

"I have the utmost faith in my irresistible charm."

She shook her head at his retreating back, then said with a spark of mischief, "You were wrong back there at the mine, Garrett."

He stopped and looked over his shoulder. "Wrong?"

"Yeah." She walked toward him. "I *have* seen you without your pants." Grinning widely, she sauntered past him, enjoying the stunned expression that froze his face.

Nick hadn't exaggerated the climb to the plateau. At times their path rose so steeply it seemed impossible that trees could cling to the crumbly earth. Lee's arms ached, both from the effort of dragging herself over rock-strewn ledges and from the indignity of being hauled up stretches of mountain where, she would have sworn, even a bird couldn't have found a foothold.

They'd been climbing for the better part of an hour when Nick startled her by shoving her under a spindly fir and holding her there. She marveled at his acute hearing; he had detected the sound long before she had.

"Is it a motorcycle?" she said as her ears caught the muffled whirring of an engine.

Nick shook his head, his forehead creased in a frown. "Helicopter. They fly supplies into the camps two or three days a week, but they don't usually come up this high."

"Well, this one is," Lee said as the whirring grew more pronounced.

"Yeah." Nick peered up through the branches. "That's what's bothering me."

"Do you think it's got anything to do with the tracks?" Lee asked, wishing her stomach would stop fluttering.

"I don't know." Nick ducked, dragging Lee down with him as the big machine roared overhead, then swung away to the right before gradually fading into the distance.

Lee found herself clutching Nick's arm, her fingers digging into his firm flesh. She let him go and stepped around him without looking at him. She couldn't afford to get that close to him again. She was only too aware of her vulnerability when it came to Nick Garrett. She knew that if they hadn't been interrupted that afternoon, she would have forgotten reason and enjoyed what Nick was offering her. And that, she assured herself, would have been a big mistake.

She had no illusions about Nick's intentions. Or his feelings for her. It was a natural reaction. They were alone, she was not unattractive, and he was a normal, healthy, virile male. She wished she could be as casual about her feelings toward him.

Nick stood with his face turned toward the sky, his brow furrowed in concentration. "I didn't see any markings on that chopper," he murmured. "I'd like to know where it was going."

"Maybe it's one of those tourist flights, like they do around Mount Saint Helens," Lee suggested.

"Maybe." He lowered his head and smiled at her. "Whatever it is, it's gone now. You ready to go on?"

She nodded. "As ready as I'll ever be."

"We have to keep moving," Nick said. "We have to find shelter before dark."

"Another cave?" Lee asked as casually as she could manage.

"Nope. Not this time. At least, I don't know of any." He held out his hand, and she grabbed it, wincing as he jerked her up the steep slope. "We'll have to make do with a friendly crevice tonight, if we can find one. You'll be sleeping under the stars."

Wherever it was, Lee thought with a measure of certainty, it wasn't going to be easy to spend another night with this man.

The sun had dipped behind the mountain when Nick told her to rest. She collapsed on the ground and looked up at him with a plaintive smile.

"Do you think," she said between gasps, "this will have a permanent effect on my legs? I'd hate to develop jock muscles."

Nick grinned and squatted beside her. "Lady, I wouldn't let anything happen to those gorgeous legs of yours."

She squirmed as he smoothed her hair back. She'd forgotten just how much he'd seen of her legs.

"While we're on the subject," Nick went on, "when did you see me without my pants?"

Lee swallowed and took an intense interest in a piece of rock, which she picked up and turned over and over in her hand. "Er, it was this morning, when we washed in the stream. I came back and you . . . weren't quite ready."

"I see."

Lee's breath seemed to be permanently trapped in her lungs.

"And how long did you stand there watching?" Nick asked in a silky voice.

She dropped the rock. She wasn't going to let him do this to her. She raised her chin and met his eyes, which were dark with amusement and with something else that started her pulse racing. "Long enough."

He smiled. It was a slow smile, full of promise. "Sooner or later, when the time is right, I'm going to even the score."

He leaned forward and dropped a light kiss on her lips, testing her self-control to the limit.

Not if I can help it, she vowed. The thought of him looking at her naked body was too evocative to contemplate.

Nick stood up and squinted into the darkening sky.

"Is it much farther?" Lee asked, staggering to her feet.

"No. It's on the other side of this bluff." He looked down at her. "We might as well camp down here for the night. There's a wide crack in the rocks over there. It should give us some shelter. It'll get cold when the sun goes down."

She couldn't stop the little cry of dismay. "Can't we go on, if it's not far?"

"How did I know you were going to say that." He sighed and looked up at the bluff. "Okay. We'll leave the packs here and go up and take a quick look. But that's all. Soon it'll be too dark to see anything, anyway."

She nodded eagerly and slipped out of the straps. "We should be able to see the ghost town from the top, shouldn't we?"

Nick sighed again. "You're going to be disappointed, Lee. It's just a flat area of ground, with a few trees. No ghost town, I promise you."

"I still want to see it."

He gave her a long look, then took off his pack and dropped it on the ground. "Okay. This is your trip. Let's go."

She didn't know she had the strength left in her to climb those last few feet. Only the thought that they might be close to Simon kept her feet moving forward, her arms propelling her up. Nick was slightly ahead of her when he stopped so suddenly she almost lost her footing.

"For crying out loud!" The words were uttered in a harsh whisper, and Lee shoved herself up, anxious to see what he was staring at. As her head rose above the top of the bluff, she saw the plateau flowing away from her, its vast, flat field of wheat grass looking strangely out of place, bordered by the jagged outline of the mountain's summit.

The pale yellow weeds swayed in the evening breeze, rippling in massive waves toward the thick stand of spruce and firs that clustered at the foot of the next rise. On the other side, the grassy field came to an abrupt end as the mountain dropped away at a sharp angle.

But it was the trees that held Lee's attention. Sandwiched among them, like macabre ghosts of the past, the weathered walls of half a dozen buildings stood sentinel.

"I don't believe it," Nick muttered. "It's impossible. They weren't there six years ago. I swear."

Lee was hardly conscious of his words. Her face bright with excitement, she gazed across the wavering grass. "He's there. I know he is." She wasn't aware until Nick answered her that she'd spoken out loud.

"I hope you're right."

She pulled at his arm. "Come on. Let's look." She would have jumped up, but he held her down.

"Whoa! Not so fast. We can't go barging down there in full view. We don't know what could be waiting for us."

"Nick, I have to go and look."

"Okay. We'll look. But we'll circle around and come down by the trees. That way, if anyone's there, they won't see us coming."

Lee's eyes clouded. "You still don't trust him, do you? You still think Simon is a threat to us."

"Simon, Midge, the bikers—I don't trust anyone or anything at the moment." He pushed his hair back with his fingers. "All I know is that something really strange is going on, and I don't like it. I especially don't like dragging you into the middle of it."

Lee smiled. "You seem to be forgetting something, Mr. Garrett. I hired you to bring me here. This was my idea."

"Don't remind me." He slid down a few feet and pulled her after him. "We'll keep out of sight as long as possible, but we'll have to move fast. It'll be dark soon, and you wouldn't like having to feel your way around here.''

The thought of that gave Lee an extra burst of energy as they half slid, half scrambled around the edge of the bluff. They were almost at the line of trees when Nick stopped and pointed at the ground. A track had been worn over the edge of the bluff, obviously leading down to the ghost town. Deep grooves rutted the hard ground to the width of a large car.

Lee glanced at Nick's face questioningly, and he nodded. ''Bikes,'' he said quietly.

Lee squeezed her lips together. ''Do you think they're here?''

''There's one way to find out.'' He cautiously raised his head above the lip of the bluff and looked down. ''Come on,'' he said, reaching for Lee's hand. ''Keep your head as low as you can.''

With hardly a sound they slipped over the edge and began the steep descent through the trees. A jay screeched above Lee's head, flapping noisy wings and screaming its annoyance at being disturbed. She tightened her grip on Nick's hand and was reassured when he returned the pressure. They moved forward, bent almost double, until they reached the flat ground.

''You stay here,'' Nick whispered when they paused beneath a clump of bushy firs.

''No. Not this time. I'm coming with you.''

To her surprise he gave her no argument, but trod quietly on, towing her behind him. When he halted, she peered around his shoulder and caught her breath. Not fifteen yards away, the building loomed above them, its coarse-grained walls of pine blending into the trees.

The beams were withered with age but still supporting the sagging roof. The windows were glassless, the door hinges corroded with rust.

Motioning for Lee to stay where she was, Nick eased forward, crouching low on his heels, until his head was below one of the windows. Lee held her breath, her teeth clamped together, while Nick raised himself inch by inch and then looked inside.

Disappointment cut into her as he dropped back and gave a quick shake of his head.

He pointed into the trees farther on, and when she looked, she saw another house a few yards away. She nodded in reply and watched him slink away from her, his body huddled close to the ground.

The shadows crept in around her, and she could just make out his outline as he reached the second building and repeated the procedure. She watched him drop back on his heels, and she clenched her hands in frustration.

Nick was coming back fast. She would never get used to seeing him move in that swift, effortless motion, like a natural inhabitant of the forest. His face gave nothing away as he reached her, and before he spoke, he drew her back, away from the buildings.

When he did, it was to give her a rush of exhilaration that intoxicated her.

"I guess," he said calmly, "we've found Simon."

Chapter 6

Lee's cry of joy died in her throat as Nick shot his arm out to restrain her. She looked up at him to protest, but his expression froze the words before she formed them.

"What is it?" She clutched at his shirt with nerveless fingers. "Nick, he's not..."

Her eyes telegraphed fear and despair, and he pulled her into his arms. "No, he's all right. But there's someone with him. A guard. And Simon's tied up." She shuddered against him and he held her closer, wishing he knew the right things to say.

"Did you recognize the man with him?"

Her voice was muffled against his shoulder, and his heart turned over. "No, I've never seen the guy before. I didn't get a good look. He was just sitting there, reading. The guard, I mean. Simon looked as if he was asleep."

"Asleep?"

He caught the urgent question in her voice and hurried to reassure her. "I saw him move, Lee. He's alive and, as far as I could tell, unhurt."

"What are we going to do?" She'd stopped shuddering, but her hands twisted the front of his shirt, and he took hold of them, hugging them to his chest.

"We're going to find a shelter for the night, and we'll talk about it then. There's nothing we can do right now."

She pulled away from him, her eyes pleading. "I have to see him, Nick."

"Lee, it's too risky. If they see us, we won't be able to help him." He took her face in his hands. "Believe me, I know how hard this is for you, but we have to be sensible about this."

She nodded, her face pinched with worry, and he touched the tip of her nose with his lips. "It'll be all right, Lee. Trust me."

She did trust him, more than was wise, perhaps. She was counting on him, and somehow she knew he would come through for her. She allowed him to lead her back to the bluff, confident that with his strength and remarkable resourcefulness, he would know what to do. Hugging that comfort to her, she concentrated on the climb back through the whispering trees.

She would have been completely lost without Nick, Lee decided as they crept down the other side of the bluff to where the packs lay. The moon was not yet high enough to give them light, and Lee expected to step off any minute into bottomless space.

Nick's hands placed her feet in niches she couldn't see and her hands on shrubs and ledges she'd had no idea were there. He moved with the efficient ease that she never failed to admire, even at times like these with the darkness swallowing her sense of direction and her mind in a confused fog.

She was weak with relief when she felt the rugged but wonderfully flat ground beneath her feet.

"Over here," Nick said. She followed him blindly, her hand in his, until the moon obliged by spreading a cold, pale light over the mountainside and she was once more able to function independently. A few minutes later Nick squatted on his heels, and she realized he'd found the packs with apparently little effort.

"I wish I knew how you do that," Lee said when Nick dug the flashlight out of his pack.

"Do what?"

"See in the dark."

"It's one of the many useful talents one develops when living in the mountains." His teeth flashed in the moonlight as he handed her the pack, and she took it from him, hugging it in her arms. "Just a few more feet, then you can rest."

It no longer surprised her that he'd found adequate shelter for the night; that was something she expected of him now. He switched the flashlight on, revealing a natural crack in the rock. The shelter was maybe eight feet high, widened by time and the ravages of wind and rain. Though roofless, the walls were close enough together to provide a barrier to the night breezes, and they would keep each other warm in the sleeping bags, Lee observed. They would have to practically sleep on top of each other in the narrow crevice.

Any other time the prospect of lying that close to Nick's body under a starlit sky would have filled her with excitement and a certain amount of anticipation. But then any other time she wouldn't be in this position.

Simon's face swam in front of her as she helped Nick unroll the sleeping bags. If only she could have seen him, even for a second, just to prove to herself that he was all right. She sighed, smoothing out the fabric beneath her. She had to trust Nick's judgment, though it was hard to imagine how he was going to get Simon out of there.

"I hope you're not a restless sleeper," Nick said when they'd finished the task.

"I'm not going to sleep at all until I know what we're going to do about Simon." She plopped herself down on the sleeping bag and eased her legs out in front of her.

"I figured that." He dropped down next to her, crossing his legs. "We'll have to conduct this conversation in the dark. I don't want to waste the battery. We may need it later."

Her heart lurched with hope. "We're going to rescue him?"

"Not we. Me." He flicked off the light, enveloping them once more in darkness.

"You can't do it alone. That's crazy."

"Exactly. I'm glad you pointed that out." She heard him moving around and jumped when his arm touched hers.

"Sorry, but you'll have to get used to it. There's not much room in here."

She heard the dry note in his voice and was instantly annoyed with herself. "It's okay. I guess I'm a little jumpy."

"I know."

She waited, afraid she already knew what he was going to say next. Her hands were clenched painfully in her lap.

"Lee, until I know what's going on in that place, I can't make any decisions. I wouldn't be much help to Simon if I went charging in there and got into trouble myself."

"Do you think it's the White Devils?" She shuddered, remembering Ben's face when he'd talked about the gang.

"I don't know who or what yet. I couldn't see much from where I was, and I didn't want to risk anything with you there."

She made a small, impatient sound, and he sighed. "Lee, I've told you before, you don't know what you're up against in these mountains. There are men out there who would kill if they thought someone was after their gold. Maybe that's what Simon got tangled up with."

She knew by the way he hesitated that there was more. "Or?"

"Or," Nick said carefully, "Simon could be involved with something heavier and got in a little too deep. Even crooks fight among themselves once in a while."

"I see. You're still not prepared to give my brother the benefit of the doubt." She heard his sigh and wished she could see his face.

"As long as there is a doubt," Nick said quietly, "I think I should find out before we make any wrong moves. I'm going to go back in there and take another look around, see what I can find."

"Now? Without me?"

His hand found hers in the dark. "Without you. The sooner we know, the sooner we can act." He squeezed her fingers, then let her go, and she blinked as the light flashed on again.

She watched him pull up his pant leg and check the knife lodged in his boot. She felt a sense of unreality, as if she were watching a bad movie. Only she and Nick were the actors and neither of them was pretending.

She thought she was past surprises, but she couldn't hide her little gasp when Nick hunted in his pack and withdrew something hidden in his hand, then with a slight movement of his thumb revealed the thin, deadly blade of a switch knife.

"I always carry a spare in tight places," he said, noticing her expression. "It's quieter than a gun and a lot more accurate."

She watched in silence as Nick pulled his jacket on and zipped it up. She didn't know this man at all, she told herself. He was an unpredictable, even dangerous man who gave away nothing of himself. And she was sitting here, desperately afraid that he wouldn't come back to her safely. What kind of sense did that make? She'd try to fool herself into thinking that it was because she was terrified of being alone and lost in the mountains, but she knew better. There was a lot more to it than that, and that was what worried her. She was being unrealistic and heading for a painful let-down, but she didn't seem able to help herself.

"I'll have to leave you without a light," Nick said as he stood up. "Once your eyes get accustomed, you'll be able to see by moonlight."

"Of course." She was proud of her calm voice. She rose, attempting a smile. "Be careful, Nick."

He didn't answer but stood looking at her, his eyes holding hers, then he curled his arm around her and dragged her up against him. He dropped a hard, swift kiss on her mouth, then he was gone, and she was alone in the silent darkness.

In spite of her torturous thoughts, she had a hard time keeping her eyes from closing. She delayed putting on her sweater as long as possible, hoping the cold would keep her awake, but when her teeth started chattering, she gave in and wrapped it around her.

She thought about singing out loud but immediately dismissed the idea. Anyone could be creeping around out there in the dark. She regretted that thought at once. Her imagination took off with it, and she spent the next hour starting at every sound. She tried not to think of Nick creeping through the darkened forest, perhaps risking his life in an effort to save Simon.

She couldn't bear to think of Simon, a helpless prisoner, afraid and alone. She concentrated instead on memories. The family picnics and the fishing trips. Christmas in the West Hills, with Father playing Santa, and Mom... She rubbed her arms and hugged them closer to her body. It had been so different after their mother had died. She had tried to keep her promise and take care of them both, Lee thought despairingly. She had really tried.

And now Father was practically a recluse, and Simon... What was Simon? When had he begun to change from the carefree, fun-loving boy to the sometimes unreachable person he'd become? She and her brother used to be so close. At times they still were, but there were the other times, when

she had sensed his inner torment and been hurt by his refusal to admit that anything was wrong.

If it hadn't been for the anniversaries, she reflected, she
might have lost touch with him altogether. At least he had
always kept their pact. Until now.

An owl hooted deep in the forest, and the melancholy
sound touched her heart. Her eyes clamped shut, she leaned
back against the wall and tried to get comfortable.

She was jolted awake by a small sound that momentarily
stopped her heart, then started it pumping wildly. She was
on her feet when Nick's broad shoulders filled the opening
of the crevice. She longed to throw her arms around his
neck, but warned by the depth of her racing emotions, she
held back, afraid of revealing too much. The moon was
much higher now, so she could see fairly well without the
flashlight, and Nick's expression did nothing to calm her
fears. She waited until he sat down on the sleeping bag, then
she knelt beside him.

"Did you see Simon?" she asked breathlessly. "Did you
find out what's going on? Tell me what happened!"

"Let me get my breath back first," Nick said, "then I'll
tell you everything."

"I'm sorry." She realized he was breathing heavily, and
she reached for her pack. "Do you want a drink?"

He shook his head. "Later."

He leaned against the wall and closed his eyes. She studied him anxiously. "You're not hurt, are you?" She was relieved when he opened one eye and gave her a small grin.

"No. Just getting old." He opened the other eye. "You
all right?"

"Fine. Anxious to know what happened, that's all."

He sat up and ran his fingers through his hair. "I got a
good look around the buildings. One in particular in the
middle of the row. The windows were covered, so I couldn't
see in. But I didn't need to. Judging from the smell and the

contents of the garbage cans outside, I've got a good idea of what's going on."

Lee stared at him. "Smell?"

"Yeah." Nick unzipped his jacket and leaned back. "A couple of months ago I read an article about the manufacturing of illegal drugs. It described the smell and named some of the ingredients used. One of them was phenylacetic acid. There was an empty drum of it in the garbage cans. That little outfit up there is a laboratory for manufacturing speed."

Lee's eyebrows shot up. "In the mountains? Where would they get the power for electricity?"

"Propane. I saw the empty canisters."

Lee caught her breath. "Then Simon..."

"It's pretty obvious he's a prisoner of the White Devils."

The thought of Simon in the hands of dangerous criminals was almost too much to bear.

"But why here? How do they transport it?"

"By helicopter, I'd guess." Nick rubbed his eyes wearily. "There've been several labs raided in California lately. It's probably getting way too hot down there, so they're moving up to Oregon. What better place to run an illegal lab than the mountains? Not many people go that high up, and those who do would just think it was another ghost town."

"Until they took a closer look," she suggested.

"I doubt anyone would get that close." Nick dragged his pack toward him. "The prospectors around here are being scared off. That's what all the raids are about. Or they could just be rumors, put out to make the miners jumpy enough to mind their own business. As for the occasional hiker—" his face hardened "—they've got that nicely covered, too."

She knew he must be thinking of when he'd been shot at. It must hurt him, Lee thought, to believe he was betrayed by a friend. She watched him dig out a packet of beef jerky and rip it open with his teeth.

"You're convinced that Midge is the man who shot at you? You could be wrong, you know." She said it more in order to take the look of betrayal off his face than out of convictions she might have.

He bit savagely into the jerky, offering her the packet with his other hand. She shook her head, and he shrugged.

"Don't you find it strange," he said when he'd finished chewing, "that Midge didn't mention the White Devils? They're common knowledge around here, according to Ben, and nothing gets by Midge. He had to know about them, so why didn't he mention them?"

"Perhaps he didn't want to scare me," Lee said, fully aware that that was nonsense.

Nick gave a short laugh. "Come on, Lee. He did his damnedest to persuade you to turn back. That's why I gave him the impression we were going back to town. Obviously he didn't fall for it."

Lee sighed. "It doesn't look good, I admit."

"It sure as hell doesn't. Especially when you consider the fact that he knew Simon's your brother. The only person who could have told him that was Simon himself. And Simon must have told him after I left."

"But Midge said he didn't see Simon again."

"Yeah. What does that tell you?"

Lee sighed. "It doesn't make sense. I just can't believe that Simon would talk to someone like that about his family. He didn't even tell you. Why would he tell Midge?"

"I don't know. That's something we'll have to ask your brother. Maybe they're a lot friendlier than we think."

"That's crazy. If Simon was friendly with those people, why would they tie him up?"

Nick pushed the empty jerky packet into his pack and found a beer. "Maybe Simon got greedy and decided to run his own show. It happens."

Lee bit back her quick retort. There was no sense in arguing about it at this point. "So, what do we do now?" It would be a relief to do *something*.

"What we should have done in the beginning." Nick flipped the tab on the can of beer. "This whole deal is more than I can handle on my own. There's someone watching Simon. I can't get near him. And there's a bunkhouse crawling with men. Luckily they were partying when I got there. Even so, enough of them were snooping around the woods to make it too risky." He tilted his head and poured beer down his throat. "We'll have to call in the sheriff," he said when he lowered the can.

"But it'll take us at least a day to get back to town," Lee said in dismay.

"Us, yes." He looked at her steadily. "I can do it alone in a few hours. It's faster going down, and if anyone's out there looking for me, I'll have a better chance of giving them the slip."

She swallowed hard. She could see the sense of it, but it didn't make her feel any better. "You want me to stay here."

"Not here. With Ben. At least he'll have a gun to protect you, if anything happens while I'm gone."

She thought about that for a long moment. "Will I have to go down the mine?" she asked in a small voice.

"Not if you don't want to. Not unless something goes wrong, anyway."

She nodded. "All right. When will you leave?"

"Just before dawn." He looked at his watch. "That's about six hours from now, so you'd better get some food in you and try to sleep."

She didn't think she could eat anything, but the granola bars she'd been saving till last tasted better than she'd expected. She opened a packet of punch, noting that there was only one left. That would do for the morning, she decided; then, if all went well, Nick would be back before nightfall.

"How will the sheriff's men get up here?" she asked Nick when she'd finished her meager meal.

"Helicopter. We should be back by midday." His smile was encouraging, and her spirits rose.

"As soon as that?"

"Just as soon as possible." He uncrossed his long legs and stood. "I don't want to leave you up here alone any longer than I have to."

"I won't be alone," she reminded him with a grin. "I'll have Ben to protect me."

He studied her in the shadowy light. "You're a gutsy lady," he said at last.

"It must have rubbed off." She tried to make light of it, to ignore what was happening between them again, but it was there, that inescapable pull that joined them as surely as if they were physically entangled. Even in that half-light she could see the muscle moving below his cheekbone and the darkening of his eyes. She had to stop it now, before she was caught up again in the irresistible seduction of his touch.

"I'm exhausted," she said, and gave an exaggerated yawn. "I won't have much trouble sleeping tonight after all."

She couldn't read the expression on his face. He stared at her for a minute longer, then turned abruptly and disappeared into the night.

It seemed an eternity before he came back, but it could only have been a few minutes. She was tempted to pretend she was asleep, but she knew she wouldn't fool him for a minute.

She kept her eyes clamped shut, willing herself not to look as he undressed quickly and slid into the bag next to her.

"You comfortable?" he said as she tried to ease her body as far away from him as possible.

"As comfortable as I'm going to be." She wiggled her back against the hard ground. "You need a tougher skin than mine to be comfortable in these circumstances."

He laughed. "You'd be surprised how fast people can toughen up. Look at you—you're getting to be a regular mountain goat."

"Is that supposed to be a compliment?" Lee asked, pummeling her sweater into a more comfortable pillow.

"In my book it is." He yawned. "You're doing all right, Ms. Coulton."

"Thank you, Mr. Garrett." She smiled in the semidarkness. "It's nice to know you can be wrong about some things."

"I seem to be getting a track record when it comes to people." He shifted his body, sending tiny shivers up her back. "But as I said once before, you're an enigma."

"You were wrong about the ghost town, too," Lee pointed out.

"Yeah. That still puzzles me. I know those buildings weren't there six years ago, yet the timber is genuine nineteenth century. I'd stake my reputation on that."

"Your reputation?" She turned her head. She could see the strongly chiseled outline of his features as he lay on his back, staring up at the strip of sky above them. He was so close. She could feel the warmth of his body, hear the gentle whisper of his breathing. She wanted to snuggle up to him, to feel the comfort of his arms around her, and knew she dare not even think about it.

"Are you an expert on antiques, then?" she asked, shutting off her treacherous thoughts.

"Some people think so."

She propped her head on her elbow and contented herself with looking at him. At least she could enjoy that for a little while.

"You're a strange man, Nick Garrett," she said. "You live in a backwoods town—in a tavern, of all places—yet you know antiques, and your taste in reading is cultured and amazingly varied."

He turned his head, and his eyes found hers in the dark. "You don't miss much, do you?"

She grinned. "It's intriguing to find a man who enjoys Hemingway and also reads something as heavy as *Canterbury Tales*."

He looked back at the sky, placing his hands behind his head. "It fascinates me to read works that were written centuries ago. Even in that world, so far removed from ours, people loved and hated and strove for happiness in the same way we do. The human condition hasn't changed much at all."

"And Hemingway?" She hardly dared to breathe. For the first time she was seeing the layer beneath the one he presented to the world, and she found it utterly fascinating.

"Hemingway." He sighed. "'A man can be destroyed but not defeated.' It's a hell of a theme."

"And one you relate to?"

"Maybe." He pulled his hands down and closed his eyes. "Go to sleep, Lee. You're going to need it."

She lay back, frustrated by his refusal to tell her more and grateful for the small glimpse he had given her. Before she said goodbye to him she would know it all, she promised herself.

She was shaken by the pain that sliced through her at the mere thought of leaving him and turned her thoughts to Simon in an effort to escape it. Was Simon as innocent as she so desperately wanted to believe? Or was there some truth in Nick's suggestion that Simon had been working with the criminals and had somehow alienated them? She stared up at the patch of sequined sky, knowing she could not accept that. Not as long as there was the slightest doubt.

She drew in a long breath of cool night air. Tomorrow she'd have the answers, if all went well. And by tomorrow night she could be saying goodbye to Nick.

She listened to the steady rhythm of his breathing and waited for the ache to go away.

Nick woke up early the next morning and, after switching on the flashlight, glanced at his watch. He was satisfied to find that the automatic clock in his brain had worked again. It seldom let him down. Then he realized that the solid warmth at his back was Lee's soft body.

Desire like fanned embers burst into white-hot heat. He was made acutely aware of his need as his body reacted with predictable speed. What had happened to his control? he wondered in frustration. He'd never wanted a woman so much in his life, not even during those interminable months in the moist heat of the Southeast Asian jungles.

What was it about Leanne Coulton that caused his libido to go on a rampage every time she came near him? He shifted his lower body away from the enticing softness, but she followed him, tucking her knees behind his.

He bit back a groan of agony. There were two layers of quilted fabric between them, he thought, and there might as well be nothing at all. He shoved his body against the wall and slid out of the sleeping bag. Pulling his pants on, he staggered out into the predawn darkness, ignoring her murmured moan of protest.

Lee's eyes opened slowly, then widened as her sleep-fogged mind cleared. She felt as if she were missing something, but she couldn't figure out what it was. She turned her head, her heart skipping as she saw the empty, rumpled bed beside her. Surely he wouldn't ... Even as the thought formed, his silhouette darkened the crevice.

He was bare-chested, and she was instantly wide awake, disturbed again by the sheer force of his masculinity.

"What time is it?" she asked, and followed him with hungry eyes as he reached for his shirt and tugged it over his head.

"Time to go. I'll go out again and let you get dressed."

"No need." She stretched and sat up. "I didn't undress, except for my shoes." It had seemed safer, somehow. She watched him push his feet into his heavy boots and lace them up. His shirt was black and made him look all the more powerful, for some reason. She watched as his long fingers worked expertly at the laces, and the tension coiled deep in her stomach as she imagined them caressing her skin.

"Will we have time to eat before we leave?" she said, certain that he must have seen the shiver that shook her body.

"What have you got left?" He opened his pack and frowned at the contents.

"Three granola bars, two bananas and one packet of punch," Lee announced, holding them up one at a time.

"No croissants?" He grinned, and she wrinkled her nose at him.

"No. You can bring me some back when you come. They're one of my favorite foods."

"Don't tell me what the rest of your favorites are. My stomach couldn't stand it." He lifted a can of beer in the air and raised a questioning brow. "Last one. Want to share? Then you can save your punch till later."

She shuddered. "Warm beer? At this unearthly hour?"

"You might be glad you did. It could be a while before you get the chance to buy more of that jungle juice."

There was something in his voice that sobered her at once. "I guess if you can do it, so can I," she said.

"That's my girl." He flipped open the tab and handed her the can. "Pretend it's hot coffee being served at the Royal King."

"Even I don't have enough imagination for that." She shut her eyes, tilted the can to her lips and swallowed the warm beer with an agonized expression on her face.

"It may be all right for you, Mr. Garrett," she said, "but it's not something I'd recommend to my customers."

"You disappoint me. I figured you'd start a whole new fad." He laughed at her, and she pulled a face.

"It would more likely start a riot." She managed to get a couple more gulps down before she handed him back the can. "I think I'll stick to punch in the future," she said with a look of distaste that made him chuckle.

"There's just no pleasing some folks. I'll bring you some back with the croissants."

She looked at him, unaware that her heart was in her eyes. "Just bring yourself back, Garrett."

He reached out and touched her face. "I intend to. I still have a score to settle, remember?"

"With Midge?"

"No. Something much more personal. Something that's not going to wait a whole lot longer."

His fingers brushed her cheek in a soft caress that traveled the length of her body.

"Let's go," Nick said softly. "The sooner we get this over with, the sooner you and I can take care of our problem."

Problem is right, Lee thought as she rolled up her sleeping bag and strapped it to her pack. She had no doubts about his intentions. Would she have the strength to refuse him? If she had any sense at all, she would. The problem was she wasn't too sensible when it came to Nick Garrett.

She followed him out into the crispness of dawn, shivering more from her provocative thoughts than from the fresh morning breeze.

The sun spread banners of pink and yellow across the brightening sky as they began the climb back to the mine. Going down wasn't all that much easier than going up, Lee discovered as she slid over a steep incline and landed awkwardly. It was just faster. She was certain she would wear out the seat of her jeans before she'd gone much farther. It was just as well that she'd packed a spare pair.

Nick managed the descent with the same graceful ease he'd displayed on the way up. If she hadn't been convinced of the wisdom of his plan before, she was now. It was obvious he would make better time without her.

Although she was constantly on the lookout for anything that moved, as she knew Nick was, they reached the final slope to the mine without incident. By now the sun had risen enough to warm her shoulders, though streaks of pale gray cloud marred the sky.

Nick looked up as she reached him, his hand shading his eyes. "Looks like we may be in for a storm," he said. "I hope it waits till I get back."

Fear touched her. "What if it doesn't?" she said, already knowing the answer.

He looked at her, his smile denying the concern in his dark eyes. "It will." He held out his hand. "Come on, Ben will be happy as a skunk to have your company for a while. Let's go give him the good news."

His hand, big, warm and comfortingly strong, held hers the rest of the way.

Ben did look happy to see them. Nick left Lee at the entrance while he went inside to find the old man, and when they both came out, Ben was chattering, his arms flying in all directions. He seemed relieved to see Lee, and greeted her with an enthusiasm that she found embarrassing. It was as if she were a long-lost child, she thought as he grasped her hand in both of his.

"I've been thinking about you two all night," he told her in his gravelly voice. "Sure glad you didn't run into any trouble. I guess you're on your way back to town."

His face changed as Nick explained briefly that he was going back for more supplies and intended leaving Lee in Ben's protection.

Ben looked from one to the other. "How come you're not going back, too?" he demanded, frowning ferociously at Lee.

Taking her cue from Nick's omission of their discovery of Simon, Lee shrugged. "I've decided to go on looking for my brother a little longer."

The prospector turned on Nick, his face screwed up in alarm. "You can't leave her here alone. What if the White

Devils come? There's nowhere to hide—they come right into the mines. They'd just keep following her till they got her."

"Ben." Nick laid a hand on the old man's frail shoulders. "I know you'll take care of her. There's no reason to expect trouble. No one knows she's here. As long as she stays out of sight, everything will be fine. I'll be back late this afternoon, okay?"

Ben wouldn't give up that easily. "Your brother's probably back in town by now." Lee saw an entreaty in his eyes. "Why don't you go back and look for him there?"

Lee shook her head. "I think he's somewhere in the mountains," she said gently. "I have to keep looking for him, Ben."

For a moment she saw real desperation in Ben's lined face, then he turned away with a shrug of defeat.

"I tried," he muttered.

"Come on, Ben," Nick said, giving the prospector a hearty slap on the back. "You know you'd enjoy the company of a beautiful woman."

Lee smiled. "Well, thank you, kind sir."

Nick winked at her. "Don't worry," he said meaningfully. "You will."

She was still trying to deal with her fluttering stomach when Nick dragged his pack from his shoulders and lowered it to the ground. "I appreciate this, Ben," he said, walking over to Lee. "I know I can trust you to take care of the lady."

"Sure," Ben mumbled. "I'll take care of her."

"Right." Nick helped Lee off with her pack and set it beside his. "I'm going to need some privacy for my goodbyes," he said to Ben. "We'll be back in a couple of minutes."

Lee's face warmed as Ben shot her a startled look, then she forgot about him as Nick took her arm and propelled her toward the trees. She glanced up at him, her mouth going dry as she met his eyes and read his intention.

"You didn't think I was going to leave you with a quick peck on the cheek, did you?" he said, grinning. "I want to leave you something to remember me by."

Her heart seemed determined to burst through her rib cage. She was trembling when he found a couple of sturdy firs standing close enough together to hide them from view.

He braced his legs apart, his back against a tree trunk, and pulled her into his body. His hand moved to the small of her back, pressing her to him, and she felt the heat of him against her stomach.

"I wish we had more time," he said huskily.

She echoed the wish as she met the warm promise in his midnight eyes. She leaned into him, and his arms tightened around her in a possessive gesture that intensified the longing that tormented her.

"There will be a time for us," Nick said softly. "That's a promise. I'm not a patient man, and I want to make love to you. But I want the time to make it good for you." With a finger he gently traced the low neckline of her shirt, his eyes following the movement. Lee, her knees growing weak, gripped the muscles of his upper arms for support.

"I want to know every inch of your body," Nick whispered. "Intimately. And I want you to know mine."

Lee found it impossible to breathe. His voice mesmerized her. She was intensely aware of his body: the hard muscles of his thighs, his firm stomach pressed against hers, his powerful chest crushing her breasts. She was intoxicated by his musky, male scent as her mind was seared by the visions his words had conjured. When he lowered his mouth to hers, she met it eagerly, thrilling at the groan that came from deep within his chest. He crushed her to him, and she dug her fingers into his back, loving the feel of his strong muscles bunching beneath the shirt.

His stubbly chin grazed her, but she only became more inflamed as his mouth took possession, his tongue plunging in and out in an erotic symbolism that swamped her senses.

She felt an acute sense of loss when he lifted his head and held her away from him. His eyes burned into hers as he stood there, breathing heavily. The look of naked passion on his face was so intense it scared her.

"I hope you know what you're unleashing here, Lee," Nick said with difficulty. "I'm not sure I can be a gentleman much longer."

She sent him a wobbly smile. "I hadn't noticed you were one before."

His answering smile was grim. "Lady, I've been a saint compared to what I can be if I'm given the chance. You'd better remember that before you trust yourself alone with me again." His eyes roamed over her, possessive and hungry. "I'd better go," he muttered, "while I still can."

Lee's throat contracted, and she tugged at his shirt, drawing him close again. She dreaded the thought of being without him, not knowing what was happening to him, or whether he was safe. "Hurry back to me," she said urgently.

His kiss was hard and brief, and infinitely sweet. "It'll be my number one priority," he promised.

She had to be content with that, and she allowed him to lead her back to Ben. Her head was reeling from the force of her emotions, and her body ached for satisfaction.

When they reached the mine, they saw that Ben had disappeared. "He's probably gone back down," Nick said, squatting by his pack. He hunted in it, found the flashlight and handed it to Lee. "Here. Stay close to the mine, and at the first sign of trouble, get down the shaft as fast as you can."

He looked at her, his eyes narrowed against the sun. "Can you shoot a rifle?"

"No."

He sighed. "Well, Ben can shoot well enough to put them off." He saw her expression of anxiety and stood quickly, reaching for her and drawing her close to his body. "I don't think any of this will be necessary. As I told you once before, I like to cover all my bases. I figure on being back in a few hours, together with a couple of helicopters and a few of the sheriff's sharpshooters. You'll be fine."

He rested his head against her forehead, wishing he could rid himself of the cold feeling in the pit of his stomach. His instincts were on full alert again, an insistent warning in the back of his mind that he couldn't suppress.

He'd considered every angle of this thing, and he couldn't see a better alternative. He knew she'd slow him down, and anyway, she was safer here with Ben. Still, his uneasiness was a persistent voice in his head, and he couldn't shake it. He'd always been so sure of himself, so confident in his decisions—even when they were split-second decisions, and even when they meant the difference between life and death. First in Nam and then in the mountains he'd trusted his sixth sense implicitly. What was it warning him of now? And why couldn't he hear what it was telling him?

He gave himself a mental shake and moved back to look into Lee's eyes. They were so warm, so soft, and they held a promise that made him weak. Maybe that was his problem. His body was still yearning for her; he would be uncomfortable for quite a while. He was amazed at his lack of control when he was near her. If he'd had the slightest suspicion that he'd end up feeling like this about her, he would have backed off immediately. He still couldn't get past who she was and where she came from. That put her on the other side of the street, no matter how strongly he was affected by his physical desire for her.

He dropped a light kiss on her soft, warm mouth, sweet pain twisting in him again as she responded eagerly. He'd forget that part of it, for it didn't change the way he wanted her.

"One more thing," he said softly as he put her away from him. Digging into his pack, he found what he wanted. He put the pearl-handled knife into her hand and pressed her thumb on the catch that released the blade. "Just in case."

Anguish tore at his heart as he saw the fear reflected in her eyes, and he forced himself to lift the pack onto his wide shoulders.

"I'll be back," he said, and after a last, long look, he turned and strode quickly toward the trees. It was hard for him not to look over his shoulder. Move fast, he told himself, and you'll be back before you know it.

He cleared his mind of all thoughts of her, calling on all his experience and expertise to concentrate on moving with the silent speed he knew was necessary.

He knew he'd finally outrun his sixth sense when, less than an hour later, a shadow moved abruptly in front of him, blocking his path. Fear raised the bile in his throat as he stared at the cold barrel of the rifle trained on him and the hands that held it—large, beefy hands covered with pale red hairs.

"I figured I'd run into you right about here," Midge said.

Chapter 7

Long after Nick's dark head had vanished among the trees, Lee stayed where she was, staring after him. A small part of her kept hoping that he would change his mind and come back for her. She felt cold and terribly alone, more alone than she'd felt since her mother died. She gripped the knife he'd given her and hugged it to her breast. At least she had something of his, even if imagining how he might have used it gave her shivers.

She slipped the knife into the back pocket of her jeans and wandered over to her pack. She could still feel the burning pressure of his mouth, and desire unfurled in her again when she remembered how his body had betrayed him and shown how much he wanted her.

If only she could take what he offered and enjoy it for what it was. She'd never been able to understand women who could fall into bed with someone they hardly knew. Until now. She wanted him with every fiber of her being, knowing they were worlds apart, knowing he wanted her for all the wrong reasons. She had to be crazy. He'd walk away from her as easily as he had a short while earlier, and she couldn't do that. Not without a lot of pain. Still she wanted him. And she'd go on wanting him, she knew, for a very long time.

She sighed and lifted her face to the sun, seeking comfort from its warmth. Even that was denied her as a filmy gray cloud blurred the bright rays. She watched it drift across the sky, chased by a bigger cloud, and wondered uneasily if Nick would be back before the weather broke. A storm, he'd said. Would they be able to fly a helicopter in a storm?

With a determined shake of her head she knelt on the ground and searched her pack for her comb. She dragged it through her hair, her thoughts on the man who had made such an impact on her life in such a short time. How Simon would laugh at her, she thought ruefully. Sensible, predictable, unemotional Lee. She hadn't even cried when her mother had died. Not in front of anyone, at least.

Absorbed as she was, she failed to connect the sound at first. After years of living in the city, such noises were part of the background. Only this wasn't the city. By the time that thought had occurred to her, the erratic buzzing had swelled to a muffled roar.

Lee leaped to her feet, the comb's teeth digging into her palm unnoticed. Her lips formed a silent word: *motorcycles*. Her feet remained fastened to the spot as her mind floundered. The ground seemed to tremble with the vibration; the roar became thunderous as the mountain caught the echoes and tossed them back, magnified and distorted.

Again Lee's lips moved in an agonized plea. "Nick!" But Nick was far away, and couldn't help her. She could see the dust now, smell the fumes of the engines, and her mind focused and took control. She grabbed at a strap of her pack, swung it off the ground and raced for the mine, praying that she hadn't been spotted. Once inside the suffocating blackness, she kept going until she'd left all traces of daylight behind her.

It wasn't until she'd bumped into a beam, scraping her arm on the rough surface and sending a shower of dust down on her head, that she stopped long enough to look for the flashlight. It was then that she realized something else. The noise outside had changed; it was more subdued. And constant. They were sitting outside the mine.

With her fingers she found the cool metal cylinder of the flashlight and closed her hand shakily around it and lifted it out of the pack. Dared she put it on? Would they be able to see the beam of light? Where on earth was Ben? He must have heard the motorcycles. As if in answer, light splashed the walls from around the curve, and she heard the shuffle of his feet. She rushed forward to meet him and almost ran into him.

The lantern swung crazily in his hand as he stared at her, almost as if he'd forgotten about her.

"Ben," she whispered urgently. "The bikers—they're at the entrance."

He searched her face while his lips moved soundlessly. Lee stared at him. How could this frail, old man possibly protect her? Or himself? She looked at the rifle clutched in his hand. She didn't know the first thing about firing a rifle, even if she could have brought herself to try. She was startled when Ben spoke, his voice quite steady.

"You stay here, Mrs. Coulton. I'll go deal with them."

"No, you can't." Lee grasped his bony arm and shook it. "Not by yourself—they'll hurt you."

He shook his head impatiently as he pulled out of her hold on his arm. "Now don't you worry none. You just sit here and don't move. Just wait here till I get back. I know how to handle people like that."

She watched the light bouncing off the walls like a deflating balloon as he shuffled off, leaving her alone in the dark. Her jaw ached, and she unclenched her teeth in a conscious effort to relax. Why had she let him go? What would they do to him? Or to her, if they found her?

She deliberately shut her thoughts down and waited, listening to the steady drone of the motorcycles, gripping the flashlight like a weapon. She almost fainted with relief when, after minutes of balancing on her toes, ready for flight, the shaft resounded with the explosive roar that signaled the dirt bikes were moving again. There were a few bad moments when she thought they might have taken Ben with them, then her face relaxed in a smile as the lantern he was carrying once more painted moving shadows on the rough walls.

She would have hugged him if he hadn't been holding the rifle. "How on earth did you manage that?" she asked breathlessly when he reached her.

"They were looking for someone," Ben said. "When I told them there weren't anyone here but me, they took off."

He edged past her, and she followed him, conscious of the uneasiness nagging at her. "Who were they looking for?" she asked.

Ben shrugged. "One of their cronies. Probably fell off his bike somewheres."

They'd reached the work area, and Ben stopped to prop the rifle against the wall. The shaft had widened considerably, and boxes of supplies were piled in one corner, while a sleeping bag and a garbage bag stuffed with what appeared to be clothes lay close by.

Lee shook off the niggling doubts. It was probably the effects of being underground. "Do you sleep down here, too?" she asked, aghast at the thought of this subterranean existence.

"Nope." Ben set the lantern on an upturned crate and took hold of the pickax leaning against it. "I sleep outside when it's warm, inside a ways when it's cold." He lifted the pickax and began to tap at the wall with it.

Lee watched him in silence for a while. He picked carefully at the rock, dislodging a small stream of stones and dust into a chute that fed into a wheelbarrow. Lee had no-

ticed the odd-looking contraption outside the mine, a long
table on some kind of springs, driven by what looked like an
old car engine. That must be what sorted the gold from all
the rubble.

She tried to imagine Nick doing the same thing, hour after hour, day after day, and wondered again what had driven
him to incarcerate himself in this depressing environment.
No wonder he loved the fresh air and the freedom of the
mountains. After spending all that time down here, he
probably couldn't get enough of it.

Thinking of Nick brought her back to the present, and she
felt a sudden urge to be back out in the daylight, within sight
of the sky. She wanted to watch for him. Already she missed
him, couldn't wait to hear his deep voice again and see his
eyes, warm and intense, promising her unimaginable plea-
sures,

"I'm going back out," she told Ben. "They must be far
away by now. I can't hear the bikes."

He gave her a sharp look and lowered his pick. "That
wouldn't be too bright, ma'am. Someone may still be out
there, snooping around, and it sure wouldn't be a good idea
for him to see you."

"But I can't stay down here," Lee protested in dismay.
"It could be hours till Nick gets back. I'll go crazy if I have
to stay down here that long."

Ben laid down his pick and stood watching her, his eyes
hard and bright as crystal. "I don't want to scare you,
ma'am," he said slowly, "but I wouldn't want to be in their
clutches. No, sir, 'specially if I was a good-looking lady like
you. Those devils ain't human. I heard some talk about the
things they done to people, and it ain't pretty. Best you stay
here with me, where it's safe."

Lee felt sick. Simon. What had those monsters done to
Simon? Had they hurt him? Alive, Nick had said. At least
he was still alive. She hugged her arms around her body and
moved over to where she'd dropped her pack. After tuck-

ing the flashlight inside, she sat down, using the pack as a cushion. The only way she'd survive the long wait down here was to keep talking, to prevent her mind from making too many detours.

"Tell me, Ben," she said, "why do you spend the best part of your life underground?"

She listened, fascinated in spite of herself by Ben's ramblings. Born into a large family, he told her, and hit by the Depression when he was a young boy, he'd been forced to scramble for what food he could find to survive. He painted her a picture of such vicious poverty that she felt almost ashamed of her own childhood. She'd taken so much for granted, and perhaps still did.

Ben had never lifted himself out of those deprived conditions; they'd followed him all his life. He'd taken menial jobs and had always been at the mercy of somebody's beckoning finger. He'd spent his years longing for his freedom. It had come, he said, when he'd met Nick.

"Yeah," Ben said as Lee's interest took on new life. "He's the one who changed things for me. Came across me in a storm and brought me down here, he did. Asked me if I needed a job. Hired me right away. I was working down here with him maybe a couple of months when he just up and said he had enough. He was getting out. Time he went back to the real world, he said."

Ben paused to wipe his forehead with a grimy arm. "Damn near gave me a heart attack. Then he said he'd sell me the mine, sign the claim over to me. I told him I didn't have no money, only a banged-up Jeep I bought cheap and fixed up."

Ben turned and looked at Lee, giving her a toothless smile. "Know what he said? He said, seeing as how he didn't have no car, that was the very thing he needed. He took it for the mine, paid in full."

Lee knew her rush of emotion must show on her face. "He still has the Jeep," she said softly.

Ben gave a dry chuckle. "He does? I'm surprised he didn't get rid of that old clunker years ago." He swung back to the wall and began picking at it again. "He should've," he muttered more to himself than to Lee. "He should've dumped it and everything else to do with this mountain. He shouldn't have come back here, getting in their way." He jabbed at the wall, bringing down a cascade of rocks around his feet.

Lee stared at his hunched shoulders. "In whose way? What are you talking about, Ben?"

"Them White Devils!" He was becoming agitated, smashing at the wall with his pick as if trying to fight his way through it.

Alarmed, Lee jumped to her feet. "Ben, what's wrong? You said they'd gone. You said—" She broke off, pictures flashing through her mind. Yesterday, only yesterday, Ben saying he'd never seen the bikers. A frightened Ben clutching his rifle, swearing he would shoot the lot of them. Yet a few minutes earlier he'd gone calmly up to talk to them. *As if he knew them.*

She became aware of her heartbeat as she struggled to clear her mind. She had to be mistaken. This harmless old man, who had just acknowledged that Nick had changed his life, wouldn't do anything to hurt him. *He shot at him twice,* her mind reminded her. By mistake. This had to be a mistake.

"Ben." Her voice shook, and she tried again. "Ben. What exactly did you say to the White Devils just now?"

"I told you."

He turned on her, and she was shocked by the wild look on his face.

"Don't go asking so many questions," he shouted. "It's better you don't know. It'll just get you into trouble. Like your brother. He kept asking questions. Wouldn't give up even when I told him he'd end up in trouble. Now they got

NO COST! NO OBLIGATION!
NO PURCHASE NECESSARY!

PLAY "LUCKY 7"
AND GET AS MANY AS SIX FREE GIFTS...
HOW TO PLAY:

1. With a coin, carefully scratch off the three silver boxes at the right. This makes you eligible to receive one or more free books, and possibly other gifts, depending on what is revealed beneath the scratch-off area.

2. You'll receive brand-new Silhouette Intimate Moments® novels, never before published. When you return this card, we'll send you the books and gifts you qualify for *absolutely free*.

3. And, a month later, we'll send you 4 additional novels to read and enjoy. If you decide to keep them, you'll pay only $2.49 per book, a savings of 26¢ per book. And $2.49 per book is all you pay. There is no charge for shipping and handling. There are no hidden extras.

4. We'll also send you additional free gifts from time to time, as well as our monthly newsletter.

5. You must be completely satisfied, or you may return a shipment of books and cancel at any time.

SILHOUETTE® "NO RISK" GUARANTEE

- You're not required to buy a single book—ever!
- You must be completely satisfied or you may return a shipment of books and cancel at any time.
- The free books and gifts you receive from this "Lucky 7" offer remain yours to keep—in any case.

If offer card is missing, write to:
Silhouette Book Club, 901 Fuhrmann Blvd., P.O. Box 9013, Buffalo, NY 14240-9013

DETACH AND MAIL CARD TODAY

BUSINESS REPLY CARD

First Class   Permit No. 717   Buffalo, NY

Postage will be paid by addressee

Silhouette Book Club
901 Fuhrmann Blvd.
P.O. Box 9013
Buffalo, NY 14240-9963

NO POSTAGE
NECESSARY
IF MAILED
IN THE
UNITED STATES

him hog-tied, and if your daddy doesn't come through with—"

His mouth snapped shut, and the silence that followed was so complete that Lee felt as if the entire world had frozen. It was broken at last by a trickle of dust falling from the cracks that fanned out from Ben's attack on the wall.

The sound released her deadlocked mind. He knew. Ben knew about the ghost town and that Simon was a prisoner there. Had he stumbled on it, as they had? Or was he one of them? And where did Father fit into this? Surely they couldn't be holding Simon for ransom. How would they know who their father was? Unless . . .

Midge. If Simon had told him about her, it was feasible he would have told him about Jonathan King. But why? None of this made sense. Unless he'd been forced to talk. *Those devils ain't human.*

She stared at Ben, whose wary eyes watched her intently. What had he told the White Devils? She had to get out of there, try to catch up with Nick, warn him somehow. Maybe she could fool Ben into thinking she hadn't understood.

"I'm sorry, Ben. I don't feel too well," she said truthfully. "I think I'll go up to the entrance and get some fresh air. I promise I'll be careful—" She choked on the last of the sentence as Ben reached for the rifle.

"I'm sorry, too, ma'am. Afraid I can't let you do that."

With a peculiar lack of emotion she watched him lower the barrel and level it at her. So Ben had sold them out. That meant he'd realized they had found the ghost town and Simon. What had she said, she wondered, to give that fact away?

She sat down on her pack, her shoulders slumping. She knew now what Ben had told the bikers. There was only one reason they would have taken off in such a hurry without bothering to deal with her first. "You sent them after Nick, didn't you?" she said wearily. "You told them he was going back to town."

Ben nodded. "I had to. He was going for the law."

She almost lost it then. They'd probably caught up with Nick by now. What would they do with him? Take him back to the ghost town? Or would they simply take care of him there, in the woods?

The pain was so acute it doubled her over. She rested her elbows on her knees and buried her face in her hands. First Midge and now Ben, she thought. How bitterly Nick would take this latest betrayal—if he lived long enough to care.

She heard Nick so clearly, as if he'd spoken in her ear: *You're a gutsy lady*. She repeated the words in her mind until she began to believe them. All right, Nick, she promised silently, I'll do what I can.

As long as there was a glimmer of hope, she couldn't give up. Simon needed her, and now it was up to her alone. With a gesture Nick would have been proud of, she raised her chin.

"How could you betray Nick after all he's done for you?" she asked, her voice thick with disgust.

He reacted at once, as she'd hoped.

"I didn't want to. God knows I didn't want to." He fixed his eyes on her face as he gabbled his defense. "They told me they would take away the mine. My mine! I couldn't let them do that. This is my home. My world. I'd die if I didn't have this. I'm free here. No one tells me what to do."

"They *are* telling you what to do," Lee argued. She moved her hand, inch by careful inch, toward her back pocket. Ben was far too upset to notice, intent on making her understand.

"They leave me alone most of the time. As long as I keep watch for them, let them know if anyone's snooping around, they leave me alone. It's part of the deal."

"And was it part of the deal to kidnap Simon?" Lee said bitterly.

"Kidnap?" Ben's eyes were wide in his stricken face. "I didn't kidnap your brother. He came here looking for them, said he wanted to join up with them. I kept telling him I didn't know what he was talking about, but he said if I didn't tell him where he could find them, he'd stick to me like a leech till they turned up."

Coughing, Ben wiped at his forehead with his arm. "There was something mean about that man," he muttered. "I figured he was more dangerous than the Devils. I didn't want him hanging around here, so I took him."

Lee shook her head. Simon? Mean and dangerous? God, what had happened to her brother since she'd last seen him? Surely she would have known if he'd turned into a criminal. How could she have been so blind?

"You took him to the ghost town?" she said unsteadily.

"No." Ben's voice rasped, and he coughed again. "I can't get up there. The climb's way too steep for me. They can't get the bikes all the way up to the plateau, so the helicopter picks them and their bikes up, in a place below the high ground. That's where I meet them when I have something to tell them."

"And that's where you took Simon," Lee said. "That's just as bad as kidnapping him."

"I didn't know they were going to turn rough on him," Ben protested. "They were real friendly when I left him."

"Then why did they tie him up like that?" Carefully Lee felt for the opening of her pocket. "That wasn't exactly friendly."

Ben shrugged. "They said he tricked them, double-crossed them. They were going to kill him, but when I told them that his rich daddy would probably come looking for him, they changed their minds. Chambers—he's the boss—he said your brother was worth more to them alive. That your daddy would pay big money to get him back."

So her guess had been right. They were holding Simon for ransom. This will kill Father, she thought desperately. Had they already sent the demand? Was he already searching for

Simon? Thank God he didn't know she was involved in all this, as well.

As if he'd realized that he was saying too much, the prospector's face hardened. "That's enough of your questions," he said roughly. "Just you sit there now and keep quiet."

Lee's fingers had at last reached her pocket, and she closed her hand around the knife's smooth, slim handle. A wave of nausea made her stomach contract, and she had to fight to keep her expression neutral.

How could she possibly go through with this? Steady, Lee. Don't rush it. Think of Simon, helpless and alone. No matter what Ben had said, she had to hang on to her belief that Simon was innocent. Ben was as much a villain as the rest of that sordid gang. He'd say anything to justify his part in it.

And Nick. Again the pain stabbed at her. Was he in their hands by now? If so, it was Ben's doing. Remember that, Lee, she told herself. It will make it easier. There's no other way.

"I have just one more question," she said, her voice pleading. "How did you find out who our father is?"

"I read the letter," Ben said, and coughed again. "I went through your brother's wallet while he was asleep." He frowned when Lee glared at him. "Before I took him to them, I had to make sure he wasn't the law. They would've killed me for that."

His cough caught him again, and he wiped his eyes with his arm. Lee pulled her hand from her pocket and slid it onto her lap. Now all she had to do was wait for her chance.

"The letter was from you." Ben wheezed, rubbing at his chest. "You talked about the hotel, made it sound real fancy. You mentioned your daddy, and there was his name at the top of the paper, right under the name of the Royal King. Everyone knows the Royal King. Even me. Jonathan King, Simon King—wasn't hard to figure out."

The next bout of coughing robbed him of his breath, and he doubled over the rifle.

She didn't have time to think. Leaping forward, she stretched out her hand for the gun, but Ben was surprisingly quick. He twisted away from her and straightened.

As he raised the rifle, she saw his expression and knew she was out of choices. She lifted her arm, releasing the blade with her thumb, and brought the knife down hard. She saw the light flash off the shiny surface as the weapon sliced through the air.

Desperation must have given Ben strength. He threw himself sideways, and the knife passed harmlessly over his shoulder. Before Lee could raise her arm again, he crashed to the floor, overturning the lantern and plunging them both into darkness.

She couldn't hear a sound from him. She held her breath, terrified of giving her position away. Did he still have hold of the rifle, waiting for her to move? She had to get out of there, get some air. She was close to blacking out. Disoriented, she moved her head, trying to remember exactly where the tunnel was.

To her left. She hoped. She took one careful step, then another. She heard something skitter noisily away and realized it had to be the knife. She hadn't noticed she'd dropped it.

She cringed, waiting for the gunshot, and when it didn't come, she let out her breath. He must have knocked himself out. Her chest hurt, and she dragged in several deep breaths. The flashlight. It was in her pack. Somewhere on her right.

She crouched and spread out her hands, searching the unseen ground around her. Nothing. She was engulfed by an icy cloud of panic. She fought it off and moved on her haunches, forward and to the right. Her hand hit the side of the pack and toppled it.

With a sickening jolt she heard the flashlight clatter on the ground and roll away, out of reach, and her body froze as another sound came from behind her. A low moan. Ben was coming around.

The wall! Where was the wall? she thought in desperation. Her hands smacked against it, and she barely felt the pain as she began to follow it along at a stumbling run. She heard the clatter of the lantern behind her as Ben righted it; in a matter of seconds he'd be right on her heels.

Terror urged her forward at a reckless speed, and she let out a sobbing cry of relief as fingers of daylight filtered toward her.

Blinded by the sun as she burst from the mine, she didn't see him at first. He stood silhouetted against the light like an enormous, faceless shadow. She didn't need to see his features; there was no mistaking that immense outline.

Midge. She was sandwiched between him and Ben, with nowhere to go. Dimly she registered the rifle pointing steadily in her direction, and she didn't even turn her head when Ben stumbled out behind her. What was the point? It was all over.

The giant stood a few yards away at the edge of the clearing, his feet braced apart, his hat pulled low on his face. His rifle was aimed at her head, and she gave a little cry when she felt Ben's rifle prodding into her back.

"Drop it," Ben snarled, "or she gets it."

Lee's stunned brain was still grappling with the logic of that guttural order when another figure emerged from the shadows of the trees.

Tall and forbidding, his dark hair rumpled, his features grim and a dangerous light glinting in his navy blue eyes, he was the most beautiful thing Lee had ever seen in her life.

"Nick!" She forgot about Ben and the rifle pressed against her spine. She forgot about the ominous bulk of Midge facing her. All she could think about was the need to be in the safety of this man's arms.

She darted forward, calling out his name again, ignoring his warning shout.

Nick's eyes flared as Ben jammed the rifle against his shoulder. Without time to think he acted instinctively, snatching the rifle from Midge's hands and taking aim. Nick had moved fast, but not fast enough. Ben had turned his rifle toward the flurry of movement, and he fired.

Lee's scream was answered by nearby blue jays as Nick's eyes glazed and he sank to his knees. A rivulet of blood trickled down his face from the wound in his forehead, and her scream died, followed by a stricken silence as he toppled over and lay still, his body covering the rifle.

Frozen with shock, Lee could only stare. She moved her lips soundlessly, and then her head jerked up as Midge's roar set off another bout of screeching from the jays.

"Run, Lee! For God's sake, run!"

She stared at Midge stupidly as he charged forward, flapping his arms like wind-tossed sheets on a line. Completely unnerved, she threw a last, desperate look at Nick's still body and ran. Somehow her feet were moving, and she fled into the shelter of the trees, not even stopping to look back as two shots rang out behind her.

She ran until she could run no more, and she sank at last into the waiting arms of the forest's undergrowth, out of breath and, she realized with a terrible desolation, out of hope.

The pain was worse than anything she could remember. Maybe time had dulled the memory of her mother's death, but her mother had been ill for so long that in Lee the sorrow had been tempered by a sad sense of relief that she was finally at peace.

This was very different. Lee rolled onto her back and stared at the patches of gray sky visible among the spiky branches. Nick had been a healthy, virile man, with the best part of his life to look forward to, until that treacherous murderer had cut him down.

Pain gnawed at her again, and she curled on her side, her knees under her chin. Dried needles and prickly fern pressed into her cheek, but she felt nothing, save a cold sense of shock and disbelief.

He had seemed so invincible. Never had she felt more protected. She'd been willing to trust her life to him. He was so strong, so capable. Her throat tightened, and she swallowed painfully.

All the people she'd loved had depended on her. Her mother. Her father and Simon. Steven, too. She'd always been the strong one with the shoulder to cry on, the ear always willing to listen. Nick's strength and dependability had given her something she'd never had before. And now he was gone.

She lay for a while longer, letting the misery engulf her, until the insistent chattering of a squirrel above her head reminded her where she was. She sat up and brushed the needles from her shirt. Who was she kidding, anyway? She'd never had Nick to lose, not in any permanent sense.

Given time, she might well have fallen in love with him, but it would have been pointless. She sighed, dusting off her jeans with her hands. The attraction between them had been strong, but that impenetrable barrier had always been there. She'd sensed Nick's contempt for her life-style, and now she would never know the reasons for it.

She rose. Whatever demons had driven that tough, perplexing man could hurt him no more.

She squared her shoulders and took a good look around. Giant firs, their branches stilled, stood watching her in silent contemplation. Scattered among them were baby Christmas trees, ferns and bushy weeds, encircling her like children on a playground. Nowhere in all that dense foliage could she see a path or trail of any kind.

Her stomach muscles contracted on a rising wave of panic. She was alone, in a maze of wilderness, without the slightest idea of direction. Think, Lee. Think hard. Simon was still in danger. She had to get back to town, to the sheriff.

What had Nick told her? Find the stream and follow it. It would eventually lead her back to the road. The memory of his deep voice stabbed at her in a rush of pain, and she hugged her body with her arms. If only the sun hadn't disappeared behind the clouds, she might have been able to gauge the right direction.

She tilted her head to listen. The air was so still; not a sound whispered from the branches above her. Only the faint chirping of birds disturbed the silence. The ground sloped away from her at a gentle angle, and she chose that direction, knowing she had to go down the mountain.

She tried desperately to keep her mind off the scene at the mine. She was still confused about Midge's part in it. She only knew that he had saved her life. She wouldn't allow herself to think about the two shots fired behind her. Nor would she think of the lifeless body of the man she'd come to care so much for.

Instead, she concentrated on finding the stream and the road to town. She could only hope that Simon was rescued before word got back to her father. It was her only incentive to keep moving.

She heard the stream long before she reached it. Muffled by the trees, the splashing sounds seemed to come from several directions at once, and by the time she knelt beside the tumbling water, she'd exhausted her willpower and her strength. Curling up on a bed of dried pine needles, she closed her eyes and slept.

Chapter 8

Nick struggled through a heavy curtain of unconsciousness, his mind screaming warnings. He could hear voices uncomfortably close by. He forced his body to relax and lifted his eyelids to narrow slits. Pain shot through his head, and he smothered a moan, waiting until his head cleared before he lifted his eyelids again.

This time the pain was easier, and he could see Ben's back and two bearded men astride a pair of dirt bikes.

Ben talked rapidly, his hands stabbing at the air. "She took off. I didn't see which way she went—I was too busy plugging the big guy."

In spite of his rigid control, Nick's body jerked, and he clamped his jaws together. Neither biker was looking at him; their attention was riveted on Ben. Nick rolled his eyes sideways in a painful effort. Just off to his left, a large booted foot floated into his vision. He couldn't see any more. He didn't have to. The pool of blood spreading around the foot told it all.

Sick rage gripped him. He tried to open his eyes wider, but his left eye was obstructed by his eyelashes matted together, and he realized it was his blood, seeping from the wound in his head. At least he was still alive. He directed his mind toward the bikers' conversation, as anger fueled strength into his heavy limbs.

"...have to get rid of them. Once we get the woman, we'll move them all into the mine. King, too. It'll be easy enough to make it look like an accident." The speaker was the larger of the two men. It was impossible, though, for Nick to see his face, which was hidden by the Stetson tilted forward over the man's eyes.

"What kind of accident?" Ben asked, sounding close to hysteria. "I don't want the law coming down on my head."

"Don't worry. There won't be nothing left for the law to find. We got enough dynamite to blow that mine sky-high, and the four of them with it. There won't be so much as a bone fragment left." The biker gave a nasty chuckle.

"You can't do that." Ben's voice had risen even higher. "You can't blow up my mine."

"Listen, old man," the biker said evilly, "we'll do what we like. You give us any trouble and you go up with them. So shut your mouth while you still got one."

Ben made a small whimpering sound and was quiet.

"That's better," the rough voice said. "You stay here till we get back. Hal and I are going after the woman."

The other biker spoke for the first time. "What if we don't find her?"

"We'll keep looking till dark. After that, it won't matter much. Chances are she'll never make it back. And if she does, who'll believe her? We'll be long gone before anyone gets back up there. Chambers says we move now, and it's about time. The place is getting way too hot."

"Yeah. I heard we move out at dawn," the other biker said.

"Right. Can't be soon enough for me. I had enough of these damn mountains. By sunup the place will be empty. They'll all be dead."

Nick's eyelids dropped as the man gestured at him.

"And the lady?" That was the other biker.

"Her, too. I'm gonna find her." The man's hoarse laugh chilled Nick's blood. "When I do, we're gonna have some fun with her before we kill her."

The other man's chuckle was just as obscene. "Yeah. Why not? Been a long time."

Nick's hand clenched against his ribs. Let them lay one finger on her...

"I guess these two are finished," the biker added. "Maybe we should pump a couple more shots in them, to make sure."

Adrenaline surged as Nick strained to hear the sound of the rifle's safety. He'd have a split second to roll away from them, then maybe a second or two before they could get another shot off.

Relief made him weak as the other man grunted.

"Come on, save your ammo for when we catch up with the girl." The bikes exploded in a roar as the men kicked the engines to life. One shouted at Ben as he wheeled away, but Nick doubted the old man heard him. Even through the narrowed slits of his vision, Nick could see Ben's expression. He looked bewildered. Stunned. Nick could well imagine what the man was feeling. He knew only too well what the mine meant to Ben. If the bikers carried out their threat to blow it up, the old man wouldn't take the loss easily.

Nick watched as the prospector mumbled something at the sky, then shuffled off toward the mine. He waited until the bowed figure had disappeared, then sat up, biting down on the groan that erupted from him as pain slashed through his head.

He carefully explored his skull with his fingers and winced when he touched the graze. He'd been lucky. A quarter of an inch closer and he'd never have seen another sunset. He turned his head to where the massive body lay in a heap. One look was enough.

Midge was sprawled on his back, his vacant gray eyes staring sightlessly at the clouds. Blood soaked his shirt from neck to waist. Nick reached out unsteadily and gently closed the eyes.

His first instinct, when he'd stared into those pale eyes, just a few short hours earlier, had been to tear the man apart with his bare hands. Only the rifle trained on his stomach had held him back. They'd faced each other, unspeaking, until Midge had broken the silence with a short laugh.

"What's up, ole buddy? You look as if you'd seen the Devil himself."

"That's not surprising, seeing as how I'm staring right at him," Nick said with deadly calm.

Midge's eyes narrowed beneath the wide brim of his hat. "What's that supposed to mean?"

"You can cut the double talk, *ole buddy*," Nick said dangerously. "I got it all figured out. You and the White Devils. What a combination. No wonder you were so damned anxious to get us off this mountain."

Something flickered in the colorless eyes, then Midge tilted his head forward, shading his face.

"You were never a stupid man, Nick," he said quietly. "Don't start being one now."

"Oh, I was stupid, all right." Nick moved his right foot forward a fraction. "Stupid to think you had too much sense to pull a stunt like this." His left foot joined his right.

Midge jerked the rifle in warning. "Nick, you don't know everything yet."

"I know enough." Again Nick slid his foot forward.

"No you don't. You..." Midge stopped and tilted his head. "Listen."

Nick had heard them, too. Off in the distance, the muffled buzz of the bike engines, behind him and high up. Lee!
His heart jerked as he thought of her up there with no one
but an old man to protect her. If anything happened to
her... He clenched his fists, and took another reckless step
forward.

"Nick. You've got this all wrong. At least hear me out."
Midge's voice was urgent. "We're wasting time. They're
coming this way. If they find us here, it'll be all over." He
lowered the rifle and grabbed Nick's arm. "Let's get the hell
out of here and I'll fill you in." He tugged, scowling when
Nick resisted him. "For crying out loud, I'm on your side."

Still Nick stood, his suspicions warring with his desperate need to believe his old friend.

The bikes were coming at breakneck speed, roaring down
the trail behind them. He shook Midge's hold off his arm,
but the big man closed his beefy hand on his shoulder.

"Nick." Midge raised his voice. "You owe me."

Nick stared at him a second longer, then, without a word,
twisted around and sprinted through the undergrowth, with
Midge crashing along behind him.

It was close. They hit the top of the slope together and
dived over, tumbling down the steep incline to land in a mess
of weeds and shrubs that obscured the dried-out creek bed.
The bikers thundered past overhead, leaving in their wake
a cloud of foul-smelling smoke.

"That was close." Midge groaned as he pulled himself
into a sitting position. "I'm getting too damned old for all
this stuff."

Nick watched him warily, flexing his ankle, which had
twisted under him on the way down. "What stuff?" His
voice still held a lethal tone, and Midge winced.

"Let me find my hat first," Midge said, looking over his
shoulder. "I feel naked without it."

"*Now.*" Nick leaned forward, his face threatening. "Before I decide to rearrange those ugly features of yours."

Midge puffed out his breath. "Okay. Simmer down. I'll tell you, but first, what did you do with the little lady?"

"She's safe."

The big man nodded. "Good. I wouldn't want anything happening to her."

"So I noticed." Nick controlled his temper with an effort. "Now let's have it."

"There's not a lot to tell." Midge pulled the front of his shirt away from his body and extracted a broken twig from inside. "I guess you know about the White Devils."

"Only what Ben told me."

Midge looked up sharply. "What did Ben tell you?"

"That they're a gang of bikers, raiding the mines, stealing gold and anything else they can get their hands on."

Nick decided to keep quiet about the lab for now. Until he knew exactly how Midge fitted into this thing, he wasn't going to give away anything unnecessarily.

"Yeah, that's about it." Midge rolled his shoulders. "Only it may not be all of it."

"What do you mean?"

"About four weeks ago," Midge said, "the sheriff came up to see me. Told me they'd heard a lot of rumors flying around, nothing concrete, but enough to get them interested. I guess everyone they talked to on the mountain clammed up. Afraid, I guess. You know how things are up here."

"I know," Nick said grimly.

"Anyway, all they knew was this gang was operating up here, but they heard there might be a lot more to it than just a bunch of punks. They'd been investigating for some time, but this is a big mountain. They'd found bike tracks, but when anyone followed them, the tracks ended up in a clearing and then just disappeared."

Midge shifted his bulk to a more comfortable position. "They also found what they think are helicopter tracks, and

they figure the bikes are picked up and put down somewhere else. What they don't know is where.

"Seeing as I know the mountain probably better'n anyone else up here, the sheriff asked me to keep a lookout, ask
questions, see what I could find out. He reckoned that since
most people know me up here, they'd tell me what they
wouldn't tell the law."

Nick could feel himself begin to relax. It all seemed feasible, yet there were still some unanswered questions. Much
as he wanted to believe Midge, he wasn't going to let up just
yet. "So, if the sheriff found the clearing, why didn't they
keep watch?"

"They did." Midge grunted and slapped at the side of his
head. "Damn bugs. Only someone was always ahead of
them. They kept changing the pickup spot. It's hard to spot
a stray helicopter. With the supply choppers and the Forest
Service, not to mention the joyriders, the sky is full of
them."

"I saw it," Nick said. "Winging over the mountain. Big
baby, unmarked—an S-61 by the look of it."

"That'd do it." Midge's gray eyes gleamed with excitement. "Did you see where it landed?"

Nick frowned. "Midge, why did Simon tell you about Lee
being his sister?"

There was a long silence while the two men stared at each
other.

"Oh, ho," Midge said softly. "So that's it. You found out
that King's in with them, and you figure I have to be, too,
seeing as how I know so much about him, right? That hurts,
ole buddy. I thought you knew me better than that." He
pushed the straggly strands of thinning hair off his forehead.

"Look," he went on, "I'd been asking questions for
days. No one wanted to talk. Then you brought King up to
the camp. There was something about him that bothered
me, especially since he wanted to go up to the high ground.

Tourists don't usually mess with the mines up there. So I followed you both."

"You seem to be doing a lot of that." Nick could feel his suspicions slipping away, but he was still wary of letting his relief overpower his judgment.

"Yeah. Sorry, ole buddy, but it was necessary."

"Why the hell didn't you tell me all this right at the beginning?" Nick said angrily, remembering his tortured doubts.

"Couldn't." Midge shrugged. "Sheriff made me swear I wouldn't tell anyone. Didn't want the Devils tipped off. I tried to talk you into going back to town, but I could see that little lady had you by the—"

"No one had me anywhere," Nick said, scowling. "You could've trusted me. I thought we were friends."

"You, maybe. But you were towing King's sister around with you. We already had him figured. How did I know that pretty face hadn't turned your head, talked you into changing sides?"

Nick ignored the insinuation. There was something more important to deal with. Something he'd have to tell Lee, and he didn't know how he was going to do that. "What makes you think Simon King is mixed up in all this?"

Midge shifted again, grunting as he pulled a small branch out from under him. "This is not the most comfortable place for a chat," he grumbled. He caught the impatient glint in Nick's eye and lifted his hands.

"Okay. I followed you and King to your mine. Saw you go down. I couldn't follow you in—you know how I am about mines—so I camped outside and waited. I got even more curious when you left two days later without King, so I hung around for another day."

There was a peculiar feeling settling in the lower half of Nick's stomach. It didn't help that his warning voice was whispering, telling him something he still couldn't hear.

"I finally hit pay dirt," Midge said with a smug grin. "I saw King leave, and Ben Matthews was with him. I followed them up to this clearing, and guess who they met up with, all friendly-like."

His heart jerked into a rapid beat. Why hadn't he seen it? Why, for God's sake, hadn't he heard what the voice had been telling him all along? "The White Devils," he said desperately.

Midge thumped his knee. "Bingo! I tried to get closer to hear what they were saying, but I slipped on some gravel and they heard me. There were a dozen of them, too many for me. They came at me, so I got the hell out of there and—"

He broke off and peered at Nick. "Something wrong, ole buddy?"

"Ben swore he'd never set eyes on them," Nick whispered. "My God, Midge, I left her there with him." He scrambled to his feet, looking around wildly for the rifle. Somehow Midge had lost it on the way down.

"Dammit, man!" Midge roared. "What the hell did you do that for?" He staggered upright, clutching his head.

"How was I to know he was the enemy?" Nick stamped down the undergrowth in a fury of impatience. He wrenched at the long weeds and tore at the shrubs, swearing when his efforts failed to reveal the rifle.

Muttering an oath, Midge joined in the search, hauling aside handfuls of greenery with his big hands. "It was Ben who told me about Lee," he said, panting. "Sheriff told me to go back and talk to him but not to let on I knew he was in with them. He was hoping to get a lead on where they were camped out. His boys had been combing the mountain for days, but those bikers are sharp. Somehow they always manage to stay out of sight. Today was only the second time I've seen them."

Nick listened with half an ear. For the first time in his life he knew real terror. He thought he'd experienced every kind of human emotion, but this fear clawing at his insides was something new. Fear for the safety of someone he cared about, he discovered, was far worse than the fear for his own survival.

He was shocked at the intensity of his emotions. He hadn't realized it had gone that deep. His frustration intensified as the rifle remained hidden, and he began searching the steep incline, knowing that without it, his chances of rescuing Lee would be minimal.

Midge was still talking between grunts as he kicked at the undergrowth. "Ben was real chatty," he said. "Nervous, like. Told me he and King had become good friends. Told me all about the family and how rich they were, trying to impress me."

Midge grunted again. "The minute I started asking questions, though, he shut up tighter than a bear trap. Got real hostile when I mentioned the bikers. I was about to give up on the whole deal, then you turned up again with King's sister. I figured she wasn't about to give up, so I followed you. Then he shot at you and I went after him. I figured it had to be a snitch planted in my camp, and I was real anxious to find him."

Midge's foot slipped, sending him sprawling, and he swore. "I can't move like I used to," he continued as he struggled back to his feet, "and I lost him. I figured then you had to be in the clear, but by the time I got back, you'd left, too. I didn't pick up your trail again till this morning when I saw you coming back down. I just wish I knew what the hell's going on."

Nick spun around as Midge's mutterings ended in a shout. The big man stood, feet braced apart, the rifle held triumphantly over his head.

"I got it," Midge roared. "Now let's go get her!" He began charging up the bank, with Nick plunging after him.

Midge had insisted on coming back to the mine, ignoring Nick's protests, Nick remembered now. On the way, Nick had told him about the plateau and the lab and that Simon King was a prisoner of the gang.

"All right," Midge had said. "First we get Lee back, then we go see about King." But Midge wasn't going anywhere, ever again.

I'll be back, Nick promised silently as he gazed down at his friend. I'll see you get a proper burial. If anyone thinks they're going to blow you to pieces, they'll have to get through me first.

He pushed himself onto his feet, his face grim. He had to get to Lee before those thugs found her. He shook his head, trying to clear it. The pain bothered him less now, but he felt light-headed and more than a little hazy. His left eye wouldn't open properly, and he couldn't wait to find the stream and get cleaned up.

He held that one advantage over the bikers. He'd told Lee to follow the stream. If she'd remembered and followed his instructions, it would narrow his search considerably. If she remembered.

He took several steps toward the trees, testing his balance. A little weak in the knees, but otherwise he seemed to have it all together. It took him no more than a moment to find his pack, which he'd dropped earlier just before he'd stepped out beside Midge and seen Lee's terrified rush from the mine.

He remembered little of what had happened after that. He would have to trust to Lee's common sense and hope she'd stay low and move slow and easy. With mounting confidence, he quickened his stride.

He chose to stay well away from the trail. If his guess was right, the bikers would stick to it until they got well below Lee, then they would search for her on the way back up, relying on her inexperience to disclose her progress through the trees. It was what he would have done. His blood ran cold when he thought about those animals catching up with her. The vision of what might happen to her before they killed her was too horrible to contemplate.

He pushed himself harder, his strides lengthening as his strength returned. He had to get there first. Hold on, Lee, he urged silently. I'm on my way.

He hit the stream at the nearest point, wasting little time washing the dried blood from his face. Soon after that he heard the bikers.

They passed close by his hiding place behind a large thicket, and his heart pounded with relief when he realized they were on their way back to the trail. They had either given up or decided Lee had gone in a different direction.

His jubilation was short-lived when, a half an hour later, he had found no trace of Lee's tracks himself. Surely she wouldn't have doubled back to the mine.

He kept seeing her face, those huge eyes looking so solemn, her mouth warm and inviting, those silly diamonds sparkling in her ears. He remembered her body moving against him with a fervor that had taken him by surprise. He had never in his wildest moments imagined that the cool, elegant woman would turn out to be such a tiger. Or that she would arouse such scorching responses in his body.

Or had he? Hadn't he sensed the passion concealed behind that indifferent smile? Wasn't that what had prompted him to agree to help her? Be honest, Garrett, he told himself. You saw it from the beginning. You just wouldn't admit it.

He skirted a clump of bushes and scrambled over an enormous tree trunk that lay across his path. He could see her vividly in his mind. The tilt of her stubborn chin, the way her hair curved into her neck, the soft curves of her firm, high breasts.

He'd had trouble keeping his hands off those tempting mounds of soft flesh. His control amazed him. He knew how willing she would be once he touched her. He wasn't stupid. Yet something had held him back. Had he been afraid to take it further? He'd never been bothered by that problem before.

He thought of the last time he'd held her, of the torrent of hot, hungry need that had roared through his body when he'd kissed her. The memory stirred his passion, and he swore as he brushed a low-hanging branch out of his way. He'd warned her what would happen the next time. Maybe he should warn himself. For he was certain of one thing. If he found her—when he found her—he would satisfy that hunger once and for all. Then he'd be able to put her out of his mind. It had always worked before. He didn't analyze the pulse of doubt in the back of his mind. He was busy worrying that he'd never get the chance to carry out his intentions.

He was close to despair when he finally caught sight of her curled in a tight ball beneath the protective branches of a lush green fir.

His heart jerked painfully at first when he saw how still she was, then his pulse quickened as she stirred with a soft moan. He reached her on silent feet and stood looking down on her, his heart thudding with relief and with a deeper emotion that he didn't want to define.

Her lashes lay dark and feathery on the smooth curve of her cheek, and even in sleep her mouth curved invitingly. Her arm covered her breast, sheltered by her knees, and Nick's eyes moved to the enticing curve of her hips and buttocks. The inevitable stirring at his groin intensified his resolve. He dropped his pack on the ground and knelt beside her. He reached for her shoulder and shook her gently awake.

Lee had been dreaming. A muddled, confusing dream. Someone was chasing her, a huge man on a bike, his face covered by a gruesome mask. She tried to run, but her legs wouldn't move, and then she found herself at the edge of a bottomless abyss. She wanted to jump, but someone was holding on to her shoulder, shaking her....

She opened her eyes and stared at Nick's smiling face. She blinked, convinced she was still in the dream, and her eyes shifted to the branches overhead and the sky above them. They looked so real. But they couldn't be. Nick was dead.

Slowly, not daring to believe, she moved her eyes back to the face in front of her. It couldn't be. And yet... She watched her hand lift and touch his cheek, then, heady with incredulous joy, she heard his rich, deep laugh, which filled her heart.

"Oh." She tried to say more, but her voice refused to cooperate, and she could only stare at him, her throat working soundlessly.

He reached for her, crushing her against that marvelous, solid warmth of his chest, and she clung to him, her hands moving over him in an urgent need to reassure herself that he was real. She felt his arms holding her, safe and unbelievably comforting. She felt the heat of his body warming her and heard him crooning her name as he rocked her.

The revelation came slowly but was nonetheless indisputable. She loved him in a way she'd never imagined. The discovery brought bittersweet pain, and she pressed her lips together, her face buried against his shoulder.

As if sensing her emotion, Nick drew back to look at her. To Lee's utter dismay, the unfamiliar sting of tears filled her eyes and, though she struggled to contain them, spilled down her cheeks to cling precariously to her chin for a second before dropping into her lap.

It was Nick's undoing. If he'd had any doubts, they were swept away as desire built an unbearable pressure in his loins. Whispering her name, he took her face in his hands and brushed at the tears with his thumbs.

"It's all right," he murmured. "I'm here now."

She managed a tremulous smile, and he captured it with his mouth, his body catching fire as she melted against him. He dragged her into his arms, and she went hungrily, her mouth seeking his with an urgency that fanned the hot, greedy flames eating at him. It was time.

Lee moaned a protest as he pulled away from her again, then gave a small sound of distress as she saw for the first time the raw, angry groove in his forehead. She lifted her hand, but he caught it and brought it to his lips.

"It's okay," he said. "It's just a graze."

She studied him and saw the lines of strain on his cheeks and the deep furrows above his dark brows.

"Are you all right?" she said. She was only slightly reassured when he smiled.

"I will be," he said softly, "as soon as I take care of one small problem."

The expression in his eyes warned her, and Lee's mouth went dry. With his unshaven chin and his thick hair tousled and windblown, he looked ruggedly male, and infinitely dangerous.

She watched as he stood, moved over to his pack and leaned down to unstrap the sleeping bag with an expert flick of his fingers. Her heart began to drum a slow tattoo against her ribs when he unzipped the bag and laid it out flat. Without looking at her, he sat down and removed his boots and socks, then stood again, facing her, his eyes dark and intense on her face.

Her lungs stopped working as he raised his hands and began to unbutton his shirt in unhurried movements that made it all the more erotic.

"Nick?" Her voice sounded strange to her.

"I'm sorry, Lee." He released the button above his belt and tugged at his shirt, pulling it free from his pants. "This isn't the way I would have chosen, but there are some things that just won't wait." He took off his shirt and let it drop. "I want you."

She found it impossible not to gaze at his bared chest, the dark hair narrowing down over his flat stomach to the heavy brass buckle of his belt. Tiny quivers radiated up from the base of her stomach to her throat. "I want you, too."

His eyes burned into hers. "I was hoping you would."

The rushing water of the stream pounded in her ears as all her senses heightened into crystal awareness. The air around them seemed to close in, engulfing them in a warm, scented stillness that was more intimate than any bedroom. The song of the birds swelled like the most romantic music Lee had ever heard, and she knew that if her life spanned a century, she would always relive this memory with an intensity that would never fade.

Her body was coming alive, pulsing with urges that couldn't be ignored. She could feel the tips of her breasts straining against the fabric that contained them, as if impatient to be free. Her skin tingled with the anticipation of his touch, and she devoured him with her eyes, no longer shy about looking at him.

The beauty of his body awed her. His powerful shoulders and chest were in perfect symmetry with his lean hips and flat belly, and as he moved toward her, she was struck once more by his supple grace, which had reminded her so often of a sleek wild animal.

He reached down for her hand, and she gave it willingly, rising to her feet at his gentle tug. She stood, outwardly passive, as he took hold of the hem of her shirt and pulled it over her head, though her insides were a turbulent mass of liquid heat.

"Do you know," he asked in a husky voice, "how long I've wanted to touch you like this?" His finger traced the lacy edge of her bra, burning a path across the swell of her breasts. "You are beautiful, Lee. Elegant, fragile and beautiful."

She gave him an unsteady smile. "I don't feel elegant, or fragile."

He moved to the back of her bra and unfastened it with expert ease. Her breath stilled when her breasts were freed at last, and he cupped them in his warm hands. "I think I can make you feel fragile again," he whispered.

He bent his head and touched the straining tip of her breast with his lips, and Lee's hands clutched at his shoulders, her fingers digging into the muscled flesh. The tug at the base of her stomach became a gnawing ache as his lips pulled gently at her swollen peak, and she leaned into him.

The movement unleashed all the hunger Nick had been holding under control for so long. He wrapped his arms around her and dragged her against his chest, the feeling of her soft breasts on his bare skin sending him out of his mind. He took her mouth in a frenzy of need, passion exploding through his body as she answered with a desperation that matched his.

He couldn't seem to get enough of her. Again and again he plunged his tongue deep into the soft recesses of her mouth, the smooth skin of her back an inviting playground for his hands. He ground his hips against hers and shuddered when she returned the pressure.

He was losing the battle. Her fingers were implements of exquisite torture, kneading his back, then sliding up to his neck to hold him while she explored his mouth with her tongue. A part of his mind registered surprise that she had destroyed his control so easily, then he forgot about it as the torment became unbearable, and he lowered her to the ground, covering her with his body while he tugged the rest of her clothes off.

Nick's impatience added fuel to Lee's already raging desire. She could hardly bear to wait while he rid himself of his pants and briefs, and then he lowered the length of his naked body on hers.

The contact of his warm flesh sent myriads of sensations sparkling down her body. She was conscious of every inch of him: of his body hair grazing her breasts, her stomach and her thighs; of his hand moving between them in slow, sensual circles over the sensitive skin of her belly; and of his mouth, finding erotic places she never knew she had.

Her body was a fiery torrent of need. She pushed her hips into him, seeking release from the unbearable tension, and knew a moment of triumph when he shuddered and gasped her name.

"Lee! I can't wait any longer."

"Then don't," she whispered back. With his knee he parted her thighs in a quick, impatient movement, and she wound her legs around his hips, crying out as he drove into her and eliminated everything else from her mind. The forest melted away as the momentum of his thrusts built the pressure inside her to an agonizing pitch.

There were only the two of them, in a maelstrom of sensations and emotions that were far beyond anything she'd known before. He was part of her, and she part of him, joined in a rising tempo of passion that had to be satisfied. She heard him shout her name hoarsely, and she called out to him. She felt the pulsing strength of him inside her, filling her, intoxicating her, then, with a final, savage thrust, he took her with him to the limits of her endurance and on, to the ultimate ecstasy of release.

She found herself floating down in a haze of wonder and disbelief. Her marriage had been brief, but until now she had never suspected that there had been anything lacking in the physical side of it.

How could she have known that with the right person it could be so wonderful, so terrifyingly wonderful? How could she possibly have envisioned her own abandonment and the incredible exhilaration that held her breathless now?

The mere touch of Nick's bare skin against hers was more sensual than anything she'd even remotely experienced. She moved under him, sliding her stomach across his, and felt the rumble of his groan against her breasts.

He lifted his head and looked at her, his eyes still burning with the depth of his passion. "I'm sorry," he said in a rough voice.

She stared at him, trying to understand. "Why? You know it was what I wanted."

"What I wanted, too. That's the trouble. I wanted it too damn much." He brushed her lips gently, his mouth warm and soft. "I promised you time. Time to make it good for you, and instead I rushed it like some teenager." He smiled, though his indigo eyes were serious. "That doesn't usually happen."

Lee sighed in pure contentment. "Personally, Mr. Garret, I found the whole procedure entirely satisfactory."

His grin finally reached his eyes. "You did, hmm? Well, lady, it might interest you to know that I can do better." He moved his hips in a highly erotic gesture. "Much better. And I intend to prove it when we get back to civilization."

Her breath caught, and she reached up to pull his head down to hers. As their mouths met, her mind spun. There would be another time. He didn't intend to walk away from her the second this was over. Was there some hope for them after all? She was afraid to explore the possibility, but a small part of her couldn't extinguish the soaring excitement that maybe, just maybe, there was a chance.

Nick's mind also whirled as he returned the kiss. What the hell was he doing? he thought. Okay, so the intensity of his feelings had taken him by surprise. Stunned him might be a better description. Not only had he lost control—an unprecedented event and one he wasn't at all happy about—but he'd just reached a new height of sexual satisfaction. Considering his experience, that was as disturbing as it had been unexpected.

He moved his lips to the silky warmth of Lee's neck. He hadn't anticipated this. He'd meant only to satisfy his hunger, to get Lee Coulton out of his system once and for all.

Instead, he'd opened the door just enough to allow a glimpse of a fantasy that scared the hell out of him. How could he have walked into this with his eyes wide open? He'd sensed she was trouble from the beginning.

There could be no future for them. Lee came from a world he would die rather than go back to, and she sure as hell wouldn't fit into his. The best thing he could do was forget his damn ego and call it quits the minute they hit town.

Lee chose that moment to run her hands over his bare back, over the swell of his buttocks, and his body mocked his conviction. He cursed his potent appetite and raised his head.

"We'd better get dressed," he murmured, "before we both get pneumonia."

Lee's protest went unheeded, and he rolled off her. She sat up and reached for her clothes, shivering when the air chilled her body. She dressed quickly, intensely aware of the man at her side. The warmth of their union still caressed her, and she felt proud that this indomitable, intense man had wanted to make love to her.

She watched him pull his pants up his long legs and imagined she could feel his body on hers once more. Her sudden surge of need astonished her. It scared her that he could arouse such primitive feelings in her, and at the same time she rejoiced in the knowledge. He was awesome, sexy, and for a short while at least, he was hers. She would make the most of every moment. He stood, towering above her, and a smile spread across her face as she met his gaze.

"You look like a climber who's just reached the top of the mountain," Nick said, and stretched out his hand to help her to her feet.

She took it, clinging to the warm strength of his fingers when he pulled her up. "That's a little bit how I feel," she said softly.

"Me, too." He opened her palm and placed a kiss in the middle of it. "I just wish we'd had more time."

He gave her a long, serious look, and Lee felt a flutter of nerves.

"What is it?" she asked quietly.

He told her everything he'd overheard between Ben and the bikers. He explained Midge's part in everything and held her when her face crumpled with the realization of what the big man had sacrificed for her. The only thing he didn't tell her was Simon's involvement with the gang. He knew it wouldn't change her mind about rescuing him and that it would only distress her more.

"We don't have a lot of time, Lee." Nick lowered himself onto the sleeping bag, and she dropped down beside him. "They said dawn," he went on. "If they wait that long, we could go back to town and hope to get word to the sheriff in time. It would take us most of the night to get there—I'm not leaving you here alone again—and then the sheriff has to get everything organized. We could go back to Midge's camp for help, borrow one of their bikes. But we don't know who we can trust. It's quite likely Midge had a traitor in the camp."

Nick ran a hand through his hair, wincing as it grazed the wound. "We could hit the trail and hope to run into a backpacker who could get word back for us, but this is a big mountain, and there are hundreds of trails. We're still way above the Forest Service area, and few hikers venture this far. We've been here for days and seen no one. We could try one of the other mines, but again, we don't know who we can trust. This sounds like a big operation. Besides, we still have a couple of goons to worry about."

Lee felt as if her face were carved in stone. "So where does that leave Simon?"

He gave her another long look. "That's up to you. Either we go back to town and pray for a miracle, or we try to get him out of there ourselves."

Her stomach plummeted. "Can we do it?"

"It won't be easy. To be honest, I don't give a hell of a lot for our chances. Even if we get him out, we still have to get off this mountain, and we don't know what kind of shape he's in."

He leaned forward and laid his arms across her shoulders. "If I go in there, you'll have to come with me. You'll be risking your life for a slim chance at best." His eyes begged her. "Give it up, Lee. I know how tough that would be for you, but it isn't worth the risks."

Her chin lifted without hesitation. "I'm not going back without Simon. If there's a chance, no matter how slim, we've got to take it."

His smile eased her tension. "I knew you'd say that," he said, "but I wanted to make sure."

She found it difficult to return the smile. "Nick? Thank you."

He answered with a quick kiss on her nose. "As I told you once before, don't worry. You'll have your opportunity to thank me properly. And I'm looking forward to it." He let her go and leaned over to grab his pack.

"I've got some beef jerky left," he said, "and a box of trail mix. That'll have to do us. I guess your pack is still at the mine."

Lee nodded. "I don't think I can eat anything, anyway."

"You'll need to keep your strength up," Nick said grimly. "This could be a long night."

She took the packet of jerky from him, trying to steady her bouncing nerves. She wouldn't think ahead. She would take it one step at a time and trust in Nick's judgment and strength. She was surprised at how calming that thought was.

Dusk began to settle among the trees, deepening the shadows and quieting the squabbling jays. She and Nick packed up quickly, unconsciously hurried by the faint rumble of thunder in the distance. Nick hauled the pack to his shoulders and draped his jacket around Lee.

"You're going to need this before the night is out," he told her.

"What about you?" she said with a quick frown of concern.

"I'm tougher than you are." He tilted her chin and brushed her lips with his. "And I'm used to the elements."

His kiss came close to making her forget the danger facing them. She clung to him with quiet desperation and then stepped back and gave him a bright smile. "All right, Mr. Garrett. Lead on."

He touched his forehead in a mock salute and twisted on his heel. With a sensation that was half fear, half excitement, Lee followed.

On the long climb back to the bluff she was grateful for his jacket. Darkness closed over them swiftly, thickened by the angry clouds sweeping across the sky. A cool wind sprang from out of the quiet stillness and rushed clumsily through the protesting firs, and the occasional crackling of lightning lit up the tossing branches.

The darkness hampered their progress, and although she tried to limit them, Lee's frequent rest stops slowed her and Nick down. It took them several hours to reach the bluff, and Lee sank to the ground in breathless relief when she finally managed the climb to the rim. Twice the helicopter had zoomed over their heads, and now, as lightning seared the sky and lit up the plateau in a split-second blaze of light, Lee caught a brief glimpse of the huge machine, which stood at the edge of the dark smudge of trees.

"Our two friends are probably back there by now," Nick said close to her ear. "They probably got a ride in on the chopper."

Lee looked at him as excitement gripped her. "Can you fly one of those things?" She could barely make out his silhouette against the sky, and the wind whipped her hair against her face as she peered at him.

"Yeah. I guess I could. If I got the chance." Lightning illuminated his face for a second or two, his teeth flashing white as he grinned. "You know, we might just pull this off yet."

Lee grinned back. "I'm counting on it, Mr. Garrett."

He was shaken by his surge of admiration for her. He knew she was operating on sheer determination, and his feelings at that moment were overwhelming. She was quite a woman. It was too bad they couldn't have gotten it together; they might have made it. Pushing his regrets into the recesses of his mind, he felt for her hand and found it cool and steady in his.

"We're going in," he told her, keeping his voice low and calm. "I want you to stay close to me, and if I yell an order at you, you obey instantly, without question."

"All right." Her voice shook, and he squeezed her hand.

"Swear to me, Lee. No matter what happens, you'll obey my orders."

"I swear."

This time her tone held a note of impatience, and he was satisfied. "Let's go get your brother."

He rose, her hand still clasped in his, and the two of them paused at the brink of the incline, buffeted by the wind as lightning took a sizzling dive to the ground. In the ensuing darkness, they slipped over the edge and began the descent through the restless forest.

Chapter 9

Nick found it difficult to keep his mind off the woman who followed him through the menacing darkness of the wind-tossed firs. His body was tormented by flashes of remembered passion as vivid and as startling as the spasmodic lightning. He was on unfamiliar ground, but his instincts were fast becoming second nature again. He and Lee had barely reached the level of the plateau when the first faint prickling at the back of his neck warned him.

Thunder rumbled closer now, and he drew her back against a thick tree trunk, signaling to her with a finger at his lips when lightning gave them momentary vision. She'd looked scared in that brief explosion of light, he thought, her face ghostly, her eyes wide and staring.

He wanted to hold her, to keep her safe from whatever was waiting out there, and obliterate that look on her face forever. He was overwhelmed by the intensity of his need to protect her, and he folded his arms around her. Feeling her body tremble, he felt a moment of panic.

What if she were hurt, or killed? How could he live with himself after that? He'd been an idiot to bring her into this. He should have ignored her protests and forced her to go back to town. That would have meant certain death for Simon, though, and he couldn't have lived with that, either. And he'd be haunted for the rest of his life if he didn't keep his vow to Midge.

Nick closed his eyes and rested his chin on Lee's silky head. He knew he hadn't had any real choices, but that didn't make him feel any better. The wind caught at Lee's hair and brushed the soft strands across his cheek. He tightened his arms around her slender body, caught in a spasm of tenderness that tied his stomach in knots.

If they were going to pull off this rescue, it was essential that he keep a positive attitude. And they would pull it off, he promised himself with a fierce determination. He would do it for her, and then maybe he could let her go, knowing he'd given her all that he could.

He put his mouth close to her ear. "Move as quietly as you can—we may have company around." He felt her arms creep around his waist, sorely tempting his tenuous control. His body warmed, and he moved his lips to her brow and pressed them against the satiny skin.

There was no time for this, he told himself. He was putting them both in danger. He held her away from him and felt the wind chill his body where her warmth had been. When he found her hand, it felt cool and disturbingly fragile, and he rubbed his thumb across the back of it, smiling in the dark when she returned the pressure.

With careful steps he moved forward, and the thunder growled again. When it receded, his ears caught the quiet snap of a twig somewhere on his right. He reacted immediately, on reflex, pushing Lee into the shelter between two small, bushy firs.

"Stay there." Though his whispered words were swept away by the wind, he knew she'd heard. He dropped his pack on the ground beside her, gave her shoulder a reassuring squeeze and edged away from her and toward the betraying sound.

He had gone a dozen steps when he was cruelly prodded in the back by the hard, round barrel of a gun. With a sick sense of resignation, he realized he'd done the unforgivable. He'd allowed his emotions to distract his concentration. He knew they'd pay dearly for his mistake, and his stomach knotted in fear for Lee.

"You look real lively for a dead man."

Nick recognized the voice the minute he heard it. He was one of the men who'd been talking to Ben at the mine. The tough one. His hopes plummeted. The man was a butcher. There would be no mercy. He forced into his voice a casualness that he was far from feeling. "Ben always was a lousy shot. Lucky for him. He'll have only one murder rap to beat when the cops get here, if they're not already." He knew it was a long shot, and it was obvious by the coarse chuckle behind him that the biker wasn't buying.

"You never had time to get word back to town, Garrett, so quit bluffing. We been waiting for you. The minute we got back to the mine and saw that you walked, we figured—"

He was cut off by a shrill scream that turned Nick's blood to ice. The chuckle behind him tortured his raw nerves. Get hold of yourself, Garrett, he ordered silently. What the hell was the matter with him? Where was all that cold detachment he'd always displayed in times of danger?

"Looks like Hal found your girlfriend," the biker said with smug satisfaction.

Nick's fists closed as he was suffused by a murderous rage. "You let her go or I'll—" The sharp blow to his head threw white spots dancing in front of his eyes. The pain vibrated off the wound in his forehead and brought the taste of bile surging to his throat. He shook his head, blinking, as lightning flashed again, followed by an angry growl of thunder.

"Keep your lousy mouth shut, Garrett, or I'll finish you right here," the biker snarled.

Nick forced his body to relax. Light spilled onto the trees on either side of him, and he could hear Hal cursing above the noisy scuffling. The light swung violent shadows bouncing all around, then was still.

"She's a wildcat," Hal said, then yelped. He let out a string of curses as Lee spat at them.

"Get your filthy hands off me, you stinking animal!"

"For crying out loud, Jerry. She bit me!" Hal's howl of protest brought a smile to Nick's grim mouth.

"So punch her out," Jerry said gruffly.

To Nick's intense relief, Lee subsided at once. He desperately wished he could see her, give her some sign of encouragement, though right now he didn't have a whole lot of confidence himself. They were in a hell of a mess. And it was likely to get worse.

Hal must have dropped the flashlight on the ground, for the beam was at an odd angle, but it was powerful enough to light a large area around them. Nick saw the branches of the firs bouncing in the wind, showering needles like fine sea spray, and the more slender trunks swaying lazily. He could see something else.

Apparently Hal hadn't deemed it necessary to take his rifle when he'd gone after Lee. It was propped against a tree a few yards from where Nick stood. If only he could get his hands on it . . .

As if he'd read Nick's thoughts, Jerry jammed his own gun hard between his shoulder blades.

"Bring her over here where I can see her," he demanded in his harsh voice.

Nick's heart leaped as Lee stumbled into his vision, helped by a rough shove from Hal. Nick saw that she held her chin in that typical pose of defiance, but even in the limited light, he saw her bottom lip trembling.

Only too aware of that telltale sign of her panic, Lee pressed her lips together as she faced Hal, who still held her arm in an agonizing grip.

"Let me go," she insisted, though more calmly this time.

"No way, lady," said Hal with a nasty leer. "You should've kept going when you had the chance. Your boyfriend was crazy to bring you back here."

"He didn't bring me back," Lee said, wrenching her arm in a hopeless effort to break Hal's grip. "I brought *him*."

"That so?" Jerry's voice came from behind Nick, low and sinister. "You must be some kind of woman to boss Garrett around. He has a reputation in these mountains. You must be slipping, Garrett, letting her lead you around by the nose."

His laugh was insulting, and Lee rose to the bait. "I don't—" she began hotly, than caught the sharp flick of Nick's head, and snapped her mouth shut.

"I'd like to see just how much woman you are." Jerry's tone sent shivers of horror crawling up her back. He watched her from around Nick's shoulder, but in the darkness she couldn't see his eyes. She could sense them, though, and had a horrible premonition. The feeling intensified when she saw him draw his thin lips back in an ugly grin.

She glanced at Nick. His harsh features were drawn into a grim mask; only his eyes seemed alive in that stony expression, and they locked on hers with a message that sent her hopes soaring. He could get them out of this, somehow. She knew it. But her confidence was badly shaken when Jerry snapped an order.

"Come here and hold this gun on Garrett." As Hal looked uncertainly at Lee, he added, "Let her go. She ain't going nowhere, not if she wants her boyfriend with no parts missing."

Fear settled in her stomach like a cold, hard rock. She watched Hal take the rifle and jab it into Nick's back, distress knifing through her when she saw him wince. Then her eyes flew to Jerry's face. He was moving toward her, and his thin, cruel smile filled her with terror and loathing.

She curled her fingers into her palms, and her nails broke the tender skin, but she felt nothing except for the icicles of fear that stabbed at her. She stood her ground, refusing to give in to the panic washing over her.

Jerry walked to within a few inches of her and stopped, pulling off his hat. Patches of bald skin lay beneath the greasy strands of pale hair above his forehead. His small eyes, spaced far apart, gleamed with a vicious anticipation, and Lee fought the waves of revulsion that darkened her vision. She could feel cold beads of sweat popping out all over her face, and she choked back a terrified moan when Jerry smiled.

"All right, beautiful," he said. "First you're gonna give me a little kiss. Then we'll see what that sexy body of yours looks like without clothes. I may keep you around a while."

His laugh goaded her more than anything he'd said, and she lifted her hand in a reflex action. He caught it in midair and twisted it brutally, forcing a gasp of pain from her lips that was echoed by Nick as he made an involuntary movement forward and received another crashing blow to the head.

Lee shot him an agonized glance. "I'm all right," she said quickly. She clenched her teeth as she watched Nick shake his head, as if trying to clear his vision.

Jerry chuckled. "Yeah, Garrett, she's all right. For now." He let go of her wrist and stepped back. "I changed my mind," he said, his voice dropping to an offensive drawl. "The clothes come off first, then the kiss."

"I'd rather die," Lee said, her voice thick with loathing.

Jerry's grin faded. "Oh, you won't die," he said softly. "Not until I'm done with you. But your boyfriend will, if you don't do what I want. And it won't be pretty. Ever see a man die from a bullet in his gut?''

Lee tasted the metallic tang of blood on her bottom lip. She sent a last desperate look at Nick and saw his eyes swivel to a spot somewhere behind her, then back to her face.

Her pulse quickened, and she frowned. Again he made the movement with his eyes, and she understood. She raised her eyebrows in scant acknowledgment, then she jerked her face around when Jerry barked sharply, "Look at me, not at him. Start stripping, or you'll watch him die."

She made an exaggerated turn toward him, bringing the area behind her into her peripheral vision. Her blood froze when she saw the rifle leaning against a tree less than three yards away.

Nick wanted her to go for the rifle. She had no idea what she was supposed to do with it. She jumped when Jerry gave her shoulder a savage push.

"Hal, if she doesn't start stripping in three seconds, let him have it."

Lee took a faltering step backward. How many steps before she was close enough to grab the gun? She would have to play it carefully, or one of them would realize what she was doing.

"All right!" She didn't have to fake her nervousness; her voice shook with it. If she could just hold their attention long enough, maybe Nick could make a move, and give her a chance to go for the rifle. She prayed that he would make it soon before she had to go too far with this.

"One!" Jerry snarled as she still hesitated. Hal gave a nervous giggle, and a quick glance told her that he was watching her as avidly as his friend.

"Two!"

Lee shrugged out of Nick's jacket and let it slip slowly down her arms.

All three men had gone so still that she could almost hear them breathing, then a sizzle of lightning lit up the trees, followed immediately by the crash of thunder.

Lee gave a startled cry and jumped back, the jacket hanging behind her, still anchored by her wrists.

"Come on, lady," Jerry growled. "I'm fast running out of patience. Maybe I should give you a hand."

"No!" Lee shook the jacket free, and it fell on the ground behind her. She stepped backward over it, then bent to pick it up.

"Let it be. Get on with it before I rip it all off myself."

Jerry took a threatening step forward, and again Lee retreated, pretended to trip and took another step back to recover.

"No! I'll do it." With shaking hands she grasped the hem of her T-shirt. She dared not look at Nick but kept her eyes fixed on Jerry's leering face. Hal's high-pitched giggle assured her he was still absorbed in what she was doing.

Nick's muscles tensed. For the past few moments the pressure of the rifle in his back had slackened, and now it had disappeared altogether. It was now or never. He couldn't stand to see that sick look on Lee's face a moment longer, and his hands, drawn into tightly closed fists, were itching to smash that unpleasant grin off Jerry's face.

Lee was no more than a couple of feet from the rifle. He knew she'd interpreted his signal, but knowing how she felt about guns, he couldn't be sure if she would follow through.

It was a chance he'd have to take—their only chance. He saw Lee's hands go to the hem of her shirt, heard Hal's low, appreciative sigh and made up his mind.

He stepped sideways, twisting his body and bringing the edge of his hand down hard on Hal's forearm. The sickening crack was drowned by a scream of pain, which was cut off sharply as Nick's clenched knuckles contacted with Hal's jaw.

Hal was tall but slightly built. He dropped like a discarded marionette.

Lee had been primed for this moment for several minutes, but when the scuffle broke out she froze. It seemed like an eternity that she stared at the rifle, then Jerry lunged for it, jolting her out of her stupor. He was fast, but she was closer.

A strong shudder shook her body as she closed her fingers around the cold, smooth barrel. She swung it away from Jerry's outstretched hand and managed to jam the stock against her shoulder in an awkward imitation of how she'd seen it done.

With a sickening jolt she saw Jerry smile. She hadn't fooled him for a second. He stepped forward, his hand held out to take it from her, and she scrabbled for the trigger, though she knew she'd never be able to pull it.

His fingers had actually touched the barrel when a dark shape loomed up behind him and crooked an elbow around his throat. Jerry's startled shout dissolved in a gurgle, his eyes glazing as his slack body fell to the ground.

Lee stared in fascinated horror at the limp figure at her feet, only half conscious of Nick prying her locked fingers from the rifle. When he gathered her into his arms, she buried her face in the hard muscles of his shoulder, drawing strength from the reassuring security of his embrace.

"Is he dead?" Her voice, muffled against Nick's shirt, trembled.

"No. It was only a choke hold. He should be out for a while, though."

"What about the other one?"

"Out, too." He tightened his hold on her. "I'm not a killer, Lee. Not unless I have to be."

"I know." She sighed and drew back to look at him. The beam from the flashlight fell across his face, illuminating his strong, indomitable features. Every line of that granite face reflected his character.

He was so competent, so reassuring. She had never doubted his ability to handle the situation. Her unqualified trust in him disturbed her. It was unnerving, as if she'd lost control of her capabilities and could no longer think for herself. She shivered, and he hugged her closer.

"You," he said unsteadily, "were sensational."

"I was scared to death. I was terrified I'd actually have to go through with it."

"I would never have let that happen."

"I know." She wound her arms around his waist. "That was the one thought that kept me going."

He brushed her forehead with his lips. "But I'm not saying I wouldn't have enjoyed it if we'd been alone," he said lazily.

"Why, Mr. Garrett." She drew back again and looked up at him. "Surely you don't think I'm that kind of woman."

His dark eyes studied her, warm and challenging. "What kind of woman are you?"

"I don't know." Her voice was softened by that peculiar breathlessness his gaze always invoked. "I seem to have changed a few of my attitudes lately."

"Is that good or bad?"

She gave him a slow, provocative smile. "I guess that all depends on what kind of woman you like."

He lowered his head. "I like you." The words were whispered against her lips, then his hand caught the back of her neck as his mouth opened and captured hers.

How could he do this to her, she wondered, just by kissing her? Every nerve in her body sprang, tingling, to life. She savored the taste of him, yielding to the insistent pressure of his tongue. She pushed her hips forward and was rewarded by the hard, heated column of his need.

"Lee," Nick groaned against her mouth, "you do this to me at the worst times. If you keep this up, I'm going to be permanently disabled."

"Yeah." She looked up at him, her eyes dancing. "But what a way to go." She gasped when he nipped at her neck.

"You're becoming positively decadent," he murmured. "Your brother won't recognize you. He'll probably put all the blame on me and punch me out for leading you astray."

She sobered instantly. "It's not going to be easy, is it?"

"Nope." He nuzzled her ear. "But with the combination we've got, we can handle anything."

He let her go and bent to pick up his discarded jacket. "At least we have a couple of rifles now."

Lee looked at him with a nervous frown. "A couple?"

"Yeah." He stroked her cheek with a feathery touch. "But first I'm going to teach you how to use it. For one thing, you have to learn to hold it the right way up."

"Right way...?" Lee buried her face in her hands. "I very nearly blew it for both of us, didn't I?"

He took her hands and held them in both of his. "No. You didn't. You did just fine. You were in a tough spot and you came through. You managed to get their attention, and that was what counted." His slow grin warmed her in spite of the cool wind.

"You never quit surprising me, Ms. Coulton," he said softly. He touched his lips to her hands before letting them go, then draped his jacket around her shoulders. "I'd better take care of our friends here first before they decide to wake up."

"What are you going to do?" She couldn't bring herself to look at the unconscious men.

Nick dropped to his knees beside Jerry and lifted the corner of the biker's jacket. "Tie them up. Belts and shoelaces come in very handy at times like these."

Lee pushed her arms into the sleeves of Nick's jacket and hugged it around her. It smelled of woodsmoke and an earthy muskiness that she knew she would carry in her memory for the rest of her life.

So many memories. If they all came out of this alive. She sighed when she felt Nick's arms come around her from behind, and she leaned back, closing her eyes as she came in contact with his chest.

"Ready for your lesson?" he asked.

She nodded. "As ready as I'm going to be."

It wasn't so bad after all, once she got past the initial revulsion of the cold steel beneath her fingers. Nick was a patient teacher. When they were finished, she reassured herself, at least if anyone threatened her again it would look as if she knew what she was doing.

She even allowed herself a small smile when she was once more following Nick through the shadowy trees, helped now by the flashlight as well as by the increasing lightning. She had a mental vision of herself striding manfully along, rifle clutched in one hand, and agreed with Nick's observation. Simon would never recognize her. As for her father, she thought ruefully, he would probably disown her.

Thunder rumbled directly over her head, following close on the jagged streaks of lightning. The storm raged all around them, though the air was dry. Lee expected to feel heavy drops of rain any minute, but they were within sight of the first building, and there hadn't been so much as a sprinkle.

Nick assured her that the ramshackle structure was still empty, and she watched him go on ahead of her to check it out. The men's sleeping quarters were at the other end of the town, Nick had told her, which in reality was nothing more than a half-dozen buildings erected in an uneven row in the large spaces between the trees. The second one, the one in which Nick had seen Simon, appeared to be a small house.

Its porch hung by one rusty hinge and squeaked noisily as the wind played with it. The tiny square panes in the windows were broken, and on one corner of the roof, tar paper flapped in a monotonous rhythm.

Lee obeyed Nick's signal and took shelter behind a tree, her eyes following him as he sidled along the wall to the window. He waited until the lightning gave the forest a semblance of daylight, then darted a look inside. Lee tensed. He drew back, waited, then took another, longer look. Uneasy, she watched him glide back to her.

"What is it?" she whispered. "Is the guard still there?" She saw his grim expression in a vivid flash of light, and her heart sank.

"No. Neither is Simon. He's gone." Her cry of dismay was drowned out by a crash of thunder.

"We'll find him," Nick said quietly. "He's got to be here somewhere."

"What if...?" She couldn't finish, and looked at Nick helplessly.

"We'll find him," he repeated with determination. "We'll search every building. They don't know we've eliminated their guards. They're probably all sleeping like babies."

"Not for long," Lee looked past Nick's shoulder to where the outlines of the trees were faintly visible against the sky. "It's getting lighter."

"There are only five more buildings to look in, and one of them is the lab," Nick said. "I doubt that they have him stashed in there. Keep close behind me, and get a good grip on that rifle. Don't forget, if I say run, you run."

She followed him without answering, her heart jumping with every roar of thunder. If anyone were sleeping in all this noise, it would be a miracle. How could they hope to get Simon out of there when they didn't even know where he was? What would happen to Father, she wondered, if neither of them survived this? Or if she had to go back without Simon? Would he blame her for not going to the sheriff in the beginning? She'd gone through all this to spare her father the worry, and perhaps disappointment, in case Simon was engaged in something dirty. It had been a bad mistake, she realized. He could have handled Simon's failings, but he would never be able to handle Simon's death. And neither would she.

She pulled up sharply as Nick came to an abrupt stop. Peering around him, she caught her breath. In a ragged, awkward row, like uninvited guests at a cocktail party, stood two small houses like the one behind them: a long, low building and two taller ones.

"Stay with me," Nick ordered her under cover of the thunder, "and keep your eyes peeled."

She answered with a brief nod, anxiety catching at her when she realized she could see his face. They were running out of time.

It seemed to take them an eternity to skirt the first house, waiting for the lightning to allow them to see inside. Lee's hopes took another beating when Nick shook his head no. The closer they got to the end building, the less room they'd have for escape. She found herself praying as they crept across the open space between the two houses.

The eruption of noise took them both by surprise. It came from the far end of the town, in a lull between thunderclaps, which made it all the more startling. Someone was shouting, loudly and hysterically, and then the staccato burst of gunfire punctuated the low roll of subsiding thunder.

The door to the house flew open, and three men tumbled down the rickety steps. Lee gave a gasp of pain as Nick hurled her, face up, against the side wall, flattening her to the ridged siding with his body. The rough, splintery wood bit into the knuckles of her hand that held the rifle. She was aware of Nick's heartbeat against her back, and of her own answering it. Footsteps pounded away from them as the men raced toward the noise, and then they could hear a voice they both recognized.

"You're not gonna blow up my mine! I'll see you in hell first, you double-crossing . . . !"

"Ben," Nick breathed. "The fool's gone crazy. Wait here." The pressure of his body eased, and then he slipped away from her around the corner and out of sight.

Thunder grumbled again, farther away now. The storm was passing over. Lee eased herself away from the wall and shifted the rifle to the other hand. She stretched her fingers and clenched them again to ease the stiffness. She could hear Ben's voice above the sporadic gunshots, and she hunched her shoulders, wondering if Simon was in the middle of all that pandemonium. What was Nick doing? She almost dropped the rifle when he appeared in front of her.

"Come on," he said urgently. "I've found him."

Giddy with relief, she followed him around the corner and up the steps of the house.

Tobacco smoke and the musty odor of damp wood met them when they went through the door. The room was empty of furnishings except for several sleeping bags strewn across the floor. Nick swept the flashlight's beam over to the far corner of the room, and Lee's breath caught in her throat. A man lay on his side, his hands and feet bound by ropes, his eyes blinking as light splashed over his bearded face.

"Simon!" She dropped the rifle with a soft thud on the nearest sleeping bag, then bounded across the cluttered floor and dropped to her knees beside him.

He blinked once, and then his eyes widened in shock. "Lee? What in God's name...?"

Lee made a choking sound and flung her arms around his neck, hugging him as if she'd never let him go.

"I hate to break this up," Nick said gruffly behind her, "but we've got to get out of here. The reunion can wait." He pushed the flashlight into Lee's hand, lifted his pant leg and drew the knife from his boot.

"How many are there?" he asked, hacking at the ropes that held Simon's ankles.

"Eleven." Simon grunted, his face twisted in pain. "Twelve, counting Chambers."

"Are you hurt?" Lee asked, her voice rising with anxiety.

Simon shook his head. "Circulation. I've been tied up for days."

"You're going to have a hard time walking," Nick said grimly.

Simon grunted again as his wrists were freed. "It doesn't make much difference. They have bikes. We won't get far."

"We will in the helicopter." Nick turned the knife back into his boot and stood. "Give me a hand, Lee."

She did so at once, holding the flashlight in one hand while she tugged at Simon's arm with the other. Between them she and Nick got him onto his feet, though he was swaying unsteadily.

"You can fly a chopper?" Simon sounded skeptical.

"I flew them in Nam. Can you walk?"

"I'm going to have to." Simon tilted his head to one side. "The shooting stopped. Was that your doing?"

"No." Nick picked up the rifles and handed one to Simon. "Is there a back door to this place?"

"Yeah." Simon jerked a thumb over his shoulder. "Through that door."

Nick looked at Lee. "You go on ahead with the flashlight. When you get the door open, go through it. Don't look back, and don't wait. Go back the way we came. Got it?"

"But—"

"That's an order, Lee."

She gave him a resigned nod. "All right. Got it."

"Man, Lee," Simon said, "you're a mess. What the hell are you doing here, anyway?"

"Rescuing you." She glared at him. "You don't look so hot yourself."

"Get going," Nick said sharply. "They're coming back."

The sound of arguing voices drew rapidly closer. Lee scrambled for the door and yanked it open. The flashlight showed her the long, narrow hallway, and she wrinkled her nose at the black smudges of fungus that clung to the walls. Remnants of flowered wallpaper hung in mournful strips, and she fled past them on creaking floorboards to the door at the end.

It led into another small room that had a door at the far end. She dived for it and realized it was bolted. Frantically she tugged at the resisting metal, and dropped the flashlight when it jerked back. The door swung open on noisy hinges, letting in a blast of cool morning air.

Lee heard Nick and Simon stumble into the room behind her, as well as the shouts of the men as they reached the front door.

"Go!" Nick roared.

With a last, frantic look at him and at Simon, who leaned heavily on Nick's shoulder, she hurtled through the door. Her feet smarted with the force she put into hitting the ground. She heard shots behind her and her own whimper of fear as a bullet whined over her head and ricocheted off a tree trunk ahead of her.

With a fresh stab of fear for the safety of the two men behind her, she kept her head down and ran. When she stumbled for the second time and landed heavily on her knees, she knew she'd finally reached the limit of her endurance.

It seemed to take an incredible effort to get back on her feet. The gunfire had stopped. At least she couldn't hear it. She couldn't hear much at all, except for the wind buffeting the branches of the firs.

Where were they? She thought of the deafening exchange of gunshots and felt cold and sick. When the sound of soft, shuffling footsteps reached her ears, she tensed. Torn between hope and fear, she looked around for a hiding place. A graceful fir, its branches sweeping the ground like a crinoline skirt, provided the answer. Trying to make as little noise as possible, she crawled between the pungent, prickly branches and waited.

When the uneven footsteps were close enough, Lee carefully separated the needles and peered through. It was amazing what the intense relief could do for her exhausted body. She surged out of the tree, heedless of the scratches inflicted on her face, and fell into Nick's arms.

"Thank God!" was all she could say, over and over again. She ran her hands over his back and shoulders. "Are you all right? You're not hurt?"

"I'm not hurt." He smiled down at her anxious face. "Your brother is a crack shot. He took two of them down before the third one gave up and ran off."

She hadn't thought anything would surprise her again. She'd been wrong. She moved out of Nick's arms and looked at her brother. He was watching her with a speculative gleam in his ice-blue eyes, his rifle resting confidently on his shoulder. He was thinner, she noticed, and his hair and beard were stringy and filthy, but his eyes were as sharp as ever.

"Where did you learn to shoot a rifle?" she asked carefully.

His expression became guarded. "It's a long story, Lee. We don't have time for that now."

"We have time for one thing." She had to know. She would know if he was lying. "How did you get involved with these men. Were you part of this setup?"

He shook his head, not quite meeting her eyes. "Not in the way you mean."

"What's that supposed to mean?" Doubt swarmed over her like a cloud of angry bees. She felt Nick's hand on her arm and shook it off. "Damn it, Simon. Don't lie to me. I heard you that night on the phone. You had this all planned. I heard you tell them to keep the police away from you. Why, Simon? Why would you do that?"

She knew that closed look only too well. She'd seen it too many times before.

"Garrett," Simon said in a voice she didn't know. "Get her on that chopper—now. The rest of them won't be wasting any time, so you'll have to move fast." He transferred his gaze to Nick's face, his eyes cold and unrelenting. "Get her home in one piece." His tone brooked no argument.

"Don't worry," Nick said, his voice hard. "I intend to. If I have to knock her out to do it."

Simon nodded and turned away.

"Wait!" Lee pulled on Simon's arm, forcing him to look at her. "You're not coming with us?"

"No." He shifted the rifle into the crook of his elbow. "There's something I have to take care of first."

He looked at her with the face of a stranger, and the knot in her stomach tightened.

"I'm not going home without you," she said. "I didn't go through all this to leave you here now. Whatever you've done, we'll take care of it, Simon. Father can—"

"For crying out loud, Lee, stop mothering me." He seemed to realize how much he'd hurt her, and his eyes softened. "I'll be all right. I promise. Now get going." He looked at Nick. "You shouldn't have any trouble with the chopper. I doubt it's locked. They weren't expecting anyone to take off with it."

"We'll wait as long as we can," Nick said, studying Lee's stricken face. He hated to see her like that—hurt, bewildered, with that awful lost look.

"Don't wait too long. Remember, I'm holding you responsible for getting her home." Simon's eyes rested briefly on Lee's face. He looked as if he wanted to say something, then changed his mind. Without another word, he spun around and walked off with a slightly unsteady gait that betrayed the stiffness in his legs. Within seconds he'd disappeared.

Nick swung his rifle under his arm and took hold of Lee's hand. Her lack of resistance worried him. It was almost as if she were in a trance, following him obediently as he pulled her along, her feet dragging.

He wished he knew exactly what Simon was up to. So many questions. How they must be tormenting Lee right now. Yet something told him Simon King was playing it straight. Whatever the man was hiding, Nick was pretty sure he wasn't a criminal. It was only a gut feeling, but Nick had learned to trust his hunches. For Lee's sake, he hoped this one was no exception.

They reached the edge of the clearing without seeing any sign of movement. The helicopter stood several yards away.

Lee stared at it with total disinterest. She was going back without Simon after all. She'd failed. She'd failed Simon and her father. Most of all, she'd failed herself and the promise she'd fought so hard to keep. She was hardly aware of Nick's hand on her arm, steering her toward the heavy gray machine.

She felt so tired. So weak. Everything seemed to be enveloped in a weird kind of haze. She stumbled and would have fallen if not for Nick's strong grip.

"Lee."

His voice sounded urgent, and she looked up, weary beyond belief. Whatever he was going to say was drowned by the horrendous explosion that slammed into her ears and shook the ground. She stared in dazed disbelief as the silvery sky beyond Nick turned pink, then red, then black.

Smoke billowed from the forest in a thick red-tinged cloud and spread rapidly over the trees. They'd covered only half the distance to the helicopter, and Nick lunged forward, dragging a protesting Lee behind him.

A second explosion seared the air and sprayed burning material into the long grass at the edge of the trees. Nick swore and tugged at the door of the aircraft.

Lee looked over her shoulder fearfully, horrified to see flames leaping across the grass, each small fire reaching ravenously for the next, until the edge of the forest was one endless sheet of flame.

Nick's efforts paid off, and the helicopter door swung open, but Lee's eyes were on the fire, her heart racing like an overheated engine. Above the crackling of the burning forest she had heard another sound.

Nick heard it, too, and turned his head. The roar of the bike grew louder, and beyond the flames a dark shape approached the inferno at breakneck speed.

Nick took hold of Lee's waist and tried to shove her into the helicopter, but she fought him.

"No!" she screamed. "Wait! It's Simon."

"Get in, damn you!" Nick roared, and heaved her onto the floor of the cabin. He looked back and saw Simon break through the fiery barrier, and then the shots rang out, loud and deadly. Lee's screams reverberated in Nick's ears. In helpless frustration, he watched Simon's bike rear up, hover for a heart-stopping moment in midair, then crash to the earth. Simon lay crumpled over the bike, motionless.

A bullet zinged off the side of the helicopter, and Nick ducked. He twisted his body to haul himself up into the aircraft and then saw Lee's face. She was staring past him, her eyes wild with desperation.

"Nick. You've got to help him."

He risked another look back and saw Simon stagger to his feet and fall again. Another barrage of shots erupted from the other side of the flames, and Nick shoved Lee to the floor.

"Stay down," he yelled at her, then grabbed the rifle and dropped to the ground.

Lee dragged herself to the doorway and looked out. It seemed as if the whole forest was on fire. She couldn't believe how fast it had spread. Driven by the winds, the spitting flames leaped from tree to tree, turning each into a fiery torch. Inside the helicopter, the acrid smell of burning vegetation and smoke stung her nose and eyes.

There was a solid wall of fire between the bikers and Simon, but they continued to fire wildly. Lee gripped the edge of the cabin floor, her heart jumping when a bullet smacked into the body of the aircraft, then another and another.

Her eyes searched for Nick and found him. On his belly, he moved at a fast crawl to where Simon lay huddled on the ground. She saw Nick reach out and turn him over, and then drifting smoke swallowed them up and she couldn't see either of them.

The revving of the engines caught her attention. The bikers had stopped shooting. She pushed herself forward and leaned out just in time to see a half-dozen bikes, chased by the leaping flames, roar up the ramp to the bluff, then disappear, one by one, over the top.

They'd given up! She jumped out of the helicopter, astonished when her legs promptly gave way and deposited her on the ground. Then she forgot about her own predicament as a shout lifted her head.

Nick was staggering toward her, supporting a badly stumbling Simon. She opened her mouth to answer and choked on the smoke swirling around her. It smelled different, like burnt fuel. She turned her head, and her stomach nose-dived. Liquid dripped steadily from the belly of the helicopter and splashed onto the flattened grass. A bullet must have hit the fuel tank.

She stared stupidly at the trickle of gas, aware of what would happen if one spark reached it yet unable to do anything about it. She felt rough hands grab her and pull her to her feet.

"Lee," Nick said hoarsely, "come on."

Her legs wobbled dangerously but supported her, and she lurched away from the aircraft, only half conscious of Nick hauling on her arm and dragging Simon along with them.

It was like the nightmare where she wanted to run but her legs wouldn't move.

There seemed to be an endless stretch of grass, swaying at alarming angles before flattening out again. When the explosion came, she felt only relief that she could lie flat on the ground, instead of trying to walk on it.

She heard Simon's voice, slurred but audible.

"What the hell was that?"

"Chopper," Nick said curtly. "It blew."

Simon swore viciously.

"Where'd they get you?" she heard Nick ask him.

Lee tried to raise her head when Simon answered groggily.

"In the shoulder. I'll live."

Lee's moan was more like a sigh when strong hands lifted her head and brushed the hair back from her eyes.

"Are we safe?" she mumbled. It was too much trouble for her to open her eyes.

"For the time being." She didn't like the guarded note in Nick's voice and forced her eyes open. His face swam in front of her, and she closed them again.

"They knew what they were doing when they took off," Simon said. "If they'd waited any longer, they wouldn't have made it." He paused. "I guess there's a way off this damn field."

"Yep." Lee felt the hard muscle of Nick's thigh as he pillowed her head on it. "If you're a mountain goat."

She knew then what the guarded note had meant. They were out on the plateau, with a raging fire between them and the bluff. Their only escape lay behind them, down the sheer drop of the precipice. Her nightmare was complete.

From far away she heard Simon's voice. He was talking to her, trying to tell her something. But it didn't make any sense. It was something about agents and the government and narcotics. What was he talking about? What did it matter, anyway? Nothing mattered anymore.

She felt for Nick's hand and curled her fingers weakly around it. There was so much she wanted to say. Her lips moved, but she couldn't form the words. With the last ounce of her strength, she whispered his name.

"Nick." She never heard his answer. The darkness swept in, smothering her in the voluminous arms of oblivion.

Chapter 10

At first she thought she was still dreaming; voices whispered, faded and whispered again, and were mixed up with the terrifying roar of the flames and the bike engines. Bike engines?

Lee wrinkled her forehead in an effort to remember. Engines. She remembered engines, louder, closer, right on top of her. Simon pleading with her, telling her something that seemed gravely important. She couldn't remember anything, save the whispering voices that were part of the dream.

Other wisps of dreams floated through her confused mind: gentle hands bathing her, a pretty face, calm and reassuring. And always the voices, whispering, sometimes urgent... It occurred to her suddenly that she wasn't dreaming now, that the voices were real.

Carefully she opened her eyes, but shut them again when the sunlight blinded her with a stab of pain. Something rustled close to her ear, and a faint, familiar smell teased her senses. Pine. And disinfectant.

"Mrs. Coulton?" The voice was soft, feminine and insistent. "Are you awake, Mrs. Coulton?"

Lee, knowing it would hurt, didn't want to open her eyes. She tried to tell the voice that, but all she could get out was a meaningless moan. She was tired and wanted to go back to sleep. And she was incredibly thirsty. She tried harder to move her lips.

"Drink." At least that came out pretty clearly. Gentle hands lifted her head and something touched her mouth. Something cold and deliciously wet. She drank greedily, making a small sound of protest as the water was removed.

"That's enough for now, Mrs. Coulton." The voice sounded brisk, efficient. She felt the soft pillow beneath her head and sighed. It was wonderful to be lying on a soft bed again after sleeping on the hard ground for— Her eyes flew open and, in spite of the pain, stayed open.

Memories, frightening, terrifying memories, crowded into her mind. The last thing she remembered was lying in the burning grass with Simon and Nick. Nick! Her heart turned over, and she swiveled her head and met the concerned blue eyes of her brother.

"Hi." He gave her a lopsided smile. "Welcome back. You gave us quite a scare."

"Us?" Her voice was more like a croak, and she wet her lips. When she turned her head, a young, attractive woman's face, framed in auburn curls, smiled back at her. The white cap sat at a jaunty angle, and the nurse looked at Lee with friendly warmth.

"How are you feeling, Mrs. Coulton?"

Lee recognized the voice and smiled back. "Better, thanks." Where was Nick? Surely he couldn't be . . .

The nurse caught her change of expression and leaned forward to pat Lee's hand. "You're fine. Just a bad case of exhaustion, lack of food and a little smoke inhalation. Nothing serious."

Lee whispered her thanks and turned back to Simon. He looked different. His shoulder was heavily bandaged, and a sling supported his left arm, but there was something else. She frowned. "You shaved off your beard."

Simon rubbed at his jaw with his long fingers. "Yeah. Blame Rosie for that."

"Rosie?"

Simon's eyes twinkled, and he glanced across the bed. "Nurse Rosie. She shaved it for me. Said it made me look disreputable."

"The word I used was 'disgusting,'" Rosie said in her musical voice. "It was past saving."

"I'm glad you didn't feel that way about the rest of my body." Simon held the look for a second longer than necessary, confirming Lee's suspicions. At least Simon was back to normal.

She couldn't put it off any longer. "Is Nick all right?"

Simon's eyes returned to her face immediately. "He's fine, Lee. Nothing a good night's sleep wouldn't take care of."

"Is he here?" Her relief was crushed by disappointment when Simon shook his head. She closed her eyes.

"I'll leave you two alone," Rosie said softly. "Don't tire her out, Simon. She needs to rest."

"I won't. See you later?"

Rosie's murmur of agreement almost made Lee smile. She waited until the sound of the door closing told her Rosie had left the room, then opened her eyes again. Simon was watching her, his look guarded. She studied him for a long moment.

She'd almost forgotten what he looked like without his beard. His face looked thinner, his high cheekbones sharper. His straight nose and penetrating eyes would have given him a look of austerity if not for his mouth, which was full-lipped. All in all, Lee decided, she had a remarkably handsome brother.

"Tell me what happened," she said, pleased to hear that her voice sounded stronger.

"Look, Lee," Simon said, "maybe we shouldn't get into all this right now. You heard Rosie—you need the rest."

"I need to know what happened," Lee insisted, trying to push herself up into a sitting position. It was a little difficult for her to sound authoritative when she was lying flat on her back.

"Okay, lie still a minute." Simon leaned forward and did something to the bed. With a soft whining noise, the top part of her mattress lifted her shoulders to a gentle angle.

"Better?" His grin was comfortingly familiar, but the tension still lingered in his eyes.

"Yes." She noticed for the first time that he was wearing a hospital gown under his dark robe. As was she, she realized when she twisted her fingers together and laid them on her stomach.

"First," she said, "at the risk of sounding like a B movie, where are we?"

"Saint Martin's Hospital, in Baker."

"How long have we been here?"

"Two days."

She stared at him in disbelief. "I've been asleep for two days?"

"You could say that."

She plucked at the sheet nervously. "Where's Nick?"

Simon cleared his throat. "He waited until he was sure you were going to be all right. They wanted to admit him for observation, but he refused. He sat in this chair for half the night, Rosie said, until the doctor said you were out of danger. Then he left. He's back at the Blue Bucket, I assume."

"Oh." There didn't seem to be anything to say. She tried to swallow past the hard, cold lump in her throat.

"Lee." Simon's voice was unusually gentle. "He cares a lot about you. I know he does."

"Does he?" She fought for control, horribly afraid she was going to lose the battle. "I care for him, too."

"I know." His hand covered hers, and she stared at it. The strong, tanned skin contrasted sharply with the white sheet. "He's a lot like me, Lee. Some men need a lot of convincing."

She heard the bitterness in her short laugh. "I've never been one to beg."

"Sometimes we have to lose some of our principles to get what we want."

She looked up, her eyes bright with unshed tears. "What about you, Simon, and your principles? How many did you have to lose to get what you wanted?"

She hated to see the hurt in his eyes, but she'd remembered his words on the mountain. *Stop mothering me, Lee.* Well, if that's what she'd been doing, she wouldn't do it anymore. She watched Simon lean back. He looked as tired as she felt. A pang of remorse touched her, and she steeled herself. He had a lot of explaining to do.

"Do you remember anything I told you back there?" he asked after a long pause.

"No, not a lot." She frowned. "Wait—you said something about agents, or something, and the government. I couldn't . . . I don't remember."

He met her gaze, and the expression in his eyes made her heart jump with apprehension.

"I thought we were all going to die," he said slowly. "That's the only reason I told you. But I'm glad I did now. It's finally over."

"Told me what?"

"Lee, I've been working for the government for the past eight years. Undercover stuff. Narcotics."

She felt a number of emotions: shock, relief and regret at the knowledge that she'd never really known her brother. She listened while he explained that he'd quit the bureau a year earlier, but they'd contacted him twice since then to take other assignments.

"They never would've let me go," he said soberly, "but I blew my cover in a big way. The papers were full of it yesterday, complete with close-ups."

"The papers?" She looked at him in alarm. "The *Oregonian*?"

"Yep. 'Fraid so." He shrugged. "I called Dad, told him what to expect."

Lee groaned. "What did he say?"

"Not a lot." Simon stood up and walked over to the window. "He was just glad that we were all right. I said I'd give him the whole story when we got home."

"What *is* the whole story?"

He glanced at her over his shoulder. "You up to listening? You're not too tired?"

"No." She wasn't going to admit that she was fighting to stay awake. "Go ahead."

It was all so simple, really. Lee listened drowsily to Simon's voice, wondering how on earth she could have possibly doubted him. Maybe she wouldn't have if it hadn't been for one thing. She'd have to explain that to him later, when he was finished.

The night she'd been in Simon's apartment, he told her, was the night the bureau had contacted him. They suspected a drug ring was operating in the mountains, and they needed someone to go in undercover.

This wasn't an isolated gang that they could just raid and close down. Chambers, the man in charge, was a member of a much larger, powerful organization. The lab was only one

of several hidden in remote locations around the Northwest. The bureau wanted Simon to find these locations and
flush out the entire organization.

Everything had gone well at first. Ben had been one of the
suspects, and his association with Nick had led Simon to the
Blue Bucket.

"Nick had already been cleared," Simon added hastily
when Lee started to protest. "I needed someone neutral,
someone who knew the mountains and the people."

"It didn't matter that you were leading him into danger?" Lee asked in an accusing voice.

"I made sure he didn't hang around." Simon gave his
sister a reproachful look. "You're the one who insisted on
taking him back up there."

"To look for you," she pointed out.

Simon sighed and stared out the window. "I had a feeling you'd do something like that when I missed the anniversary. Anyway, I gained Ben's trust and talked him into
taking me to meet the White Devils. I almost made it. I had
the files in my hand when Chambers burst in on me in his
office. I thought it was all over until Ben talked them into
keeping me alive long enough to get the ransom sent. Then
they were going to kill me."

Lee shivered. "They almost did. They were going to blow
Ben's mine up, with you in it."

"I know. Nick told me. I guess Ben went berserk and decided to shoot all of them rather than let them blow up the
mine. That's when you and Nick arrived on the scene."

Simon came back to the bed and looked down at Lee.
"You'll never know how I felt when I saw you standing
there. You were the last person in the world I expected to
see. I didn't know whether to hug you or scream at you." He
frowned at her. "I was all set to give Nick hell for bringing
you, except I know how damn stubborn you can be. How
did you manage to talk him into it?"

"It wasn't easy," Lee admitted dryly. "I appealed to his better nature."

"Whatever you did, I'm sure glad you pulled it off."

He smiled at her, but his eyes told her what he found too difficult to say. In that respect, Lee thought wryly, they were alike.

"So am I." She reached for his hand and squeezed it. He looked surprised at the gesture.

He cleared his throat. "I couldn't believe that was you, standing in that crummy little house. You looked so . . . earthy."

"Earthy?" Lee's voice rose on a squeak.

"Yeah." The bed sagged as he deposited his weight on it. "Earthy. I hardly recognized you. I don't know what went on between you and Nick, but it sure changed you."

Lee made a face at him, aware of the hot flush creeping across her cheeks.

"You know," Simon said thoughtfully, "I never would've guessed that Nick Garrett was your type. It just goes to prove how wrong you can be about some people."

"You're not wrong." She found it difficult to hide her pain. "You don't share the kind of danger we did without becoming emotionally involved. But we're very different people, with different backgrounds and different ways of looking at things. It just wouldn't have worked."

Simon looked disappointed. "Too bad," he murmured. "Nick's a great guy."

"You haven't told me how we managed to get back here," Lee said, determined to change the subject. "The last thing I remember is the forest burning around us and nowhere to go."

"Right." Simon's face was grim. "It was pure luck, really. I guess the storm the night before had set off a few small fires on the lower slopes, and the Forest Service crews were checking things out and directing the firefighters. One of the chopper pilots decided to check around the high ground, saw the smoke and came in to investigate. It was close. Another ten minutes and there would've been nothing left but ashes."

Lee shivered. "I must've passed out. I can't remember anything."

"Nick was going crazy trying to get you to come to. I swear, Lee, that guy was practically in tears when the chopper came in. For someone who isn't serious about you, he gave a pretty good imitation."

Lee's heart began to beat a little faster. It was foolish to hope, she knew, and so very hard not to. "How did the fire start?" she asked quickly.

Simon looked sheepish. "That was me. They were getting ready to leave, and I wanted to give you and Nick time to get away. I figured I'd create a diversion. I don't know what they had in that lab, but it went up like a fireworks factory."

All at once she was incredibly tired. It hurt to think. She just wanted sleep. Maybe after a good rest she'd be able to sort out her chaotic feelings.

"If you don't mind, Simon," she said faintly, "I think I'd like to sleep now."

"Oh, sure." Simon stood, his face creased in concern. "I'm in the next room if you need me. The doc said that if you check out all right, he'll release us both in the morning. I've arranged for your car and luggage to be brought here from your motel. I don't know what happened to my car—Nick said it wasn't in the parking area on the mountain."

Lee shook her head wearily. It seemed like months since the day she and Nick had arrived on the mountain. She felt a sudden, fierce longing to see him again, and she closed her eyes quickly before Simon could see the tears threatening.

"Lee."

The tension in Simon's voice made her open her eyes again.

"I'm sorry. You could've been killed. I never meant for you to get mixed up in all this."

She frowned, sensing there was something else he was trying to say. "What is it, Simon?"

"It's hard to thank someone for doing what you did. Especially when you thought I was some kind of a crook."

"I didn't." Her voice faded, and she struggled to stay awake a moment longer. It was important. "Not until Nick said you were a crack shot. You always said you could never use a gun, not even on an animal."

Simon shrugged and gave her a rueful smile. "Circumstances can change your way of thinking."

Lee yawned and closed her eyes. "We were never very good at talking to each other about things that mattered to us," she said sleepily. "One of these days you'll have to tell me how you got involved with the government in the first . . ." The effort to talk had become too much for her. She heard Simon whisper, "One of these days," and then the room faded as sleep claimed her.

When she woke again, the nurse was standing by her bed. The tray Rosie held looked promising, Lee thought, realizing that she was ravenous.

"You're looking much better, Mrs. Coulton," Rosie said, and pulled a small table around in front of Lee. The whirring sound accompanied the lifting of her shoulders again. Someone must have lowered the bed while she was asleep, she realized.

"What time is it?" she asked as Rosie whipped the lid off a bowl of marvelously aromatic chicken soup.

"It's six-thirty. I let you sleep a little longer, but now you need to eat. You must be starving."

Lee picked up the spoon and sighed. "I am. It seems days since I ate."

"We fed you intravenously last night, but since this is the first solid food you've had in a couple of days, go slow with it."

Lee took a mouthful of soup and made a sound of appreciation. "This is great." Memory bit into her, of a fire crackling in the midst of the forest, smoke wreathing above a dark head and a plate of stew in her hands. She had used those exact words to Nick....

She looked up to smile at Rosie, and a flash of color caught her eye. Turning her head, she saw a huge bouquet of chrysanthemums and daisies, a riot of yellow, gold and white, standing on the small dresser. Her eyes widened in pleasure.

"Oh, how lovely. Where did they come from?"

"Read the card and find out." Rosie picked up the tiny white envelope and handed it to Lee.

Her fingers shook as she opened the envelope, hardly daring to breathe. The words scrawled on the card blurred, then cleared, and her heart leaped to her throat.

Glad you're feeling better. If you need anything, let me know. Yours, Nick.

"Must be someone special," Rosie said softly.

Lee looked up and met curiosity in the nurse's bright green eyes. "A good friend." She laid the card down and resumed eating her soup. That's exactly what the card had sounded like—from a good friend. The flowers were lovely, but the card was polite, impersonal. Her heart ached.

"Well, I'm off for the evening," Rosie said. "I'm just going to check on your brother before I leave." She flipped the lid on Lee's water jug. "Try to drink two or three glasses of water," she said. "You're still a bit dehydrated."

Lee nodded. "I will." She looked at Rosie's flushed face. "Give my love to Simon," she added wickedly.

Rosie grinned. "He's quite a man, your brother," she said. "But I'm not allowed to fraternize with the patients."

Lee grinned back. "I have the feeling you won't have much say in it. Simon can be very persuasive."

Rosie's flush deepened. "So I've discovered. Good night, Mrs. Coulton."

"Lee. And thanks, Rosie. Good night." Lee lay back against the pillow as the door closed behind the nurse. It wasn't often she envied her brother. Maybe he had the right idea—stay uninvolved. It was a lot less complicated.

There was just one problem. It was a little late for that, as far as she was concerned, she thought with a sigh. She looked at the baked custard with a grimace of distaste. If this was solid food, she couldn't imagine what a liquid diet looked like.

She nibbled on a cracker, her thoughts on Simon's conversation that afternoon. Now that it was over, it was hard to believe it had all happened. Except for the unusually deep suntan she'd acquired and a few bruises that were beginning to turn an ugly purple, she might have thought it was all a long, particularly vivid dream.

She picked up the card on the table and looked at the scrawled message again. This was no dream. Nick had been real, as real as the love she felt for him now. That part of it would remain with her for a very long time.

Simon's words, never quite out of her mind, came back clearly. *For someone who isn't serious about you, he gave a pretty good imitation.*

If you need anything, let me know. Was that just a polite phrase, something you would say to anyone lying in hospital? Or was it Nick's way of leaving the decision up to her?

Was there hope after all? If she could only be sure that he really cared for her, she would move mountains to be with him, even if it meant giving up the hotel. She could be happy on the slopes of the mountain, as long as they were together.

Lee's mouth widened in a rueful smile. What would Simon say to that? She finished the custard quickly and pushed the tray away. She was determined. She wouldn't go back to Portland until she'd given Nick the chance to tell her how he felt about her.

She studied the phone beside her bed for several seconds before she leaned across and picked it up. The label stuck on the front told her to dial 9 for an outside line, and she did so, her heart fluttering like a frantic moth.

When the dial tone sounded in her ear, she punched some more buttons, and the operator answered her.

"I'd like the number of the Blue Bucket Saloon in Gambler's Gulch," Lee said, feeling sick with excitement and apprehension.

The operator rattled off the number. "Would you like me to connect you?" the metallic voice asked.

Lee looked frantically around for a pencil and, finding none, gulped. "Er, yes, please." Her heart was beating so hard she could hardly hold on to the receiver. What could she say to him? Had she read the wrong meaning into that terse message? Would he think she was throwing herself at him? Conversations flickered through her mind: his sarcastic remarks about her life-style, his words to her on the mountainside. *You were right about one thing. You're definitely not my type.*

She was about to hang up when the ringing was answered by a voice she didn't recognize.

"Blue Bucket Saloon."

Her own voice sounded strangled as she answered.

"Is Mr. Nick Garrett there?"

"He's upstairs in his apartment," the male voice said. "Just a minute. I'll put you through."

"No . . ." Lee began, but it was too late.

"Garrett." The deep voice sent the blood rushing to her head, and she gripped the phone with a hand that trembled.

"Nick? I hope I'm not disturbing you." She had attempted to sound light, casual, but she could hear the quaver in her voice echo all the way down the line. The silence stretched for an agonizing minute.

"Hello, Lee. How are you feeling?" The guarded tone of his voice chilled her.

"Much better, thanks. What about you?"

"I'm fine. When are you getting out?"

"Tomorrow." She swallowed miserably and struggled on. "I wanted to thank you for the flowers, Nick. They're lovely."

"I'm glad you like them."

The dull ache in the pit of her stomach intensified. "Nick, I owe you some money. I thought I'd stop by and drop off the check tomorrow before I go back to Portland, if that's all right."

"Lee, forget the money. You don't owe me anything. I almost got you killed back there. I wouldn't feel right taking money from you."

"And I wouldn't feel right not paying you. You did rescue Simon for me. I couldn't have done that without you."

"Without me none of this would have happened. You would've had to call in the sheriff, which would've saved us all a lot of trouble."

"I see." The lump in her throat felt as if it would choke her. "Then there's all the more reason for paying you for your trouble."

He must have heard the agony in her voice, for he relented. "Lee, please. Forget the money. I won't be here tomorrow, anyway."

The slight softening of his tone did nothing to dispel the knot in her stomach. "Oh? Are you going away?" Please, she prayed. *Not yet. Not before we've had a chance to sort things out.*

He hesitated for a long moment. "It's Midge's funeral," he said at last. "The service is being held in the morning."

"Oh, Nick." She forgot her own pain, sympathizing with his. "Is he being buried in Gambler's Gulch?"

"No. I have to go now, Lee. They need me downstairs. Take care."

She didn't know how she managed to keep her voice steady. "You too, Nick. Thanks. For everything."

"Yeah."

She held the dead receiver to her ear for long seconds, her eyes closed tightly. She was still holding the phone when her door opened and Simon poked his head in.

"Hi! How're you doing?" His face changed when he saw her expression. "What's wrong?" He came over to the bed and gently took the phone from her hand, placing it back on the stand. "Were you talking to Nick?"

She tried for a smile, and made it. "How did you guess?"

Simon shrugged. "He's the only guy I've seen you get that moony over."

It was just what she needed. Her chin came up. "I don't get 'moony,' as you so quaintly put it. I leave that distinction for you."

Simon grinned. "Ah, but I do it all the time. It's less dangerous."

"And more unsettling. Especially for your girlfriends. How's Rosie, by the way?"

Simon's sun-bleached eyebrows rose. "Now what do you mean by that?"

"Oh, don't play the innocent with me," Lee retorted playfully, grateful for this opportunity to recover her self-control. "I know the beginning of a flirtation when I see one."

"Is that what it is with Nick," Simon asked, "a flirtation?"

Lee's face stiffened. "There are times, Simon, when you ask too many questions."

She tried to evade his searching look, but he was too sharp for her.

"It is something more, isn't it?" he said softly. "At least for you." He shook his head. "Funny, I would have sworn it was for Nick, too."

"I guess we were both wrong there." Her casual tone didn't deceive him for a second.

"So, what are you going to do about it?"

Lee gave him a helpless look. "I don't know. What can I do?"

Simon dented the bed with his weight as he sat down. "Since this is the age of women's lib, you go after him, that's what."

Lee shook her head. "You know I can't do that."

"Why not?" He picked up her hand and studied it, shaking his head when he saw her torn and jagged nails. "You've done just about everything else in the past few days, haven't you? Before all this happened, who would have thought you could climb a mountain and carry a rifle as if you'd been doing it all your life?"

She gave him a wan smile. "No one. But then I didn't have much time to think about it."

"Ah." He dropped her hand. "That's the trouble, Lee. Don't think about it. Just do it. If he means that much to you, you'll do it."

She stared at him for a long moment. "You know something?" she said softly at last. "Sometimes you make a lot of sense. Do me a favor, will you?"

Simon rose and gave her a mock bow. "Anything, my dear sister. Just name it."

"Midge is being buried tomorrow morning. Nick is going to the funeral. I want to be there, too."

"Now wait a minute," Simon said, raising a warning hand. "I don't think that's a good idea. You've been through a lot the past few days. I plan on taking you home to recuperate before you go dashing off on your quest for love."

"No way." Lee looked at him stubbornly. "Once I get home, I'll never find the courage to do this. Please, Simon. Find out for me where the service for Midge is being held. With all your experience you should be able to do that for me." Her eyes pleaded with him. "Apart from anything else, I'd really like to be there. Midge saved my life. Even if Nick gives me the cold shoulder, I'll at least feel I paid my respects to Midge."

Simon sighed. "Okay. I never could refuse a pretty face. What's Midge's full name?"

Lee gave a cry of dismay. "Oh, Simon, I don't know. I don't think even Nick knew what his real name was. Midge was just a nickname."

Simon pulled at his bottom lip with two lean fingers. "You're not making this very easy, Lee. But I'll do what I can. Just pray there aren't too many funeral homes around this area. Didn't Nick give you any clues?"

"No." She looked unhappily down at her hands. "I guess he didn't want to tell me. The only thing I know is that it's not in Gambler's Gulch."

"Well, that eliminates a couple of phone calls," Simon said brightly. "Cheer up. I'll find it. I'll get Rosie to help. Between the two of us we'll track it down."

"I thought it was Rosie's night off," Lee said in surprise.

"It is." Simon laid a finger against his lips and winked. "She's sneaking in to see me later."

"Don't get her into trouble," Lee warned him uneasily.

"Who, me?" Simon's face registered outraged surprise. "Would I do a thing like that?"

"Not only would, but have," Lee said dryly.

Simon grinned. "Makes life exciting though, doesn't it?" He was still grinning when he backed out of the room.

For the next two hours Lee watched the flickering shapes on the television set above the foot of her bed without absorbing a single second of the movie. Her mind was busy replaying the events of the past few days, from the moment she'd first stepped into the Blue Bucket until she'd woken up here in the hospital room. She tried to remember every word, every expression on Nick's face, searching for clues as to his feelings for her. He'd cared; she couldn't have loved him if he hadn't given her at least a hint of that.

He had intended them to be together again; he'd said so. Or had that been the heat of the moment? Had she been just another in what was probably a long line of relationships? She had to find out one way or the other before she went home. She couldn't just walk off into the sunset not knowing why he'd changed his mind or why he didn't want to see her now.

She drifted off to sleep finally and didn't hear Simon gently open, then close, the door.

Rosie was smiling at her when she opened her eyes again. Lee was surprised to see sunlight bathing the bottom of the bed.

"Good morning," Rosie said brightly. "You should be feeling refreshed now after all the sleep you've caught up on."

"I do." Lee's heart jumped as she came fully awake. "Where's Simon? Did he find out where the funeral is?"

"He did indeed." Rosie's eyes laughed at her. "I have a hunch your brother could do anything in this world once he sets his mind to it."

"So can his sister." Simon spoke from the doorway, and Lee looked at him anxiously.

"You found it?"

Simon nodded and crossed the room, putting a slip of paper into her hand. "It's in a little town called Prairie City, about ten miles from here. The service is at two-thirty." He glanced at his watch. "That gives you at least three hours before you have to leave."

Lee nodded. "It won't take me long to dress and shower."

"You're going to eat something first," Rosie put in firmly.

Lee smiled. "If it's anything stronger than soup and custard, I'd love it. I could eat an entire cow."

"I'll find something," Rosie promised. "You slept through the breakfast, but the doctor left orders not to wake you till you were ready."

Simon's eyes lingered on the nurse as she left the room, and Lee shook her head. "Have a good evening?" she murmured sweetly.

"Yeah." Simon's eyes came back to her. "That one's going to be hard to leave."

Lee frowned. "What are you plans now, Simon? I mean, after you've been home to see Father."

The closed expression she'd dreaded seeing again swept over Simon's face. "Well, I'm out of the bureau now, so I have to make a living with my photography. Up till now I've only been playing with it."

She wasn't going to let him fool her again. This time she wouldn't ignore that look.

"Okay, Simon. What are you really going to do?"

He shrugged. "Well, I do have one little thing I want to take care of before I settle down into being a normal citizen."

Lee laughed. "That you will never be. What is this project you don't want to talk about?"

"Chambers," Simon said briefly. "I may be out of the bureau, but I have a couple of scores to settle with that gentleman. He may have eluded the police, along with half a dozen of his cronies, but I don't intend to let him off scot-free. I'm going to find every one of them and bring them in. Especially Chambers."

"Oh, Simon." Lee looked at her brother helplessly. She knew that hard look only too well. Nothing she could say would make the slightest bit of difference. Simon had made up his mind, and there wasn't a soul on earth who could stop him.

"Don't worry." The look had disappeared. "I can take care of myself. I may have run out of luck in the mountains, but I'll make sure it doesn't happen again. Anyway, we don't have to worry about that yet. I'll take you to the funeral and then—"

"No!" Lee pulled herself up in the bed and met her brother's startled gaze defiantly. "I'm going by myself."

"Now wait a minute." Simon's brows drew together. "You're not strong enough to—"

"I'm perfectly fine," Lee cut in. "I'm going alone, Simon." She looked at the address in her hand. "This Prairie City can't be all that hard to find."

"It's not," Simon said reluctantly. "It's on the main highway. A little town on the John Day River. Small town— anyone can tell you where the church is."

"Great. Then there's no problem, is there?"

Simon's reply was halted by Rosie coming back with a steaming tray. Lee looked at it with delight when Rosie lifted the lid from the plate.

"Is that real bacon and eggs?" Lee asked reverently.

"With toast, jelly and coffee," Rosie assured her.

"Who do you know?" Simon grumbled. "All I got was oatmeal and scrambled eggs."

"All you had to do was ask," Rosie said, flashing him a suggestive look.

Without taking his eyes off Rosie, Simon said, "I'll wait around here, Lee, until you get back from the funeral. Then I'll drive you back to Portland."

Lee noticed the glance being exchanged between her brother and the nurse and once more felt a stab of envy. "I have a better idea," she said. "Why don't you rent a car? Then I don't have to worry about coming back for you, and you can leave whenever you're ready."

Simon flashed her a grateful look. "Sure you're up to driving to Portland?"

"I'm sure." She grinned at Rosie, who looked a little embarrassed. "After all I've been through, I think I'd rather drive myself. It's more relaxing."

"Great." Simon made no effort to hide his relief. "What time do you get off, Rosie? You can help me find a car."

Lee coughed politely. "Would you mind conducting this conversation somewhere else? I'd like to get dressed."

"Oh, sure." Simon's big hand squeezed her shoulder. "I guess I'll see you back at the old homestead, then?"

Lee nodded. "If you get home before me, tell Father I'll explain when I get there."

Simon's brow lifted. "Okay. And good luck."

"Thanks," Lee said dryly. "I'm going to need it. I just hope I'm doing the right thing."

"In my book," Simon told her, his blue eyes regarding her solemnly, "you'd be crazy not to give it a shot."

A little more than an hour later she was still trying to convince herself that he was right. The church had been easy enough to find, situated in a picturesque setting of full-leafed apple trees. Judging by the pickups and worn-out cars parked outside, Lee surmised, the church would be full. She was right.

It was a full five minutes before she caught sight of Nick. Even so, she was unprepared for the jolt it gave her to see his dark head near the front of the crowded pews. She was several rows back, and he couldn't see her unless he turned all the way around.

She couldn't tear her eyes away from him. As he turned his head to look at the young man next to him, she saw the dressing taped to his forehead, and her stomach twisted with bittersweet memories. Would he be angry with her for being there? Would he be as distant as he'd been on the phone?

Listening to the moving tributes paid to the man who'd sacrificed his life for her, she wished she had the courage to step up and add her own thoughts.

Instead, she paid a silent homage and hoped that it would be heard. Then she turned her attention back to Nick. Now that she was actually faced with the prospect of speaking to him, her courage appeared to be deserting her. It had been a stupid idea. What if he embarrassed her, made it clear he was no longer interested?

She couldn't bear the thought of him looking at her as he had in the beginning, so coldly and indifferently. She had to admit, the circumstances were a lot different now that they were back in civilization. Perhaps it would be better to leave things as they were, take the memories, go back to Portland and put this part of her life behind her.

The service was ending. She stood, intending to creep to the end of the row and slip out of the door. As if nudged by some silent instinct, Nick looked back over his shoulder and saw her. Lee froze, her eyes locked with his, unable to move or even breathe. In a daze she watched him rise and move down the pew, then come toward her.

He indicated with a curt movement of his head for her to follow him, and she obeyed, unable to resist the command. Unaware of the curious heads turning, she reached the door and, without looking at him, walked past him and out into the clean, fresh air.

The familiar weak-kneed feeling overwhelmed her as she heard the door close behind her. The sun had reached its summit and beat down on her unprotected head. She managed the few steps to the shady trees without tripping, much to her surprise. How many times had she cursed the effect he always had on her?

She was afraid to turn around, afraid to see the expression she dreaded in his eyes. She heard his footsteps as he approached, and the last of her composure vanished. Her hands clenched as his deep voice came from behind her.

"It must be important if you've gone to all this trouble to track me down."

"It is." She took a deep breath. She would know the minute she looked into his eyes. With all her hopes balancing on the next few seconds, she turned to face him.

Chapter 11

She'd forgotten his ability to freeze all expression from his face. She gazed up at him and couldn't think of a single thing to say. Dressed in a conservative dark shirt and slacks, his hair neatly combed, he looked formidable and so unlike the stubble-chinned, windswept charmer who'd made love to her in the pine forest.

"I just wanted to pay my last respects to Midge," she stammered.

He stared at her in silence for so long she almost turned and walked away.

"You're very pale," he said finally. "Are you all right?"

"Fine." She didn't feel fine. She wasn't sure what she felt. The sun warmed her shoulders through the thin cotton of her shirt, yet inside, a cold ache was spreading.

"I want to thank you," she said with a desperate little smile. "For saving my life, and Simon's."

His laugh was bitter, and he turned from her, staring at the mountain silhouetted against the blue sky behind her. "I almost got you killed," he said. "I should have known better. My track record with women isn't exactly impressive. I usually end up hurting them in one way or another."

"Or they hurt you?" Lee asked, her voice soft.

He looked at her then, and she almost cried out at the pain in his eyes.

"Not anymore," he said grimly.

She'd never felt so helpless in her life. She wanted to touch him, to beg him to tell her what was in that stubborn, complicated mind of his. She wanted so badly to share his pain, to know what it was that tormented him to the extent that he could hurt her like this. To shut her out after all they'd meant to each other.

But that was it, wasn't it? she reminded herself. All they had meant to each other. Had it meant anything to him at all? Had Simon read him wrong? Was his concern over her just a matter of guilt? Of an inflated sense of responsibility?

She gave him one last look of despair. How could she possibly get through that barrier he'd put up between them? She'd never know how he really felt about her. Maybe he didn't know himself. Whatever had happened in his past was stronger than anything he felt now. Perhaps that was her answer.

With a sigh of defeat, she pushed her hair off her forehead. The heat seemed to be getting to her; everything shimmered in a bright haze. Past Nick's shoulder she saw people filing out of the little church, and she knew it was time to go.

With an effort she placed a smile on her cold lips. It was strange how she could feel so cold with the sun burning her skin. "I guess you won't accept my check?" she said unsteadily.

"I don't want your money, Lee." He frowned. "Are you sure you're all right? You've just got out of the hospital—

you should be resting, not standing in this sun." He glanced around as if realizing something for the first time. "Where's Simon? Isn't he with you?"

Lee shook her head, then swayed when the movement made the ground tilt alarmingly. "I'm driving myself back to Portland. He has his own plans." She gulped in some air. Maybe she should sit down; her head felt strange. "I'll be going now, Nick. Thanks again for everything." She held out her hand and was surprised to see it shaking. She pulled it back quickly and tried to smile, but it was just too much effort. Everything was too much effort. It was even too much effort to stand.

She turned and took a faltering step toward the car and felt as if she'd stepped down a large hole. The last thing she remembered was Nick's voice, swearing in his usual, vicious way, then the wonderful strength of his arms closing around her, just before the hole swallowed her up.

It was as if she were trying to push aside suffocating folds of heavy velvet. If only she could see, if only her head would stop swimming... She opened her eyes and looked straight into Nick's concerned gaze.

"Hi." His voice, low and unsteady, betrayed his anxiety, and Lee struggled to reassure him.

"Hi. I seem to be making a habit of this. I'm sorry."

She started to sit up, but Nick laid a hand on her arm, and immediately the familiar tingling shivered along her flesh.

"Lie still," he said firmly. "You have to rest. Doctor's orders."

She lay back, only too glad to do as she was told. "How long have I...?"

"Not long," he interrupted her. "About half an hour. I drove you here in your car—it's outside."

He shrugged at Lee's questioning look. "My Jeep is still in the mountains. Your keys were in your purse. I hope you don't mind."

"Of course not. I'm grateful." She was in a living room, she discovered, lying on a soft coffee-colored velour settee.

"Here," Nick said. "Drink this."

Lee looked at the amber liquid swirling around in the glass he handed her. "What is it?"

"My best brandy."

His arm slipped under her head and supported it while she took an experimental sip. Her throat burned, and she choked. Nick took the glass from her hand.

"You'll never make a boozer." He looked down at her, unsmiling. "Want to try again?"

She nodded and took a hefty gulp this time. It went down easily, and she managed a triumphant smile.

Nick shook his head. "Always trying to prove something, aren't you?" he murmured.

Lee looked at him searchingly. His features had relaxed, but his eyes were still guarded and wary. Still, there was something in the dark depths that stirred a flicker of hope.

The brandy was fueling her strength. Her head felt clear, and the dull ache had disappeared. She swallowed another mouthful.

"Whoa!" Nick took the glass from her hand and set it down somewhere behind her head. "I don't want a drunk on my hands. Feeling better?"

"Much. I'd like to sit up, though."

He examined her with a critical eye. "You do have a bit more color now. But take it slowly, okay?"

He lifted her shoulders until she was sitting upright. Lee looked around with interest. "Is this where you live?"

"Yep. You're in the Blue Bucket. Or, to be more precise, above it. This is my apartment."

It was a long room, with two large windows in one wall. The ceiling was low and heavily beamed like the tavern downstairs, but the similarity ended there. The light oak bookcase, filled to capacity, the stereo system next to it, the comfortable leather armchairs, with their pale orange cushions, added up to inexpensive but quiet taste.

Lee eyed the Tiffany light fixture above the smooth, polished dining table with appreciation. "It's an interesting mix of old and new. I like it. Did you furnish it yourself?"

"Guilty." His tone was light, but she knew he was pleased.

"You said something about a doctor?" She wondered if he'd called the hospital. She couldn't remember a thing after she'd fainted, until now.

"James Clayton. He was at the church, luckily. A good friend of mine." Nick straightened up from his crouched position beside the settee. "He looked you over and talked with the hospital. He seemed to think you'd be all right with a little rest. It's probably just the aftereffects of everything, and a little too much sun too soon."

"I see." Lee looked down at her legs and made a futile effort to pull her denim skirt over her knees. "I'm sorry to be such a nuisance."

"You're not a nuisance."

The mask had settled over his face again, Lee noticed in dismay. Now what had she said?

"Are you hungry?"

His question took her by surprise, and she shook her head. "No, thanks. I ate a good breakfast." She glanced at her watch, shocked to see it was almost five. "Don't let me stop you, though," she added hastily.

"I'm not ready to eat yet."

It was hard to believe they were the same two people. Why were they being so polite to each other? She looked down at her hands, clenched in her lap, and jumped when he spoke.

"How's Simon?"

"Fine. His shoulder is bothering him, I think, and his arm is in a sling, but he seems to be on the mend."

"He should've had more sense than to let you go off on your own like that. Why didn't he come with you?"

She didn't know how to answer that. "I wanted to come alone," she said, twisting her fingers together.

She was saved from any more leading questions by the shrill ring of the telephone. She watched him cross the room to the low table next to one of the armchairs. Even his walk affected her sexually. Everything about him affected her that way. What kind of chance did she stand against him?

How many women had felt the way she did about him? A good many, probably, she told herself. What a fool she was to have imagined she could be the one to break through that bitter wall he'd built around his emotions. And yet . . .

She watched him answer the caller without hearing a word he said. She was remembering, reliving moments that would forever be burned in her mind.

His whispered words just before he had left her alone with Ben: *There will be a time for us—that's a promise.* Then later, in the forest, again the promise. It had seemed so very right. He had cared for her then; she knew it. She'd heard it in his voice, seen it in his eyes and felt the force of it in the strength of his body when he'd made love to her.

Even Simon had seen it. And now he was denying it, to her and to himself. He'd had time to think it over, time to brood and time to once again erect that formidable barrier. She gave a rueful shake of her head. Time. The one thing he'd promised her had become her enemy.

She swung her legs to the floor as Nick hung up the phone.

"That was the doctor," he said, frowning at her. "What are you doing?"

"Standing." She did just that, pleased to find that everything remained stationary. "I feel a lot better now. Pretty normal, in fact." She wondered whether she'd ever feel normal again.

"Well, don't rush it. Jim said you should stay overnight. You certainly can't drive yourself back to Portland today."

"Oh, I couldn't. I mean—" She broke off. Why couldn't she? Wasn't this what she needed? Time. Maybe, with just a little more time, she could persuade him to talk about his past, make him bring it out in the open, where they could both deal with it.

"Perhaps I could get a room at the motel, just for the night?" The invitation would have to come from him.

"You're in no shape to be on your own. You can stay here tonight. I'll sleep out here on the settee—it's as comfortable as it looks."

Afraid of revealing her delight with her success, she looked down. "I couldn't possibly impose on you like that," she murmured. "If you'll just take me to the motel, I'm sure—"

"No." She didn't miss the grim note in his voice, and she flinched inwardly. It was obvious he wasn't happy about the idea of her staying, and the doubts rushed back to torment her. What could she possibly hope to achieve in one short night?

"I'll go down and get your luggage out of the car," Nick said, "and I have to look in on the tavern. I won't be long."

He reached the door and looked back, and Lee's heart twisted at the impassive expression on his face. What she wouldn't give to see that look of naked hunger again, the way he'd looked at her in the forest when he'd started to undress. Even at the beginning, when she'd first felt the electricity between them, even then, when he'd fought so hard to hide it, he hadn't looked at her with this total detachment, which so clearly locked her out.

"Make yourself comfortable," he said. "Feel free to turn on the television or the stereo. I'll be back as soon as I can."

"Don't worry about me." Lee leaned back against the cushions and smiled. "I'll be fine."

He looked at her for a second longer, then, apparently satisfied, went through the door and closed it behind him.

Lee stared at the space where he'd been. He couldn't have changed his mind about her with such unwavering finality. What they'd shared had been too special. No. It was this shadow in his past that was keeping him from admitting what was in his heart. Somehow, she vowed silently, before she left this town, she would do her damnedest to find the chink in that wall.

Lee stood up and walked over to the stereo. Somehow she had to get his defenses down, and she had no idea how she was going to do it.

She found the stack of albums under the stereo and idly flipped through them. She had to find a way to bring back that closeness, to make him relax enough to want to confide in her.

She discovered a singer she recognized and slipped the album from its cover. Somehow she'd have to make him remember the moments they'd shared, the whispered words that had been exchanged in the heat of their passion, deep in the wildwoods of the mountain.

She swore softly under her breath. Why didn't she just admit it? Even if she never learned his secrets, the one thing she wanted, with a hunger that shocked her, was one more night in Nick's arms.

She placed the album on the turntable and touched the switch. A low, throbbing tune filled the room. It was country music and, like Nick, raw and infinitely sensual.

Lee stared at the stereo as the smoky voice poured out the haunting lyrics. *Think of me as passing breezes sigh through every tree tonight. Think of me as lonely sea gulls cry across the sea tonight. Think of me, and as you see my face feel again the thrill of our embrace. Think of me and know the reason why you're wanting me tonight. Think of me.*

She heard Nick's voice whispering to her in the darkness, the thunder echoing his words. *What kind of woman are you?* Was she woman enough that he would want her just one more time? And if so, was she woman enough to break down the defenses he was so determined to hold on to?

If he means that much to you, you'll do it, Simon had told her. She closed her eyes, remembering Nick's face, his voice, when he'd told her she was sensational, his aroused body when he'd pulled her into his arms.

She let the music wash over her. She wanted him, no matter what the consequences. Maybe she'd finally reach the part of his soul that he'd buried so deeply, but if he still shut her out, she'd at least have this night to remember.

She turned off the stereo, leaving the record on the turntable, and switched on the television.

She was watching the news when she heard his steps outside the door, and though her fingers were clenched, she looked at him calmly when he came through the door.

"I'll put this in my bedroom," Nick said, carrying her suitcase across the room. "If you feel up to it, I'll show you where everything is."

"I feel fine," she assured him, and followed him into the narrow hallway. He came to a door and nudged it open with his foot, then stood back so Lee could enter.

The room was large, and essentially masculine. A heavy oak dresser stood in one corner and a bedspread patterned with a brown and cream geometrical design covered the queen-size bed. On the wall above the bed was an enormous painting, a panoramic view of heavily forested mountains. It was so similar to the environment they'd recently shared that Lee felt a sharp tug of nostalgia and wished passionately for a moment that they were still there, in the exotic freedom of the wilderness.

"It may be humble, but it's home," Nick said behind her.

Lee dragged her eyes away from the painting and looked at him. Surely he wasn't back on that tack again. "It's impressive, and very you," she said firmly.

He raised his eyebrow a fraction. "Whatever that means." He set the suitcase down and looked at his watch. "I'll leave you to get settled. I have a couple of steaks in the fridge, if that sounds good."

She sent him a quick smile. "Don't tell me you can cook."

He smiled back. "I'll let you be the judge of that. Give me about half an hour."

She nodded. "Fine. Would you mind if I took a shower? After everything that's happened, I can't seem to get enough of them."

The flicker of his eyes sent her hopes soaring.

"Sure. You'll find towels in the closet just inside the door. Take your time." He couldn't get out of the room fast enough.

She accepted his suggestion and took a leisurely shower, enjoying the sting of the hot water on her skin in a way she'd never appreciated before. It would be a long time before she took hot water and clean sheets for granted again, she mused as she dried herself with a soft towel.

She rummaged through the contents of her suitcase, racked with indecision. She didn't have a lot to choose from, and nothing seemed appropriate. She finally settled on a silky royal blue blouse and a pair of black slacks.

The aroma coming from the kitchen was mouth-watering, but Lee was sure she wouldn't be able to eat a thing. This was a lot different from eating over a campfire in the wilderness, and for some reason, her stomach felt as if she'd just finished a ride on a roller coaster. Considering everything she and Nick had experienced together, she wasn't handling this too well.

She examined herself critically in the mirror. Moisturizing cream had softened her skin, and the healthy glow of her suntan added sparkle to her eyes. A light touch of lipstick was all she really needed, she decided.

Her freshly shampooed hair curled smoothly back above her ears, and the diamonds sparkled in the light from the lamp behind her. In spite of everything she'd been through, she decided, she looked remarkably healthy.

The mountain air must have agreed with her. Or perhaps the man waiting for her in the kitchen was responsible for putting that radiance on her face. Taking a deep breath, she blew a kiss for luck at the mirror and left the room.

She found she could eat after all. The steak was delicious, cooked to perfection, and after three glasses of the excellent zinfandel Nick served, she began to relax. Even Nick seemed to be more at ease, smiling at her now and again, though without the intimacy she was used to.

The conversation centered mostly on the events of the past few days. Simon, it seemed, had filled Nick in on the entire story, once it had become apparent that his cover was blown.

"Did you have any idea he was an agent?" Nick asked when they both sat back, comfortably replete.

"No." Lee folded her napkin and laid it on the table. "I was shocked when he told me. I guess I should've known."

"So you were going on blind faith after all," Nick said in an odd voice. "I wonder if Simon knows how lucky he is."

"Simon doesn't give away too much of what he's thinking. I've come to the conclusion that I don't know my brother very well."

"Isn't that a little unusual for twins?"

Lee shrugged. "Maybe." She lifted her glass, which contained the last of her wine. "Have you had any word on what happened to Ben?"

He accepted her change of subject without comment. "He's dead. They got him in the exchange of gunfire when we were getting Simon out."

"I see." Feeling sick, Lee took a sip of the wine. "What about the other two, the ones you tied up?"

"Cooling their butts in the county jail. The law picked them up right after us."

"Thank goodness." She replaced the glass carefully on the table. "I couldn't bear to think that we . . . that they—"

"Lee." His eyes reflected his concern, warming her. "Don't think about it anymore. It's over. You have no reason to feel guilt or remorse. You did what had to be done, and you did it with remarkable courage."

"You gave me that courage. I'll never forget what you did for me."

There was a breathless silence, then Nick said quickly, "Your brother solved the riddle of the ghost town for me."

"He did?" Lee said, disappointed. "What riddle?"

"The reason I hadn't seen the ghost town before when I was living up there." Nick pushed his chair back from the table. "Apparently the White Devils had brought the timber up from the lower slopes and rebuilt the houses themselves. They figured that even if they were seen from the air, no one would pay much attention to old, broken-down buildings."

"I see. They thought of everything, didn't they?"

"Not quite everything. They hadn't reckoned on an enterprising agent and his stubborn, determined sister messing up their operation."

"Not to mention a tough, efficient, shrewd ex-mountain man masterminding the whole production."

His eyes darkened, stilling her breath. "We were quite a team, weren't we?" he said.

"Yes. We were." Her voice was husky with longing as she met his intense gaze.

"I think," Nick said unsteadily, "I'd better do the dishes."

"Let me." She reached for his plate, but he leaned forward and covered her hand with his, triggering jets of liquid heat throughout her body.

"I never let my guests help with the dishes." He was almost whispering, his eyes burning into her soul.

"Nick." She had barely breathed the word, sensing the struggle going on behind his midnight-blue eyes.

She sighed in frustration when he stood and began stacking dishes.

"Go sit down," he said abruptly. "This won't take long." She watched him stride into the kitchen, her confidence fading.

He was fighting her, and she knew only too well how strong he could be. Whatever reasons he had, they must be powerful indeed to govern him so completely, she thought.

If she were certain that his feelings for her were nothing more than simple animal attraction, she'd walk out of there tonight and not look back. Only she knew better. The words he refused to say were in his eyes when he looked at her. Damn him! Why was he being so stubborn!

She sighed and wandered over to the stereo. Precious time was slipping away, and she was getting nowhere. If she thought it would do any good, she'd ask him outright, demand that he tell her why he was sending her away.

Knowing him as she did, it would only make matters worse. He would probably deny his feelings, and once it was put into words, there'd be no going back. She was too insecure to take that chance. Bleakly she raised the lid of the stereo.

In the kitchen Nick slapped dishes into the dishwasher with unprecedented force. What the hell had possessed him to bring her back here? Hadn't he had enough pain without deliberately invoking more?

That long night in the hospital, he'd vowed that once he was certain she'd be all right, he'd get out of her life for good. What could he possibly offer a woman like Leanne Coulton? He'd die before he'd go back to the phony, bigoted materialism of the world of the wealthy.

True, Lee was not like that, he'd grudgingly come to admit, but even so, there were certain things she was used to that just didn't belong in his life. Sooner or later, she'd miss them, become disenchanted, bored. They would end up fighting and—

His contemplation was interrupted as the husky voice of his favorite singer invaded the room. Lee must have put the stereo on, he thought. He put the last dish in the machine and closed it, then wiped his hands on a dish towel.

When he walked back into the living room, Lee was standing by the window, staring out at the night sky. He studied her profile for a moment, his heart twisting at her pensive expression.

The singer's sultry voice filled the room, quickening his senses. He felt the fluttering where it bothered him the most and knew, too late, that bringing Lee back here had been a grave mistake.

He swept his gaze over her body, taking in the soft curves beneath the silky embrace of her blouse, the smooth, clinging line of her slacks.

The music pulsed in his mind, blotting out everything but the memory of how her body felt, soft and naked in his arms. He saw again her eyes, warm with passion, her parted lips moist with invitation.

With the desperation of a drowning man, he fought to erase the vivid memories, but his throbbing need refused to be abated. His voice was hoarse when he uttered her name.

She'd been staring at the glittering stars, remembering another night when she had watched them as she'd lain on the hard ground with Nick by her side. That was before she'd known the touch of his hot flesh combining with hers and the burning magic of his mouth on her naked skin.

How much more poignant the memories were, now that she knew how it felt to lie in his arms, spent and satisfied. Would she ever be able to look at a night sky again, she wondered, without feeling this desolate ache inside her?

She hadn't heard him come into the room. The music filled her, intensifying her dejection. *Think of me. Think of me.* Would he think of her after she'd gone?

She heard his strangled voice and turned. Her heart caught, held and then began a joyful tattoo. There was no mistaking the look on his face, the hungry need in his dark eyes.

The walls of the room disintegrated, and she could feel the mountain breezes, hear the whispering branches, as she moved slowly toward him. He stood, motionless, until she was close enough to touch him. Still he made no effort to reach out for her.

She knew the next move was up to her. Holding his gaze steadily with her own, she raised her hands and undid the top button of her blouse.

"I want you," he said huskily.

She smiled. "I was hoping you would." When he closed his arms around her, it was like coming home. She clung to him, answering the insistent demands of his mouth with a fever of her own.

Without lifting his mouth from hers, he moved back, pulling her with him into the hallway and finding the door behind him with unerring confidence. It swung open at his touch, and Lee followed him into his bedroom.

It felt so right. His body was wonderfully familiar, hard and warm beneath her searching hands. The smell of him, the woodsy, musky fragrance that was so much a part of him, heightened the excitement that was fast taking her out of the real world and onto another plane of existence.

Every nerve in her body quivered when he lifted his head and gazed down at her. It was the look she'd longed to see, the fiery hunger that made her feel desirable, sexy, beautiful—all the things she'd never felt before.

"Did anyone ever tell you," he asked softly, "that you're an incredibly sexy lady?"

She laughed in sheer delight. "No, I can't say anyone ever did." Her face grew serious again as she looked up at him. "But then, no one has ever made me feel sexy before."

She felt the pulse fluttering in her throat as he moved his hands to her blouse and undid the next button.

"Not even your husband?"

"Especially my husband."

"Ah!" He brushed his knuckles against her breasts as he slid the next button open. "That explains a lot."

"It does?" The words were hard to say, considering that she had run out of breath.

"Yeah." He released the last button, then pulled the ends of her blouse free. His hands were warm on her shoulders as he pushed the silky fabric from them. "You've never taken the time to enjoy it, have you?"

She thought of the nights she'd lain awake, long after Steven had fallen asleep, after another bout of pretense and frustration. She had blamed herself, putting it down to tiredness after long days at the hotel. It had never occurred to her that Steven's selfishness could be responsible for her lack of response.

"Time." She dropped the blouse to the floor and reached up to touch his face. "I seem to remember you mentioning that word before, somewhere."

"I did, didn't I? And Nick Garrett always keeps his promises." His lips brushed hers as he unsnapped her bra, then blazed a moist trail down to her bared breasts. She cried out, digging her hands into the firm flesh of his shoulders when his mouth teased her into a frenzy of need.

He lowered her onto the bed, then slowly finished undressing her, his mouth exploring every part of her body as he uncovered it. By the time he had reached her feet, the tension in Lee's body had built to an almost unbearable level.

"Nick! Please." She squirmed as his lips touched the sensitive undersides of her feet, and he raised his head.

"Oh, not yet. We still have a long way to go." He slid off the bed and stood looking down at her.

She felt a moment of embarrassment at her nakedness, then forgot it as he undid the buttons of his shirt and dragged it off. Now it was her turn to look, and this time she was going to make the most of it.

She watched him pull down the zipper of his slacks, then push them down his long legs without a hint of concern. Only the rapid rise and fall of his chest revealed the increasing force of his passion.

She caught her breath as he hooked his thumbs into the waistband of his briefs, then eased them over his hips and down his legs. He straightened, and she was stunned by the pure, unadulterated beauty of his body.

From his strong, narrow feet, the powerful curve of his thighs, the shattering splendor of his manhood, the awesome play of muscles in his heaving chest, all the way to his sensually parted mouth and blazing eyes, he was heated, aroused male, and he wanted her.

She managed to croak his name, her arms outstretched, then her eyes closed in unbelievable pleasure as he lowered his body onto hers. She parted her legs, her hips grinding against his, her hands clawing at the smooth skin of his back.

"Not yet. Let me make it good for you first," Nick murmured.

His mouth became a tormenting source of unbearable ecstasy. There wasn't a spot on her body he didn't find and make her undeniably aware of. Every movement he made, every touch of his tongue, his lips, his knowledgeable fingers, brought her to a squirming, writhing peak of tension, until she could stand it no longer, and at last, with a sobbing cry, he took her to the limit of her endurance and she crashed through to the waiting release.

It was a moment or two before she realized Nick hadn't reached it with her. He knelt astride her, an arm on either side of her shoulders, his ragged breath fanning her face. Her question must have shown in her eyes as he gave her a tight smile.

"I wanted you to know how it feels to be completely satisfied," he said in a husky voice.

She wanted to cry. Never in her life had she experienced such a degree of unselfishness. She felt a deep urge to return it, and nudged at him firmly until he understood and rolled over onto his back.

She'd never imagined she could be capable of touching a man in that way. It was something she never would have dreamed of doing with Steven, yet now it all seemed so natural, so incredibly wonderful.

She took him in her hands, caressing and stroking.

"Lee!" His shout was hoarse and desperate. She slid up his body, bending her knees as she lowered herself onto him, amazed to find her own need just as strong as it had been a moment earlier. She cried out as he filled her, then began moving her hips.

"Oh, Lee, Lee." He repeated it over and over, louder and louder, as his frenzied thrusts drove deeper. Lee's cries mingled with his, her fingers digging into the solid flesh of his shoulders, and then once again she felt the intoxicating moment of release a second before Nick's body shuddered on its final plunge.

"That," Nick breathed as they lay fighting for breath, "was unbelievable."

Lee lifted her head from his damp chest and grinned. "For once, Mr. Garrett, we are in complete agreement." She was still joined to him, lying on top of him, and she moved her hips, reluctant to give up the pleasurable sensation of him inside her.

"You know, Ms. Coulton," Nick said lazily, "as I said once before, you never stop surprising me."

She leaned down and kissed the tip of his nose. "Or you me," she whispered. His mouth was a temptation she couldn't resist, and she moved her lips down to taste the sweet warmth of it. To her intense delight, she felt him stir inside her.

He groaned when she lifted her head. "You're going to make an old man of me."

"And what a sexy old man you'll make," Lee murmured, and trailed her lips down the slightly abrasive skin of his chin and onto his throat.

He pulled his hands up the sides of her body until his thumbs found the velvety smoothness of her breasts. "Don't start something you don't intend to finish," he warned her, squirming as her lips traveled across his chest.

Lee smiled sweetly and began a slow, erotic circling of her hips. "I'm willing to finish it if you think you can manage it."

She gasped as he gave a low growl and with a heave of his body twisted her under him. "I'll show you what I can manage," he promised, and proceeded to do just that.

They spent a good part of the night talking, though Lee did most of the talking. She tried several times to prompt Nick into revealing his past, but he was adept at changing the subject, and apart from a fascinating account of his years in the mountains, she failed to discover the bitter secrets of his heart.

They slept and then awoke in the early hours before dawn, reaching for each other with a renewed passion that amazed Lee. Nick seemed to have an inexhaustible appetite, and she was every bit as eager as he was.

He was gentle and tender and at times demanding and physical, whispering sweet words one minute and devouring her the next. She seized it all with every fiber of her being, exalting in each moment. And not once during that long, magical night did he mention anything about love. In the morning, when she opened her eyes to the sun, she was alone.

Chapter 12

In the kitchen, Nick sat staring moodily into a cup of cold coffee. He'd slipped out of bed and showered more than an hour before, anxious to have time to himself in order to sort out his muddled thoughts.

There was no sense in fooling himself. Last night had been inevitable from the moment he'd caught Lee in his arms at the church. He had known it then, even if he hadn't admitted it to himself. The point was, what was he going to do about it?

Oh, he knew what he *should* do about it. He should send her back to that comfortable, secure, rich life, where she belonged.

He took a mouthful of his coffee, scowled and pushed back his chair. Only it wasn't that easy. After the night they'd just spent together, he doubted very much that he could find the words to send her away.

Yet he knew the gamble he'd be taking, even thinking about asking her to stay. Oh, she'd stay; he had no doubts

about that. But for how long? How long would it take fo
her to start missing the luxuries she was used to, and blam
him for the lack of them?

He dragged himself from the chair and wandered into th
living room, over to where the windows looked out onto th
main street.

She wouldn't say anything, of course. But it would b
there, the resentment, building up until it exploded and de
stroyed them both.

He stared down at the deserted main street, at the an
cient buildings warming in the morning sun. It had taken
him a long time to come to terms with his life. He was rea
sonably content. If someone had asked him if he was happy
he would have shrugged off the question.

How many people were truly happy? He had a busines
he enjoyed, friends he liked, a roof over his head an
enough money to get by. A lot of people would envy him
Most of all, he was able to live with himself. He owed noth
ing to anyone, had never cheated anyone and had neve
willingly hurt anyone.

He swore quietly and rubbed at his forehead. It would b
better to get it over with, put an end to it now, while it wa
still good between them. Better that than watch what the
had die a slow death. Sure, it would hurt for a little while
but time took care of most things; it would take care of that
too. For both of them. He heard a sound behind him an
turned sharply.

She looked even more beautiful this morning, he thought
Her huge brown eyes, still misty with sleep, smiled at him
across the room.

"Good morning. I forgot that you're an early riser."

She was wearing his shirt, baring her smooth long legs. H
almost winced when the pain sliced through him.

"Good morning yourself. Want some coffee?"

She nodded. "Please. I'll get it."

"Pour one for me, too. Mine's cold."

The beginnings of a frown drifted across her face. "Have you been up long?"

"Long enough to shower and shave."

Lee hesitated. Something was wrong. His smile was forced; his eyes were bleak. A cold lump settled in the pit of her stomach. Had she lost after all? It was hard to believe, after last night.

She'd been so secure, until the moment she'd woken up and found him gone. Then she'd sensed the first, niggling doubt. She opened her mouth to speak, then closed it again. She could think better on a cup of coffee.

All the time that Lee busied herself with the coffee, questions were running through her head. Why? It had all been so perfect, so wonderful. And yet she hadn't been able to get through to him, to the part of him that she needed so desperately to know. And he hadn't told her he loved her. She'd waited all night to hear him say it, bursting with the desire to tell him how she felt, how much he meant to her.

She took several sips of the scalding coffee, then refilled his cup before carrying both cups carefully into the living room. Nick still stood at the window, his back to her. She walked over to him and handed him his cup with a bright smile.

"Your coffee's as good as your steaks," she said cheerfully. "I'll have to take lessons from you. Father's always moaning about my dreadful coffee."

He took the cup from her, and her heart sank at his blank expression. No, not again. Please, she begged silently, please, Nick, don't shut me out. I need you.

"Your father must be wondering about you," he said carefully. "Did Simon tell you the whole story was on the front page of the *Oregonian*?"

She'd felt this pain before—when she'd thought he'd been killed. Only it was worse now, somehow.

"Yes, he told me." She swallowed with difficulty. "I'll explain everything when I see Father tonight." She waited, with increasing agony, for him to say the words that would keep her there forever. When he didn't speak, she laid a hand on his arm. "Nick."

"Lee." He moved away from her, though at least now he was facing her, looking at her with those dreadfully bleak eyes.

"I'm sorry, Lee. I know what you must be thinking, and I don't blame you. Last night . . ." He put the cup down on the table by his side and paced across the room like a restless lion.

"Last night," he went on in a dry, tight voice that tore at her heart, "was the most incredible experience of my life. I mean that. It's a night I'll never forget."

So why did those words sound like a goodbye? She waited, not daring to speak.

"It wouldn't work, Lee. It's better that you go back to the city, where you belong, and forget about me."

"I see." She put her cup down carefully, afraid she would drop it. The lump in her throat felt like the mountain itself.

Her anguish must have communicated itself to Nick. He swore and took a step toward her, grabbing her arm.

She shook him off in a violent movement that sent pain up to her shoulder. "It's all right, Nick. I understand."

"No, you don't." His voice was ragged. "There are things you don't know."

"Then tell me." Her eyes smarted, and she blinked. "You at least owe me that, Nick."

He stared at her for a long time, his pupils indistinguishable against the dark irises. She was right. It wasn't fair to send her away without at least telling her why.

"I was almost married once," he said finally.

Lee stifled the twinge of jealousy and stared at him. "What happened?" His expression shocked her.

"She was beautiful, intelligent, funny and exciting to be with, and I loved her. It took me a long time to find the courage to ask her to marry me, but when she accepted, I was over the moon." He sat down on the end of the settee.

"I lived in Portland then," he said in a curious, flat voice that frightened her. "My mother's family's been in business there for more than fifty years. My mother is a very...strong woman, used to having her own way. I often wonder why my father married her. His life was miserable for most of the time I knew him."

He pushed his feet forward and stared down at them, but Lee knew he was seeing something else. She waited for him to continue.

It was a while before he spoke again. "I thought my mother liked Laura. They always seemed to get along, but when I told her I was going to marry Laura, she tried her darndest to talk me out of it. It didn't make any difference to me. I knew what I wanted, and my mother sure as hell wasn't going to stop me. I was serving my time in the air force then, but we went ahead with the wedding plans and set it for my next long leave."

He paused, and Lee's skin prickled. She wasn't sure she wanted to know the rest of it, but she couldn't stop him now.

"Before that could happen," Nick continued, "I was sent to Vietnam." He stood up and began the restless pacing again. "I wrote every day, and at first the letters from Laura were pretty regular, then all of a sudden they stopped coming.

"I blamed the military for messing up the mail, wrote frantic letters home and begged my mother to find out what was wrong. She finally wrote and told me that Laura had met someone else and hadn't had the courage to tell me."

He stopped pacing and stood in front of Lee, staring down at her with unseeing eyes. "I went a little crazy after that. I took all kinds of risks, not caring much what happened to me. By some miracle, I made it out anyway. Th first thing I did when I got home was look up Laura.''

He seemed to realize he'd been staring at Lee, and h moved abruptly, sitting down on the settee again. ''He mother was there when I arrived, and she had a real nic story to tell. It seems my mother decided that Laura wasn' good enough for me.

''She had big plans for me in the business, and Laur wasn't the kind of girl who'd fit into those plans. She didn' have the upbringing, the class or whatever damn thing it wa that was so important to my mother. So she offered Laur money to get out of my life. A considerable sum of money apparently.''

The room had grown cold, and Lee hugged her body with her arms, trying to erase the agony of Nick's face.

''I don't blame Laura for taking it,'' Nick said tiredly ''She'd never had any of the luxuries that we took fo granted, and it must have seemed like a fortune to her. Th last I heard, she was in Hawaii, living it up with the jet set.'

''And you went to the mountains, to forget.'' Lee touched his arm, then withdrew her hand when she realized he hadn' heard her. There was nothing else to say. He'd been be trayed twice, by the two women he'd loved most. No word could ever undo the pain of that.

''Money does terrible things to people,'' Nick mur mured, as if to himself. ''It corrupts them, governs their lives and makes them forget what's really important. I swor I would never be part of that world again.''

And I'm part of that world, Lee thought, understandin at last. ''Nick, you can't judge everybody by the actions o two selfish women.'' She felt a cold fury at the thought tha anyone, let alone his own mother, could treat this man i such a callous way.

He looked at her as if seeing her for the first time. ''I'r not judging them, or you,'' he said quietly. ''I'm judgin myself. I've lived with this too long. I'm not sure I can get past that. I don't want to end up hurting you, hurting both of us."

"And if I'm willing to take a chance?" She was making a fool of herself, she told herself miserably, but she couldn't walk away without a fight. Not after last night.

He turned back to the window, and she knew she would never forget that look on his face.

"You'd be betting on a long shot. It isn't worth the gamble, Lee. Believe me."

"That doesn't sound like a gambler talking." She tried desperately to keep her voice light but couldn't quite prevent the break.

"Maybe I've got too much to lose."

"Maybe we both have." She willed him to look at her, but he kept his gaze on the street outside. "Isn't that what gambling is, though? Taking a chance? Isn't that what life is all about, anyway? Where would any of us be if no one took chances? There would be no vaccines, no moon landings."

Why was she doing this? she wondered. Why was she torturing them both by beating against a wall he was determined to preserve? Because she loved him, her heart answered, and she couldn't bear the thought of life without him.

"It all comes down to how badly you want something," she said when he still didn't answer. "I guess you're right. It isn't worth the gamble."

She twisted away from him before he could see the tears filling her eyes. "I'll go take a quick shower," she said quickly, afraid her voice would break altogether, "and then I'll be on my way."

Nick stared for a long time at the street below. He'd known it would hurt; he'd never imagined it could hurt so much. He had a sudden vision of what his future would be

like from then on. He'd never be able to look at another
woman without seeing Lee's wide brown eyes, warm and full
of promise.

His life would be empty and meaningless without her, but
how selfish would he be to ask her to give up so much? He
drove his fist viciously into the wide beam that separated the
window panes, ignoring his smarting knuckles.

He turned his back on the window and took a long look
around the home that had come to mean so much to him.
The Blue Bucket was his life. But so was Lee.

He drew in a long, slow breath and let it out on a sigh. He
had one card left to play. One ace in the hole. It wouldn't be
easy, but if she was willing, it might be the answer. He heard
the bathroom door open and made up his mind.

She looked calm and composed when she came into the
living room, dressed in linen slacks and a pink-striped camp
shirt.

"If you wouldn't mind bringing my suitcase down to the
car," she said, not meeting his eyes, "I'd appreciate it."

He winced at the cool, indifferent tone. "Of course. Lee,
I have a big favor to ask. It would really help me out."

Her face was impassive, but her eyes looked despairingly
at him when she answered. "What is it?"

"I need a lift. To Portland. Since my Jeep is still stuck up
in the mountains, I don't have any transportation. I've decided it's time I bought a new one anyway. I'd really appreciate it if you'd take me to Portland. Then I can drive the
new one back."

No, thought Lee feverishly. It was all she could do to
maintain an outward composure as it was. The thought of
being closeted with him for several hours in the intimate
confines of a car was too appalling to contemplate.

"They don't sell Jeeps in Baker?" she asked desperately.

"They do." Nick stuck his thumbs into his jeans and smiled at her. "But I have a friend who's a dealer in Portland. He'll give me a good deal."

"I thought you didn't have any friends in the city," Lee said, striving to keep the bitterness out of her voice.

"I don't. He usually drops by when he comes through here. He told me to come and see him if I ever wanted to buy a new Jeep."

"Are you sure you want to trust yourself to the big city?"

This time the sarcasm was heavy, and he flinched. "Please, Lee. I wouldn't ask if I weren't desperate. I have a lot of work to catch up on, and I don't have time to make other arrangements. If you take me today, I can be back here by late tonight."

Cursing herself for being all kinds of a fool, she found herself nodding. "All right."

Her tone clearly implied her reluctance, and Nick let out a sigh of relief when he went into the bedroom to get her suitcase. He would have applied force if it had been necessary. He was immensely grateful it hadn't come to that.

Lee was waiting in the car when he came out onto the sunlit sidewalk. She sat behind the wheel, tapping on it impatiently, her eyes on the distant mountains.

He walked up to the door and pulled it open. "I'll drive."

"I prefer to, thanks." She didn't look at him but kept her gaze straight ahead.

He threw the suitcase into the back of the car and slid into the driver's seat, using his body to force her to move over. She scrambled away from him as if he had a contagious disease.

"I'll drive," he repeated. "You can take over when I get tired."

She threw him a mutinous look but said nothing, and he switched the big engine on and pulled away from the curb.

Lee sat in miserable silence for what seemed like hours, though it had to be less than two. Nick had long ago given up any attempts at conversation, and she could hardly blame him. Her answers to his comments had been brief and disinterested, a major effort to talk past the ache in her throat and the misery tormenting her stomach.

What hurt more than anything was Nick's apparent lack of concern about their impending separation. He was tense; she couldn't help noticing the tight grip of his strong fingers on the wheel, and once, when she'd thrown a quick glance at him, she'd seen the telltale muscle twitching above his cheekbone.

Otherwise, he seemed relatively unmoved, certainly not as devastated as she felt. That hurt. That really hurt. She pressed her back into the seat and tried not to think about the time they'd spent together on the mountain.

It was obvious that now that it was all over, he was ready to put it all behind him and forget it. She'd let one wild, unforgettable night fool her into thinking he cared enough about her to make a commitment.

What an idiot she'd been, trying to convince him it could work. He was right. It wasn't worth gambling on. She hunched her shoulders and glared out the window, wishing fervently that she hadn't agreed to give him a lift back to town.

It would be at least four or five hours before they got there, and she was dying for a cup of coffee. They'd left the Blue Mountains behind them some time ago, and now Lee could see the snowcapped Cascade Range faintly in the distance.

They would pass through desert, then forest, then mountain passes before they finally reached their destination. Lee sighed, wondering how much longer she could stand this unbearable situation. The very presence of him sitting so close to her was a constant reminder of all they'd been through.

She found it increasingly difficult not to let her eyes stray to his tanned hands on the wheel, remembering how it had felt when he'd caressed her heated body. Every time he moved, the fragrance of his after-shave tortured her senses, and she was painfully aware of his strong thighs so close to hers.

She had to fight the urge to lay a hand on him, to touch him, to beg him to change his mind. But Leanne Coulton had never begged, and wasn't about to now.

She was shocked when, almost an hour later, Nick veered off the main highway onto a side road. She sat up quickly, looking around in confusion. "Where are you going?"

He kept his eyes on the road as he answered her. "I don't know about you, but I could use some coffee and a hamburger."

"But there's a town coming up on the highway. Why didn't you stop there?"

"This one's closer." He slid his gaze over her briefly, then he looked back at the road. "Aren't you ready to eat?"

"I'm not hungry," she said shortly, then, realizing how childish she sounded, said "but I would like a cup of coffee."

"Good. This won't take long."

Her uneasiness grew as he drove through a small cluster of buildings without stopping. "Wasn't that the town?" she said, her voice tight with suspicion.

"Yep. But there's something I want to show you first."

She couldn't hold it back any longer. "Nick, I'm not in the mood for sight-seeing. Now turn the car around and take me right back to the highway or I'll . . . I'll . . ."

"You'll what?" He braked, taking her by surprise. She put her hands on the dash to brace herself as they pulled to a stop on the shoulder of the road.

"I'll scream my head off," she said recklessly.

"Go ahead. No one will hear you."

For some reason, her heartbeat had begun to speed up. She stared at him, trying to analyze the look in his midnight-blue eyes. "I don't know what you're supposed to be doing," she said through her dry lips, "but whatever it is, I'm not amused. All I want is to get back to Portland as soon as possible. So please, either start the car or give me the keys so that I can drive."

"Not until I'm ready."

He opened the door and slid out, striding around the hood to her side before she had recovered. She stared at him as he pulled her door open and stood looking down at her.

"Come on, I want to show you something." He took her arm, but she shook him off.

"I don't want to see it," she stubbornly.

Nick sighed. "I really don't want to carry you, but if you insist . . ."

She shoved at him as he leaned down and slid one arm under her knees, the other under her shoulders, but he ignored her and hauled her unceremoniously out of the car.

"Put me down," she yelled, furiously.

"Not on your life."

She struggled, knowing it was a waste of energy, and pounded her fists on his chest. "All right, damn you. I'll come. But you'd better make it fast."

"I thought you'd listen to reason," Nick said, letting her feet slide to the ground. "It's not far."

"It'd better not be," Lee muttered as she allowed him to lead her by the arm toward a thin line of trees. What had gotten into him? Had he gone completely crazy?

She was surprised when they came out on the other side of the pines. Although she'd been aware of the car steadily climbing for some time, she hadn't realized how high up they were. Below them, a river wound its way through the sparsely populated forest, and on one side stood a two-story house, with a dozen or so cabins scattered behind it.

In front of the house was a small dock with several small boats tied up to it, and beyond the cabins, a ramshackle stable leaned next to a small, fenced paddock where two horses were quietly grazing.

Nice, Lee thought. Quiet and serene, though the place looked a little neglected. She looked up at Nick, who stood close to her, watching her intently.

She ignored the little jump of her heart. "So? What were you going to show me?"

"You're looking at it."

His voice sounded strange, and she narrowed her eyes. "You mean this?"

She waved an arm to encompass the scene below them, and he nodded.

"Yeah. What do you think of it?"

She shrugged. "I don't know. It's very quaint. What is it?"

"It's a resort. Or it will be by the time I'm finished with it."

She stared at him, her eyes wide. "You? You own this?"

"Not yet."

His eyes were telling her something, something she dared not even guess at, in case she was wrong.

"I've had a buyer after the Blue Bucket for some time," he said in the same odd voice. "I heard about this place a couple of months ago. The owners are anxious to move and are offering a good deal. I've been thinking about selling the Bucket and taking this over. I think, with a little hard work and some help, I can build it into something much larger, much more ambitious."

"I see." She couldn't seem to tear her eyes away from his face, and something was happening to her breathing.

"I need a manager," Nick went on, "someone with experience in hotel management. I plan to build a hotel eventually—small at first, but we can add on as we get more established."

"We?" Hope was building in her, a wild, impossible hope.

"I thought you might take on the job. It's not all that far from Portland, so you could visit often. With your experience and what little I've picked up, we could turn this place into something special."

"You're offering me a job as manager?" Lee asked carefully.

Fascinated, she watched the muscle twitching in his jaw.

"Yes. Of the Blue Bucket resort. And of me." He reached for her hand, opened up her fingers and placed a kiss in her palm. His face was serious as he closed her fingers over it.

"I'm not doing this very well," he said, "but I love you, Lee. I'm asking you to marry me."

Lee blinked back the tears as the exhilarating joy swept her up to impossible heights. "I love you, too, and you're doing just fine," she breathed.

"Is that a yes?"

It was the first time she'd ever seen him unsure of himself, and she was tempted to hold out a little longer, knowing this moment would never come again.

"You bet it's a yes," she said, and flung herself at him, nearly sending him off his feet. He lifted her off the ground, so that her face was level with his, his arms secure around her waist.

"Are you sure, Lee? I know what I'm asking you to give up."

She moved her hands to the back of his neck and caressed his jaw with her thumbs. "What about you? You're giving up the Blue Bucket, and I know how much that tavern means to you."

He gave her the wonderful, slow smile that could make the entire world disappear for her. "I'm willing to take the gamble if you are."

His mouth was warm and responsive under hers. "With the combination we've got," she whispered against his lips, "how can we lose?"

He let her body slide down his till her feet touched the ground.

"I seem to have that problem again," he said, his voice husky.

"I know." She grinned up at him. "I could tell."

"I think we should go down and try out the beds in all the cabins. Just to make sure they're up to standard."

"Now?"

"Right now." He pulled her into him, his kiss convincing her.

"All of them?" she asked breathlessly when he let her go.

"All of them."

"Right." She took his hand and pulled him back to the car. "And then you're going to buy me the biggest croissants you can find."

"Lee." Nick's voice sounded worried. "I'm afraid there are some things you may have to do without."

She stopped and faced him, reaching up to wind her arms around his neck. "Don't worry," she murmured. "I'm sure you'll find ways to compensate."

His grin warmed her heart. "Lady," he said softly, "you can bet on it."

* * * * *

*. . . and now an exciting short story
from Silhouette Books.*

*

HEATHER GRAHAM POZZESSERE

Shadows on the Nile

CHAPTER 2

Alex!'' Stunned, Jillian gasped out his name as he came closer. Her heart was beating frantically, and she prayed that he had come as a friend, not as an enemy.

"What?" the man with the scar on his face said in confusion, his knife still lying against her throat as he started to turn.

Too late. Alex was upon them, his fist raised.

Jillian let out a scream as Alex's blow connected and the man with the scar lost the knife, which went clattering into the darkness. The man spun and fell, just as his companion rushed at Alex. Jillian, her back still against the wall of the alley, screamed Alex's name again, but he had apparently already seen his attacker.

This was a different Alex from the suave man she had met on the plane. Despite the shadows, she could see his eyes, and they were dark, dangerous. She had no time to wonder how he had found her; she was only grateful that he had.

Now he backed away from the man with the switchblade, avoiding the man's first swipe. She was never sure what happened next, because Alex was just an eerily swift blur in the darkness, but somehow he spun around and kicked out, and then the second assailant was down.

"Come on!" Alex reached for her hand, and the next thing she knew, they were running. The exotic colors of the bazaar blended and swam in Jillian's vision, but he kept up the killing pace, and she followed. She really had no choice, and at least he seemed to know where he was going as they followed the twisting streets until they came to a curb where a dark sedan and a driver seemed to be waiting for them. Alex ushered her quickly inside, then followed.

As the car jerked away from the curb, Alex glanced out the window, sighed and leaned back. "We had some trouble," he said lightly, apparently to the driver.

Incredulous, Jillian stared at him, then turned her attention to their driver. "John!" she gasped. Her voice lowered suspiciously. "We *definitely* had some trouble. And what were you doing, waiting...?"

"Alex and I saw you go into the bazaar. It can be a dangerous place for a lady. All kinds of people you wouldn't want to meet hang around there."

Jillian turned to Alex again, her eyes narrowing. "You just happened to be here? The hell you did! What in God's name is going on?"

Alex sat up. "Going on?" he repeated indignantly. "You were attacked in an alley. I saved you." There was a husky reproach in his tone.

She didn't believe it was as simple as that, but she couldn't think of any other explanation that made sense. "You're— you're lying. That man kept asking me where it was. I don't even know what it is. We need to call the police."

She thought she saw Alex and John exchange glances through the rearview mirror, and then Alex shrugged. "All right, we'll call the police."

Suddenly she realized that they had reached her hotel. "Goodbye, Miss Jacoby," John said as Alex jumped out of the car and came around to her side. He opened the door, then offered her his hand, and she realized that he was going to stay with her. She hesitated, then tried to accept his hand casually. Her heart was beating too quickly again, but she wasn't sure why. After all, he was going to stay with her, and that should be reassuring.

He escorted her into the lobby, where he went immediately to a pay phone. Her eyes widened as she listened to him speak, because he was talking in fluent Arabic. When he caught her eyes on him, he broke off ruefully, paused, then continued to speak, but more self-consciously this time. He'd made a mistake, she thought uneasily—speaking the difficult language in front of her. Arabic wasn't exactly an everyday talent for the average American male to have.

Alex hung up, slipping an arm around her shoulders. She stiffened and said, suspicion tinging her voice, "You speak Arabic."

"Also French, Spanish, Italian and German," he admitted.

"You're quite talented," she challenged.

"Thank you." He didn't intend to offer more on the subject. "Let's sit in the lobby; Ben will be right here—" He cut himself off when he saw her eyes widen suspiciously. "Ben Ahmed. He's an inspector with the police. I doubt if he can do anything, but..." *But you wanted the police called, so I called them.* The words remained unspoken, but she heard them just the same. "Ben is an old friend of mine," he offered lightly.

They sat in the lobby and waited. Jillian had dozens of questions that she wanted to ask him, but she knew she wouldn't receive answers. Nor could she really find the energy to press her point at the moment. She was too keenly attuned to the man beside her: his scent; his warm, dark eyes. He was relaxed, strong, composed. She probably shouldn't trust him, but there was something honest about his hands, with their long fingers and clean, blunt nails. The same held true for the planes of his face, the square determination of his jaw.

Just as he had promised, a striking Egyptian with a sleek handlebar mustache arrived shortly. He listened intently to Jillian while she carefully described her attackers, then questioned Alex, too. Jillian thought that the two men exchanged knowing glances, but nothing was said, and she began to wonder whether her imagination had gone wild. After all, the past few years had been so empty. For the first year she had gone to work, then come home and cried. The second year, she hadn't cried anymore; she had just felt half dead herself. Egypt was providing far more excitement than she had ever begun to imagine.

After Ben Ahmed left them, promising to do his best, Alex turned to Jillian and said, "Let's get a drink, shall we?"

She gave him an assessing look. "I don't think so, Alex. I don't know what's going on, and I—"

"And you need a drink."

"I'm filthy and hot and—and *I* want to ask the questions."

"Okay, a shower, then a drink, then dinner."

She hesitated. If nothing else, he had been there when she needed him. And she did want to know more about him. "All right. A drink—and answers. Real answers. Wait here."

He took her hand as she stood. "I'll stand guard duty at your door."

Ten minutes later she was in the shower. When she was finished, she chose a black silk cocktail gown with bead work along the bodice. She forced herself not to examine her motives for choosing a dress that showed her off to such advantage.

He was at the door when she came out, and when he whistled softly, she again felt the warmth of his stare. "Five foot two, eyes of blue," he said laughing. And then he lifted a strand of her hair from her shoulder, and his fingers were electric against her bare flesh. "You're bewitching. A beautiful flower of the desert," he whispered, very close to her. So close that she could feel the steely strength of his chest beneath the fabric of his clothes.

She stepped around him. "A drink and dinner—and some answers," she reminded him.

He smiled, silently appraising her appearance again. "Oh yes, answers."

When they got back downstairs, Jillian ordered white wine, and he asked for a Scotch. As soon as their drinks had arrived, she began. "Who are you, Alex? What do you do, and what are you doing *here*?"

He laughed, catching her fingers across the table. "My name is Alex Montgomery. I'm with the Metropolitan Museum in New York, and I'm here because Egyptology is my specialty." He hesitated. "I come here frequently, not only because of my work, but because I love Cairo. That's how I know Ben. And it's how I knew that the bazaar might be dangerous."

"Oh," Jillian murmured. Was she wrong to distrust his story? Had he really just found her by accident, then saved her?

He was already talking easily again. He laughed and told her that beggars would follow her all the way to the pyramids, and that the museum in Cairo was really splendid, and that of course everyone needed to be careful these days, but the average Egyptian was warm and wonderful.

Listening to him, Jillian began to forget everything else. He loved this magic land, loved her people and her antiquities. Jillian realized that she hadn't accepted a date since Gary's death—until now. And she could do so now only because she felt as if she had known Alex a long time. She felt comfortable with him, secure in his presence and . . . excited by his touch.

After dinner they went dancing at a little rooftop lounge Alex knew, and she allowed herself to rest her cheek against his shoulder. It was nice. The scratchy fabric felt delicious and the stars above them were wonderful. She thought she must be mad to feel so comfortable with a stranger, yet she did. Perhaps it was all right to go for the magic, she told herself, to forget everything and enjoy herself, if only for the moment.

He took her back to the hotel at midnight. He brought her fingers to his lips and brushed his mouth against them. "The pyramids? Tomorrow? I'm the best guide you'll ever find."

Should she agree? He was handsome and charming, but she wasn't a fool, and she knew that no matter how wonderful he might be, he wasn't being completely honest with her. She nodded anyway, her eyes caught by his as she opened the door to her room.

That was when he kissed her.

His arms slipped around her, and her body melded to his, sweet heat washing through her veins. His lips touched hers and her mouth parted. Honeyed sensations filled her as he lifted her into his arms and pushed open the door to her room, carrying her into the sultry darkness.

* * * * *

To be continued . . .
Join us next month, only in Silhouette Intimate
Moments, for the next exciting installment of
SHADOWS ON THE NILE.

Silhouette Intimate Moments

COMING NEXT MONTH

#217 MOONBEAMS APLENTY—
Mary Lynn Baxter

Kari Kerns wanted peace and quiet, but when she witnessed a robbery, she found herself in trouble. Sheriff Nate Nelson was right there to protect her, but that created more problems. Neither of them wanted to get involved, but they couldn't seem to help it.

#218 RENEGADE MAN—
Parris Afton Bonds

Rita-lou Randall had turned Silver City upside down once, and now she was back. So was Jonah Jones, the only man with any chance of taming her. But he wasn't sure he wanted to. "Ritz" had always been wild, and something in him liked her that way—a lot!

#219 ARMED AND DANGEROUS—Joanne Pence

C.J. had to find her brother, but only one man in Hong Kong could help her—and he wouldn't! Darius Kane knew trouble when he saw it, and C.J. was definitely *it*. There was only one problem: he'd always been a man in love with trouble.

#220 KING OF THE CASTLE—
Heather Graham Pozzessere

Kit had spent one night in Justin's arms, and the memory had lasted years. Now she was back in Ireland and, before long, back in his embrace. But there was danger in loving him, a danger that threatened not only her heart, but her life.

AVAILABLE THIS MONTH:

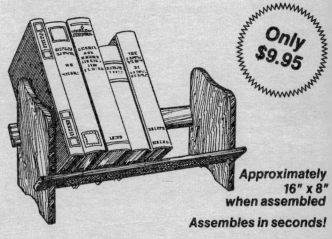

COMING NEXT MONTH

Silhouette Classics

The best books from the past by your favorite authors.

The first two stories of a delightful collection . . .

#1 DREAMS OF EVENING by Kristin James

As a teenager, Erica had given Tonio Cruz all her love, body and soul, but he betrayed and left her anyway. Ten years later, he was back in her life, and she quickly discovered that she still wanted him. But the situation had changed—now she had a son. A son who was very much like his father, Tonio, the man she didn't know whether to hate—or love.

#2 INTIMATE STRANGERS by Brooke Hastings

Rachel Grant had worked hard to put the past behind her, but Jason Wilder's novel about her shattered her veneer of confidence. When they met, he turned her life upside down again. Rachel was shocked to discover that Jason wasn't the unfeeling man she had imagined. Haunted by the past, she was afraid to trust him, but he was determined to write a new story about her—one that had to do with passion and tenderness and love.